Montana Animal Rescue Mystery, Book One

K.L. BORGES

CAMEL
PRESS
KENMORE, WA

PRESS

A Camel Press book published by Epicenter Press

Epicenter Press
6524 NE 181st St.
Suite 2
Kenmore, WA 98028

For more information go to:
www.Camelpress.com
www.Coffeetownpress.com
www.Epicenterpress.com
www.klborgesauthor.com

This is a work of fiction. Names, characters, places, brands, media, and incidents are either the product of the author's imagination or are used fictitiously.

Cover design by Scott Book
Interior design by Melissa Vail Coffman

Murder in the Crazy Mountains
Copyright © 2025 by K.L. Borges

Library of Congress Control Number: 2025937036

ISBN: 978-1-68492-256-7 (Trade Paper)
ISBN: 978-1-68492-257-4 (eBook)

To the animal rescue organizations of Montana,
whose valiant work is never done.

ACKNOWLEDGMENTS

I OWE A DEBT OF GRATITUDE TO DeeDe Baker, the awe-inspiring founder of Dog Tag Buddies, a real-life Montana organization that trains rescued dogs as service dogs for veterans. She provided information and reality checks for the book that were much appreciated.

Thank you to my early readers: Elena, who read it first, also Bob, Linda and Kim who cheered me on along with my husband, Miles, who dared to say when a scene wasn't working. This is a better book because of your feedback!

I would especially like to thank all the people at Epicenter Press who made this a published work rather than a manuscript sitting on my home bookshelf.

A final word of appreciation goes to those of you who have purchased Murder in the Crazy Mountains, I wish I could say a personal "Thank you," to each and every one of you. A portion of my proceeds will be donated to animal rescues in the Billings area, as well as to Dog Tag Buddies.

PROLOGUE

THE CHILL NIGHT AIR SWIRLED DOWN the mountain's slope, bringing the fresh scent of pine trees to the man. A jeweled tapestry of stars blazed forth overhead, undimmed by either the moon or lights from a city. Nearby, the booming hoot of a great horned owl rolled through the air as the bird of prey began its nightly hunt, but the man noticed none of these natural splendors as he stood silent in the trees. His full attention was fixed on the crumpled figure of the woman that lay at his feet.

He burned with anger and outrage at the precarious position she had put him in. She had disrupted his life as she led him on, ultimately duping him into divulging information that was not his to share. She was dead, no denying it, and if the police found out, she would cause him to go to prison. *Bitch*, he vindictively spat at her still form.

He would have to separate himself from her bloody corpse. Given enough distance and time, no future investigators would be able to link him to her demise. Instead, she would be just another unsolved missing and murdered brown woman in Montana, one of many, grist for task forces that ultimately led nowhere.

He had never been in this area of Montana before, and in a few hours would be several hundred miles away, never to return.

Hiding her body well enough to prevent its discovery for months, years, hopefully forever, that was his focus now.

Fortunately for him, nature had provided a ready-made graveyard, complete with headstones; no shovel work necessary. He had only to get her underneath the multitude of rocks that lay tumbled at the toe of the slope. He pulled on leather work gloves to protect his hands and set to work shifting stones. Soon he was sweating heavily despite the chill of the night air.

The owl had quit hunting for the night, and the stars had begun to fade in the approach of dawn when the murderer slunk unseen back through the shadowed woods, to drive furtively away from the mountains, fleeing in a nondescript passenger car of an indeterminate dark color.

ONE

MY EYES ALMOST POPPED OUT OF my head and my mouth hung open for an embarrassingly long moment at my first sight of the crazy quilt dog. He was a powerfully built dog, with a hound's deep chest, long legs and a coat of slick, short hair. His coloration was striking; the dog was covered with a unique pattern of irregular black patches and stripes, laid on top of a light gray background, but it was the dog's eyes, fixed unwaveringly on mine, that really gave me a jolt. Extraordinarily round in shape and accentuated by circles of black, as if he were wearing war paint, his eyes were a surreal electric blue, absolutely unworldly, and unreadable.

A young couple, probably in their late teens, had just arrived with the dog for a late drop off to RogerDog Rescue, a dog-only shelter located on the southern outskirts of Helena, Montana. The two of them, both dressed for the fall outdoors in lightweight hiking pants topped by fleece jackets, stood silent at the side of their black and silver Dodge pickup, protectively flanking the starved looking dog. Tearing my gaze away from the dog's eyes to glance at the man and woman, I found myself on the receiving end of hard stares from two more sets of blue eyes and belatedly realized I wasn't making the best first impression. Sheepishly shutting my mouth, and switching my attention to the two young people, I ran a hand through my silvering, pixie cut hair as I straightened up to my full height of five foot three. I gave them a warm smile in greeting and introduced myself.

"Hi, I'm Kelly Boyd. You're the ones who called earlier aren't you? About bringing in a stray dog you found in the mountains?" At their cautious nods of affirmation, I continued. "Let's all go inside the office. You can fill me in on the whole story and we'll get this guy settled in as a RogerDog."

I am a diehard devotee of Shakespeare's writings, and in the twenty-twenty view of hindsight, it's hard to believe that I failed to immediately recognize the dog for what he was—an incarnation of Hamlet's grey, grim ghost that haunts the castle ramparts, moaning from the darkness of murder most foul, crying loudly for vengeance.

As the college kids and the dog followed me inside the office, though, I didn't have the slightest foreshadowing of doom. Nope, as far as I could see, being profoundly late for dinner was the most serious outcome stemming from the dog's arrival.

I AM A SEASONED VOLUNTEER AT ROGERDOG Rescue, a shoestring shelter that houses up to twenty dogs at a time. I act as a de facto second-in-command for the place, behind the leadership of the founder, Betty Mills. I have worked here for the last two years, starting soon after retirement from a twenty-five-year career as a high school math teacher down in Billings.

I've always loved working with animals, and as a girl dreamed of becoming a veterinarian or zoo worker. I had set aside those aspirations in college; instead embracing a more practical career as an educator. Now, no longer busy with the demands of the classroom, the long-dormant dream of being an animal worker had reawakened in my heart. After my husband, known as Boyd to all except his mother, and I moved to the Helena area, I joined RogerDog Rescue working four days a week, with my duties split between office work and hands-on time with the dogs.

I fell in love with the varied tapestry of animals, people and experiences that make up life at RogerDogs. As a rescue worker, you never knew what a day would bring. Will there be glory or despair? Will you find yourself a hero, or a clown? Sometimes I tag all these bases in a single day, before lunch! The only guarantee is that the day will be interesting, never boring and at the end of it, my heart will be filled with a warm glow, lit by the love shining in the dogs' eyes and the knowledge that I have made a positive difference in their lives with my efforts. If teenage math students had provided as much daily satisfaction to the heart and ego, I would never have retired.

I also discovered early on that rescue work has a way of sucking you in beyond 'regular' hours, if you don't set clear boundaries and stick to them. Normally, I wrap up my day by four o'clock and return home to Boyd and our own two dogs, a pair of blue heelers named Sadie and Leo.

This day there were a couple of hours to go before quitting time, and I was outside the yellow, prefab metal building that houses RogerDog Rescue, taking a break to breathe in some fresh air and sunshine. It was a glorious Montana autumn day: the mid-September sky was the classic, deep blue of Indian summer and the air was simultaneously filled with both warm sunshine and air crisp enough to let you know it was indeed fall. High above, I could hear the wild, rattling calls of a flock of sandhill cranes winging south to New Mexico for the winter.

It would be a sin not to enjoy such a day while it was available. All too soon it would be the period for early season snowstorms in Montana, with winter itself coming to stay by Thanksgiving.

Betty Mills exited the building behind me and at first I thought that she was stepping outside to take a smoking break, as she is wont to do at intervals during the work day. Instead, she crossed to where I was standing by our respective cars: mine a trusty blue Subaru Outback and hers, a disreputable gunmetal gray jeep that has the dubious honor of sporting an odometer reading over

200,000 miles and that coughs out enough blue smoke when started to warrant a visit from the EPA.

"What a gorgeous day, Betty! They don't come better than this, do they?" I chirped in her direction before taking a good look at the woman.

"Jesus, here you are, I been looking for you," she replied in a raspy voice. I shot her a surprised look; and belatedly clocked her red-rimmed, bleary eyes that were set in a paper-white face. A high flush spread across her cheekbones, as if she had recently been slapped. Betty Mills continued in an especially hoarse croak of her gravelly voice, which always sounds like she has smoked a pack of cigarettes before breakfast. "I'm feeling like total crap, Kelly. I gotta go home. You think you can take over and not burn the place down while I'm gone?"

I stared at her for a moment before answering.

Betty Mills is a hard-faced woman with dirty-blonde, lanky hair, who, in previous versions of herself has been a ranch cook around the West, a long-haul trucker, and a bartender, with a stint in the military sandwiched in somewhere along the line. She looks to be in her fifties but is most likely younger; sun exposure and cigarettes do have a pesky way of artificially adding on years. Betty has maintained her military posture, standing a ramrod straight five-ten, and possesses a set of muscular arms and shoulders that are kept in shape by throwing hay bales around for her horses. Hell, maybe she bench-presses grizzly bears, too.

What she doesn't do is leave RogerDog Rescue for personal time off, ever. Betty Mills leaving the building was akin to the sun itself abruptly taking a powder during its daily sojourn across the sky.

"Sure, Betty, I can hold down the fort. Not anything special going on today, is there?" I said, feeling simultaneously concerned for Betty and filled with a secret giddy thrill. Me! I was going to be in charge! Kelly the Rescue Queen!

"Are you driving yourself home, or do you want me to call an ambulance, boss? You're looking kind of poorly," I queried her, half-jokingly. The woman looked seriously ill.

"Har-dee-har-har," Betty rasped back at me. "Thanks, but no thanks. If you remember, I don't live but ten minutes away, I think I can just about manage to get myself home. But, hey, you'll need to stay later today. I told some girlie that she and her boyfriend could drop off a dog after-hours. They called a little bit ago from down by the Crazy Mountains, said they found the dog wandering lost while they were hiking. They called the Bozeman shelter first and got spooked about the dog's long-term safety once his stray hold was up. Apparently, Bozeman's overcrowded right now, and the dog's got some sort of leg injury. They thought he'd wind up euthanized if they left him there. You got any problem staying until they get here? Shouldn't be much later than six."

"Got it," I quickly assured her. "Don't worry about it. Grace and J.J. must be almost done with the afternoon cleanup. I'll make sure everything's shipshape before they leave, then I'll hang out until the new dog gets here. Boyd's busy in his shop, working on his latest carving project. I'll text him a head's up, but I doubt he'll notice if I'm home late. Now for heaven's sake, go home before you die here, and I have to deal with the sheriff's office."

After two years of working with Betty Mills, I knew better than to offer up warm and fuzzy solicitousness to the woman, even though we were now good friends. She possesses the stoicism and hardiness of a pioneer woman and has zero tolerance for what she calls fussing and foolishness on my part.

Shooting me a rheumy-eyed glare and scowling fiercely, Betty shuffled to her jeep without any further discussion. She fired it up in a cloud of environmentally unsound blue smoke and drove off in the direction of the ramshackle property where she lives with her husband, Randy, a couple of horses, and, incongruously, a black and white miniature pig.

I texted Boyd to let him know that I was going to be late.

It was almost seven o'clock by the time the pickup truck pulled into our gravel parking lot. By then the glory of being Kelly the Rescue Queen had tarnished as I had become seriously hungry. We have snacky stuff on hand in the office, but my stomach was ready for a more substantial offering than pretzel twists and diet cola. The ebullient Grace and her silent sidekick, J.J., had offered to stay and wait with me, being eager to see the new dog arrive—but I had convinced them that tomorrow would be soon enough and they had departed before five o'clock.

Chase and Tara, the college kids who found the dog, were indeed leery of relinquishing him to a shelter. Later, after I assured them that he was safe as a RogerDog for as long as it took to rehab and rehome him, they loosened up enough to come inside and complete his intake. His ribs stood out starkly and he couldn't put much weight on his left front leg, but didn't appear to need immediate, emergency veterinary care. A visit to Dr. Rex could wait until the next day.

Thirty minutes later, the dog was installed in a kennel with food and water for the night, and I left the premises. The kids were on their way to meet up with friends in Helena, and after checking that the door was locked behind me, I fired up my trusty Subaru and pointed the headlights toward home. Time to see what Boyd, Sadie and Leo had done with their day.

Two

Boyd's shop was closed up and dark as I passed it on my way up the quarter-mile-long driveway to our house. Nestled in the low hills a mile to the west of the highway that runs through the valley south of Helena, the house commands spectacular views of Canyon Ferry Lake on the Missouri River, but the shop was the clincher to our purchase of the property.

Huh, I thought to myself, *what's up with that?*

Boyd had owned and operated a construction company for thirty-plus years in Billings and his deep-seated love of working with tools, the bigger the better, had not been dinted by retirement. He had gotten into chainsaw art last September after we attended the annual international competition held in Libby. The four-day festival included several 'quick carve' events in which men and women work with chainsaws and bare logs to create, on-the spot, detailed carvings in under an hour. He had been fascinated to see the high-speed emergence of mermaids, eagles, and bears from the six-foot-tall, two-foot diameter chunks of wood. Before the next weekend had rolled around, Boyd had scavenged up some logs of his own and had begun channeling his inner chainsaw. Initially, he had worked with pre-gridded carving patterns and YouTube videos, but quickly moved into carving his own designs.

Currently, he was working on a composition of otters and trout that he hoped would be good enough to earn him a spot as a selected competitor in a June festival over in Oregon.

Most days, Boyd would lose all track of time when he worked on his carving projects and would have to be pried out of the shop at the end of the day by yours truly, no matter the hour. Finding the shop already shut seemed ominous. It made me nervous that he worked with chainsaws when there was no one around to help if the saw carved Boyd instead of wood.

With a small frown between my blue eyes, I hopped out of the Subaru and quickly walked up the steps to the redwood deck that runs along the east side of the house. I gave the deck a quick scan before walking across; a flock of wild turkeys had recently started to hang out at the house, leaving golf ball sized calling cards behind, but the deck was free of hazards tonight. Lights were on in the kitchen, which was reassuring, but I still felt concerned.

Stepping into the mud room, I hurriedly glanced into the kitchen and felt my mouth drop open for the second time in the day. Our white-washed pine table was covered by a pretty, striped tablecloth and set with our company blue and white dishes. Our special occasion wine glasses were on the table as well, along with a centerpiece of candles.

Tall, handsome Boyd himself was standing near the stove, wearing a man-apron that I had given him several birthdays ago. His dark brown eyes glinted at me from under his thick gray eyebrows, and his brown mustache crimped upwards in a small smile of amusement as he smoothed his thick head of salt and pepper hair back from his face.

"Ah, the mistress of the house returns," he quipped. "Just in time to partake of the evening's repast." As Boyd spoke, he opened the oven door and pulled out a pan of steaming cornbread that looked as good as it smelled.

Sadie and Leo charged into the mudroom, biting at my hands in greeting. I absently petted their wiggly bodies as I continued to take in the sights and smells of the kitchen where I had thought I would be making grilled cheese sandwiches and soup for the two of us.

There was a mixed-greens beet salad gracing the sideboard in a wooden bowl, and on the stove was a bubbling pot of aromatic green chili stew. Boyd had been working on this dinner extravaganza since the midafternoon at least.

It wasn't my birthday, it wasn't our anniversary. Daniel Ryan Boyd was up to something.

I hung up my coat and pulled off my boots in the mudroom, and padded stocking-footed into the kitchen to greet Boyd with a quick squeeze around his middle. I got an appreciative pat on the rump in return.

"Dinner's on the table in five minutes," Boyd said, sporting his small smile that was creeping into an out-and-out grin. "Go get changed out of your dog clothes, woman, and I'll pour you a glass of wine."

Boyd's eyebrows waggled at me as he held up a bottle of New Zealand Sauvignon Blanc from my favorite winery. He didn't have to tell me twice!

Boyd handed me a glass of wine when I returned in clean, comfy clothes.

"Have a seat, honey, and tell me about your day," he said, a gleam of suppressed humor in his dark brown eyes.

"Well," I replied, tipping my wine glass slightly toward him as he ferried a tureen of stew to the table, to join the bowl of beet salad, and the plate of hot corn bread. "Like I texted you, Betty went home this afternoon looking like death warmed over. I bet it'll be a couple of days before she's even able to get out of bed. Guess who gets to run the show in the meantime?" I said with no small amount of pride.

Boyd's little grin now stretched into a smirk. He knew I relished the idea of being in charge.

"Everything went smoothly for today," I continued. "The only new thing was getting a crazy looking dog from two college kids this evening. They go to school in Dillon at Western and are using their fall block break to go exploring. They went hiking all the way over in the Crazy Mountains on account of the girl being nervous about running into grizzly bears if they stayed closer to Dillon. They found the dog near the trail to those falls on the east side of the Crazies; you know the ones I mean; we've gone there a couple of times. Lord knows how long he's been on his own, he's just skin and bones, and has a sore leg to boot. I'm going to need to run him to the vet's tomorrow and see what's what."

"Show me," Boyd said. "I want to see this crazy looking dog. You have pictures, right?"

Of course I do. I always have up-to-date dog pictures on my phone; same as most women have pictures of their children and grandchildren. I pulled out my phone, brought the pictures of the new dog up on the screen and handed it to Boyd. "Aren't his markings wild? And those eyes, my lord! He's a Louisiana Catahoula Leopard dog, I think."

Boyd scrolled through the pictures of the new dog and gave a loud shout of laughter. "By God!" he exclaimed. "It's Murphy, come back as a dog! Did you ever meet Murphy? Think back to the mid-nineties, he was a skinny guy who was my backhoe operator for about five years. Socially awkward and shy as hell. Always wore a greasy John Deere cap that he kept pulled low, with these curly wild eyebrows that stood out to *here*." At this, Boyd indicated a set of foot long eyebrows with his hands.

"His eyes were kind of sunk in dark circles all the time, and were pretty hidden under the eyebrows and hat, but on the rare occasions that he looked at you, Jesus! They were shocking blue, like this guy here," he said, waving my phone at me. "Literally shocking, it was like getting hit with a cattle prod when he made eye contact. But an artist with the backhoe."

I cast around in my memory for a blue-eyed, backhoe operator from the mid-nineties but came up blank. We had always thrown a company Christmas party for Boyd's Construction Services, but other than that once-a-year event, I generally didn't see the guys on the crew.

I shook my head at Boyd.

"Well, you've got to name this guy Murphy!" Boyd enthused. "Any other name would deny the karma of the similarity and bring down bad luck on us all." Boyd was openly laughing now.

"Alright, Murphy it is," I agreed. "It's a good name for him, and who needs bad karma, after all." We smiled at each other, enjoying the joke.

I reached out a leg and prodded Boyd with my foot.

"Your turn now, mister. Spill the beans; fill me in on the meaning of this decadence."

We passed dishes and dug into the wonderful food as Boyd did just that. He had received two phone calls while I was at RogerDogs that put the feast into action. The first was from Randy Mills, Betty's husband, a big, gruff man who looks like the aging motorcycle gang member that he is, and who works as a high-end automotive paint detailer in Helena.

"He called to tell you that Betty won't be back for two days, guaranteed. Claims he has her handcuffed to the bed until she's better," Boyd chuckled.

I hoped he was kidding about the handcuffs.

The second call came hard on the heels of the news that I would be spending most of my time in the upcoming days at RogerDogs. This time it was his old hunting buddy from Billings.

"Ron Duchene's going to set up a hunting camp near Cooke City for his boys. He's hauling in wall tents with some horses, just like we used to do in the old days. He wants me to join in on the fun; we'll be out for a week. We'll get to enjoy all the time in the camp and scouting in the woods and then his kids will take over at the start of the elk season."

Before I could open my mouth to weigh in on this arrangement of activities, both mine and his, Boyd held up a hand to forestall me and continued to speak.

"Have I mentioned that Sadie and Leo would go with me to keep us all in line, *and* did you notice the little something on the counter?" Boyd gestured toward a professionally decorated dark chocolate cake that held pride of place near the refrigerator.

Who could resist such blandishment and bribery? Certainly not me! "All resistance is overcome!" I laughed. "Kelly the Rescue Queen grants her loyal kitchen serf a week of backwoods freedom!"

THAT NIGHT, AS WE WERE SLEEPING after stocking up on certain bits of marital bliss that would be missed during our week of separation, a young badger moved into a moonlight filled meadow in the Crazy Mountains.

The badger was scouting for territory of its own as it dispersed away from its mother's range. The young animal had been roaming for several weeks before finding this location on the eastern flank of the Crazies. As the badger investigated the edge of a talus slope at the back of the meadow, its nostrils twitched with the sudden smell of a carrion meal hidden beneath small boulders and rocks.

Other smaller predators had attempted to access the cached food source, but the rocks had kept them at bay. A bear could've easily turned over the rocks, but none had yet discovered the site. To an animal that could tunnel as well as the badger, the rocks were just so much decoration. Within minutes, the hungry animal had burrowed under their protective layer to set up a lair.

The badger's tunnel, in turn, provided access to other small animals over the ensuing days. Slowly, bit by bit, pieces of cloth and bone travelled to the surface from the hidden grave of a young woman.

Three

THE NEXT MORNING, I STOOD OUTSIDE the rescue's big, yellow rectangular building as the sun peeked over the mountains to the east, spilling the first rays of daylight into the wide bowl of land and water that encompasses the Helena area. Rimmed by mountains on three sides, the town of Helena drapes across the slopes of the west side, while the Missouri river trails through the east, flowing northward to disappear between limestone cliffs that were dubbed the Gates of the Mountains by Lewis and Clark.

RogerDog Rescue is on the open south end of the bowl, far enough from the city limits to be on unincorporated land, thus free of pesky zoning laws that might have banned a kennel often filled with loudly barking dogs. The rescue, originally started by Betty's uncle as a board-and-train facility for hunting dogs, sits on five acres. Our nearest neighbors, a taxidermy business and a small engine repair shop are far enough away to be out of sight behind a ragtag spread of chokecherry bushes and juniper shrubs.

I stood for a moment in the cold morning air, snuggling in a warm fleece jacket while I surveyed my domain with satisfaction. Several skeins of geese crossed overhead, honking loudly as they flew away to their morning feeding grounds. Most would soon leave for warmer southern climes, not to return to Montana until the spring.

I could hear the current residents of RogerDogs, barking greetings to me, but couldn't see them behind a screen of lilacs planted years ago to soften the otherwise utilitarian aspect of the place. The bushes, still covered in rust and gold fall leaves, cut off my immediate view of the dogs in their outdoor runs. These runs, ten on each side, stick out like low wings from the building proper and provide every dog the luxury of an outdoor space in addition to an indoor sleeping area.

I walked around the building, but didn't see Scott Marsh, our morning kennel worker, anywhere outside. Scott shows up in the early morning hours every day, except Sunday, and cleans up the mess from up to twenty dogs, while simultaneously juggling them in and out of the play areas in compatible groupings of his design. It's not a job for anyone overly sensitive in the smell department but he doesn't seem to mind, and the dogs love him. He has an undefinable *something* that causes all dogs to worship the ground his scuffed boots walk on.

Each day, Scott finishes his RogerDog duties and gives a rundown of dog health and any other issues to whomever is in the office around nine o'clock, but as the new commander-in-chief, I wanted to get a jump on his report.

Most likely he was working with dogs in the exercise area at the back of the building.

I heaved open the heavy back door, and looked around the single large room, open to the peaked roof. Natural light streamed in from high windows set around the white walls. The room's floor space was soft underfoot, covered with interlocking black rubber mats laid on top of the concrete underfloor. Brightly colored ladders, inflatable balances, hula hoops and a plethora of stuffed animals, all for dog enrichment activities, were scattered around the room.

There was no Scott in sight.

Crossing the exercise room, I had the choice of three doors to check behind in my continued search for Scott. To either side, windowed doors led to hallways along the interior portions of the kennels. A quick glance through each window showed he wasn't in either corridor, leaving me to deduce that Scott was behind the middle Door Number Three, working in the storeroom.

Indeed, there he was, with his back turned to the door as he poured fresh bags of dog chow into large rubber storage bins. Scott is a wiry man in his fifties who moves with small jerky movements as if he is some sort of windup toy. He's as skinny as they come, with glittery eyes and cheek bones so sharp they threaten to burst out of his skin. Scott has shoulder length, wild red hair that floats around his head like electrified floss when it isn't pulled back into a ponytail, and he is missing a couple of front teeth. He puts me in mind of a poor man's version of Willie Nelson.

He also likes to work with his ears filled with earbuds and loud country music, and I could see the devices were in place from wires hanging down the sides of his head. I was sorely tempted to sneak up on him from behind, but startling the help into a heart attack didn't seem like a responsible way to start the day. Instead, I circled around through the dimly lit storeroom, trying to get his attention from the front.

He jumped sky-high anyway.

"Kelly, wh-what's up? Why are you here this early?" he stammered, pulling his earbuds out to dangle around his neck, where they continued to emit a thin sound of twangy music. His lids fluttered across his eyes as he looked in the direction of my shoes. Eye contact with people is hard for Scott, even at the best of times. It took almost a year for him to warm up enough with me to have a conversation, but now he and I enjoy our short daily interludes of overlapping time at the rescue, trading jokes, and pranking each other from time to time, like a brother I never had.

I held up my hands in the universal sign for 'I come in peace'.

"Sorry, Scott, I didn't mean to startle you! I just wanted to let you know that Betty's out with the flu for today, maybe even for tomorrow. She was looking pretty rough when she left yesterday afternoon," I said.

Scott's faded blue eyes met mine questioningly for the briefest of moments before skittering away to his left. He shuffled his knee high, brown and tan rubber work boots, and shifted the weight of the food bag he held in his arms.

"That's right. I've been promoted to head poohbah while she's gone," I continued, putting one hand on my hip and waving the other around in an all-encompassing swirl. "We'll stay open for business as usual, except, of course, we won't be able to do any more adoptions while she's gone." It is a firm rule at RogerDogs that Betty and Betty alone approved adoptions.

A small smile played on Scott's lips as he finished pouring the bag of food into the bin. "Well, it's lucky for us Mika went out yesterday, then. Barky little goober. He was driving me nuts, Kelly." Scott looked at the ceiling as he smiled and rolled his shoulders. Mika, a feisty three-year-old, black and white fox terrier mix, had been the most enthusiastic barker in residence, and a trial to us all. Much as we had adored him for his spunky character, no one would miss his noise.

"Hey, I thought it was way quieter in here today!" I grinned at Scott and put out my fist for an impromptu fist bump of celebration.

"Speaking of changes, Scott, did you see the new dog that came in last night? I put him in the last kennel in the back, the one we have hooked up with the nanny cam."

"Yeah, I looked in at him when I got here. Couldn't see much of him. He was too busy impersonating roadkill to pay me any mind. Is there something wrong with him?"

"That's what we need to find out. I know he was limping pretty hard on his left front leg last night, and you can tell he's starved down. I'm going to run him over to Dr. Rex's in just a minute. Anything you want me to pick up while I'm out and about?" I said, a twinkle in my eye.

"Well . . . what about the donuts?" Scott asked plaintively to the airspace just to the side of my left ear. "Betty always brings in donuts." His voice trailed off and he risked another moment of direct eye contact.

I scratched the back of my neck and looked away to hide my face as I answered, "Donuts? I don't know, Scott, Betty never said anything about donuts. I don't know if she'd want me spending money on random stuff while she's out."

At his stricken look, I broke into a reassuring grin and pointed at him as I replied. "Already gotcha covered, Scotty. You can get your fill in the office, as long you're a good boy and hose off those boots first."

Scott rocked back on the heels of his rubber boots and gave them a thorough once over, taking care to inspect both soles.

"Ah, you're funning me, Kelly. I ain't done any kennel cleaning yet, these boots are clean enough for company. Get out of my way, girly, I'm on a donut mission."

Laughing, we both walked through the storeroom to the front office to stock up on sugar, fat and caffeine.

The office area at RogerDog Rescue anchors the front of the building. The rescue's main door, emblazoned with 'RogerDog Rescue', opens directly from the parking lot to the middle of the room. On one side are utilitarian bookshelves, two beat-up metal filing cabinets and a gun-metal gray desk that holds my computer. This desk weighs approximately two tons and is government surplus of some sort. It is an unforgiving monstrosity, as unfriendly a piece of furniture that has ever existed. I had early on suggested to Betty Mills that we upgrade to a more modern wooden desk, but she had only snorted. Apparently, the behemoth was here to stay unless I wanted to personally fund my own office furniture. I had settled for painting the plain concrete floor a tasteful Mediterranean blue and purchasing the dog-themed area rug that now lies in front of the door.

A round, forest green, plastic table with four mismatched

wooden chairs sits on the far side of the room, alongside a small counter outfitted with a bar sink. A coffee pot and mini-fridge complete the ad-hoc break area for humans at RogerDogs. The day's allotment of jelly donuts was holding court in the middle of the table, to Scott's glee.

I snagged a donut as well, along with a cup of coffee, enjoying a second breakfast while watching the sunrise from two large windows that look over the parking lot. These bring a lot of natural light into the office as well as affording me a sneak peek at people approaching the front door.

On any day, the office is my special domain at RogerDog Rescue, and I love the feeling of importance I get from being the face and voice of RogerDogs to people who call or come to the office. Here, Kelly Boyd matters.

After Scott departed with his daily supply of donuts, I tried to settle in and catch up on my office work. Betty Mills is allergic to all things electronic, 'buncha horseshit', she calls it, so keeping our computerized records up to date, both for the dogs and the accounting, was the purview of yours truly, but my attention kept wavering away to Murphy.

I was able to watch Murphy on my computer via feed from a strategically placed camera and he never moved from his bed, staying curled up in a tight ball. It's not unusual for a new dog to be overwhelmed for the first few days; some even refuse to eat.

Scott's description of Murphy as a dead dog was hard to get out of my mind, though. The sooner we got him to the Dr. Rex's, the better!

Four

SMALL DARK SPOTS AND TINY FLASHES of light danced in front of my eyes, and the room seemed to tip and sway as the smell of antiseptic cleaner became overwhelmingly strong. Somewhere to my right, a voice was speaking, but I couldn't make out the words over the rushing, white noise that filled my ears.

"Uhhh," I made a low gurgle of my own as I leaned my head down between my knees in a valiant effort to keep from fainting onto the white and brown patterned linoleum of the veterinarian's exam room.

Dr. Rex Bittner broke off his discourse of Murphy's X-rays that were hanging on a light box. He quickly crossed to the corner of the small room where I sat slumped in a white plastic chair and put a steadying hand on my shoulder. "Whoa, there, Kelly," he said in a slightly alarmed tone of voice. "Keep your head down for minute, deep breaths, now." He continued to pat my shoulder as I buried my face in my cold hands and took a few deep, juddering breaths.

The rushing noise in my ears faded away, and I soon felt steady enough to sit back upright. Dr. Rex stood looking down at me with concern in his light brown eyes, slightly magnified by his black, horn-rimmed glasses.

Dr. Rex is a tall, gangly young man in his early thirties who is a modern-day Ichabod Crane. He has a skeleton-like frame, complete with bony wrists that perpetually stick out from his white exam coat, and a prominent, beak-like nose. He pushed his curly, dark brown hair off his forehead as he took a step back from me; leaning against the waist high exam table as I sat up.

"Phew," he said. "I thought I might have to use my doctor magic on a human for a second there!"

"Crisis averted," I said as I fanned my face with my hand. "All units stand down." I gave a somewhat shaky laugh and added, "Sorry, you'll have to start over from the beginning. Everything blurred out after you said that Murphy had been shot."

Inwardly, I felt sick. Apparently, I had been in charge of a dog with multiple gunshot wounds but had failed to notice that anything serious was wrong.

"Okay, from the top, then," Dr. Rex said. "If you start feeling woozy, just hold up your hand and we'll take a break." Great, now I had a reputation as a week-kneed fainter. I cleared my throat and hit Dr. Rex with a full blast of a patented, Mrs. Boyd-teacher-glare. I was gratified when he promptly jumped from his leaning position as if he had been poked with a pin.

Ha! I thought with a fierce burst of pride. *You still got it, Mrs. Boyd.*

"When we began Murphy's exam, we noticed right away that he had a three-inch-long gash along the side of his head, back under his left ear. We sedated him so we could get a better look at it and stitch it if needed.

"Once we got the area shaved, it was obvious that it had been caused by a bullet graze. All graze wounds look like prehistoric flatworms with legs off to the sides, kind of like centipedes."

Murphy had a bloody centipede on the side of his head? And I never noticed a thing? What sort of a rescue worker was I? I mentally castigated myself.

"We suspected he might have been shot in more than one place.

We completed a full set of body X-rays to look for additional gun-shot wounds."

These X-rays, now hanging up on the light boxes, showed that Murphy had indeed been shot in two other places. One intact bullet, possibly .22 caliber, was lodged along his spine.

Murphy had also been struck in his left leg, just below his chest. The bullet had broken his leg before fragmenting into small pieces of shrapnel that were now embedded in surrounding muscle.

"What's his prognosis then, Doc?" I queried, trying to maintain my composure in the face of all the medical bad news. "Does Murphy need an operation? To take out the bullet in his back, and those shrapnel bits in his leg? What about needing to keep him off his front leg while that cracked bone heals?"

Dr. Rex looked at me with a pained expression, his brown eyes expressing sympathy. "It's not that straightforward, Kelly. The wound on his face will heal fine with antibiotic cream to help things along. The bullet in his back is so close to his spine, I would suggest leaving it alone and hoping for the best."

Dr. Rex paused and took a deep breath.

"Then, there's Murphy's leg. You can see all the small fragments around the bone. Surgery to try and remove them is not in his best interests. We would probably miss some and they would cause lingering, maybe even severe, pain.

"The fracture isn't an easy one to repair, either. If you look closely, you can see some of the bone has chipped off completely, and there's a partial displacement at the break. But the real game changer is what we see *here*."

Dr. Rex pointed to an area of the X-ray near the fracture site. "See how the bone looks a little motheaten, with some shadowing?"

Well, no. Actually, I didn't. Whatever Dr. Rex was seeing wasn't apparent to my eyes. The whole X-ray was a bunch of indistinct shadows to me, but he's the doc. If Dr. Rex said there were shadows and the bone looked nibbled on, who was I to disagree? I made helpful noises to show that I was on board with what he was trying to show me, without needing further explanation.

"This is a bone infection, Kelly. That means an amputation is *necessary* for him to stay among the living. I'm sorry, but it's the only way forward for Mr. Murphy. Otherwise, I suggest that we let him go, while he's still sedated," Dr. Rex said, gently.

Let him go? What? Dr. Rex was suggesting *euthanasia*?

Dr. Rex pulled the exam room's second plastic chair over and sat down next to me. He took my hand in his and I realized that mine must still be icy because his felt so hot.

"Kelly, dogs recover very well from limb amputation, and lead perfectly happy lives as tripods. It's actually a straightforward surgery—the leg is attached to the chest with muscles only. Post-op, Murphy would stay with us for a couple of days and then be ready to go home.

"He'd need to be kept quiet, getting on his feet with a sling support, only for potty breaks, for a week post-surgery. After that, Murphy can be weaned away from the sling, but it'll be a good three weeks before he's adjusted to his new balance and body mechanics."

Dr. Rex laughed and patted me on my shoulder as he took in the glazed look on my face. "Information overload! Don't worry, we'll write it all down for you." Dr. Rex's face shifted back to seriousness as he continued. "That is, if you decide to go ahead with the amputation."

Questions about cost, RogerDog's finances, and Betty Mills' reaction when she was brought up to date about Murphy's medical drama swirled in my head—but overriding it all was the memory of my recent, heartfelt promise to Tara and Chase that this dog was *safe* with us at RogerDog Rescue.

"Do the amputation. I can take Murphy home with me when he's ready. If RogerDogs can't cover the cost, then Boyd and I will take up the slack," I said with a croak. "Boyd named Murphy, I'm sure he'll want to help." Mentally, I crossed my fingers behind my back and hoped that no stray lightning bolt would hit me on my way out to the car for putting words into Boyd's mouth.

Dr. Rex looked at me with an amused smile playing on his lips, and his eyes crinkled behind his glasses. "I'll take your word on that, Kelly. We can do the surgery this afternoon, and I'll have one of the nurses give you an update call when Murphy's in recovery. He'll stay here for the first two nights and be ready to go home with you the day after tomorrow."

We shook hands, and I went out into the cozy reception room where patients and their owners were distributed on padded benches along the walls. Kitties wailed from small carriers and dogs sat by their owner's feet, or perched on human laps. Everyone seemed to be watching me with interested eyes. Sheesh, did I still look pale, pasty and shaky-legged?

I stopped at the front desk to confer with Ellie, who rules the reception area. She is a bosomy, warm, friendly woman in her mid-forties, with shoulder length straight blonde hair and a set of crooked teeth that knew no orthodontic intervention. If she had an aura, it would be a cozy, warm maroon. Just settling up a bill with Ellie somehow makes you feel safe and cared for. In the face of bad news, Ellie and her aura give you courage and hope.

I wanted to make a few spay and neuter appointments for dogs, but Ellie forestalled me by handing me a white paper bag with 'Murphy' written on it. "Here's the collar that Murphy was wearing, we had to take it off for the X-rays."

Oh, yeah, Murphy had been wearing the dirty, flat collar from when he was found in the mountains. It appeared to be covered in dried blood and was just plain nasty. I wanted to throw it directly into the trash, but didn't, on the off-chance Murphy's original owners might still be found and want it back.

"Thanks, Ellie," I said. "I'll bring in a new collar when I pick Murphy up when he's ready to go home."

We finished up with our business and I retreated to RogerDogs where I holed up behind the protective fortress of my hulking desk. I sat slumped in silence, holding my head in my hands and replaying the visit in my mind. *Betty Mills is going to shit a brick!* I thought. I had been in official charge of RogerDog Rescue for less than a day and now we were on the hook for several thousand dollars of vet care, all on the say so of little old me.

Unexpectedly, the rescue's front door flew open to crash noisily against the metal wall and I jumped almost as high as Scott had earlier in the day.

"Whoops! Sorry about that Mrs. B!" an unrepentant girl's voice rang out.

The afternoon cleanup crew of two high school teenagers had arrived.

Grace Oberlander is one of RogerDogs' paid employees, while J.J. Shepherd is completing community service work with us as part of a judicial redirection program for young Helena miscreants.

Grace sports a short haircut that includes shaved areas, and the color of the hair itself changes almost daily, according to her whims. Today it was magenta on the top, with dark blue on the sides. With a personality that matches her loud outward appearance, Grace has enough self-confidence and chutzpah for a whole army of teenagers.

J.J., on the other hand, is a skinny boy who always dresses entirely in black, with a hooded sweatshirt perpetually pulled over his head. When he first started at RogerDogs, J.J. had slunk around like a puppy who's been smacked across the nose with a rolled-up newspaper. Over the course of time, the boy had come out of his shell with both Grace and the dogs and become a valued asset to the rescue. However, he has yet to make eye contact with either myself or Betty Mills.

Grace bounced through the door and headed straight to the donut box still sitting on the round table at the side of the office. "Oh, man, there's only two left today, Scott must have been sugared up to his eyeballs!" She took a large bite from one and inadvertently squirted red jelly across her bright yellow t-shirt.

Both J.J. and I laughed out loud at the look of vexation on Grace's face as she took in her newly redecorated front.

"Hey, Grace," J.J. snorted gleefully from under his hoodie. "Put some peanut butter on your shirt, too, why don'tcha? You'll be a PBJ! The dogs will really love you, then!"

Grace amiably joined in the laughter as she wet a paper towel at the small sink and sponged jelly off her shirt. "It would be a good way to introduce myself to the new dog, I guess. What kennel is he in, Kelly? Or is he a she? I thought you were going to send us pictures last night, but, alas, none arrived." She waggled her phone at me.

I hesitated before answering. I didn't feel up to rehashing the drama of the dog's medical status quite yet.

"Oh, sorry, Grace. I did forget to send you some. Come over here, you two, and look at the ones I took last night. Right now, he's at Dr. Rex's for a checkup. You'll have to wait to meet him in the flesh."

The teenagers were as struck by Murphy's out-of-the-world eyes and wackiness of coat coloration as Boyd and I had been. We chatted for a while about their school day, Grace ebulliently and J.J. with monosyllables. They were the only teenagers in my life now, after years of seeing dozens in a day, and I treasured the time I was able to spend with them. Sometimes they would stay and do homework when they were finished cleaning, especially if there were thorny math problems to be addressed.

J.J. hung back as Grace bounded out of the office into the storeroom, on her way to the dogs in their kennels.

"Mrs. Boyd," he spoke hesitatingly. "Are you okay?"

Startled, I looked up from my computer and found J.J. regarding me from under his black hoodie with a pair of warm brown eyes. J.J. nodded slightly at me and continued. "You look a little down, kinda worried. Is everything okay?"

I was moved near to tears at the unexpected sensitivity of the boy. Habitually hidden beneath his black hoodie, I had never felt he paid any particular attention to the adults at RogerDogs. I felt a sudden burst of warm affection toward the young man.

I took a deep breath before replying.

"Dr. Rex had some bad news about the dog, but it's nothing he can't take care of. I was feeling a little overwhelmed at being in charge, that's all. Thanks for asking, J.J., I appreciate it."

"No problem, Mrs. Boyd. I'm sure you're doing a good job. Hey, let us know if there's anything me and Grace can do to help out." J.J. gave me another shy smile and exited to find Grace.

Buoyed by the unexpected interaction, I fired up my computer and jumped into my own afternoon's work with renewed cheerfulness.

FIVE

A S IT TURNED OUT, BETTY MILLS took the news about Murphy's amputation in stride, although she couldn't pass up the opportunity to razz me, growling, "Jesus, Kelly. I go home sick, and you whack a dog's leg off. Borrowed one of your husband's chainsaws, I bet. Any other dogs missing body parts?"

She had waved off the idea that RogerDogs needed monetary help from Boyd and me for Murphy's veterinarian bill. "We've got the Dependable Dozen on tap for stuff like this. As soon as Murphy is looking better, we'll send them some 'before and after' pictures, along with a little writeup. Jerk some tears while we're at it. They'll wind up covering anything above our medical care budget." The Dependable Dozen, as Betty Mills calls them, is a handful of local people who have agreed to pay one hundred dollars per individual dog to cover non-routine veterinarian care for RogerDogs. There are actually more than twelve people we can call on. Over a year's time, each donor usually covers three hundred to five hundred dollars of extra expenses for us.

Upon his return from the woods, Boyd had unexpectedly suggested that we foster Murphy at our house while he recovered but had eventually agreed that trying to keep him quiet and still in the presence of two rowdy, rough heelers wouldn't be in his best interests. Instead, Murphy spent his days in a large crate next to me in the RogerDog office where it was easy to take him out on multiple, short exercise breaks during the day. It was also easy for us all to spoil him rotten with extra attention and treats. Murphy soaked it all up.

Murphy had recently passed his last post-op checkup with flying colors. There was no sign of infection at his flap site, and Dr. Rex had been impressed with Murphy's agility as a tripod. Murphy no longer needed any support to get up on his feet, or to navigate in and out of the car.

"He's coming along great, Kelly!" Dr. Rex said with a wide smile at the checkup. He gave Murphy a friendly slap on his hindquarters, causing the dog to cavort happily around in a tight circle, while lashing our legs with his wildly whipping tail. The hair had almost grown in enough to cover his scar, and Murphy was looking like a new dog, albeit one with only three legs.

"He's raring to go, go, go, isn't he?" Dr. Rex twinkled at Murphy with his warm brown eyes. He paused as he ran his hand through his hair, rumpling his brown curls even more and causing an extra few inches of bony wrist to extend from his white lab coat. "He's ready for anything, as long as you keep him mostly on a leash."

"No worries, there, Doc," I assured him. "Easy does it for Mr. Murphy. I've got my fingers crossed for a quick adoption for him. He deserves some good luck, don't you think?"

I thought back to my conversation with Dr. Rex as I stepped through the process of uploading Murphy's photos and bio blurb, written by Grace, to the Petfinder site, a national clearinghouse for animals in need of rescue. With his ever-happy attitude and expressive blue eyes, Murphy had become the hands-down favorite of everyone at RogerDogs in his time with us. He certainly did deserve a change of luck and I looked forward to fielding enquiries about him in the upcoming October days as I uploaded his documents by close of business on September 30th.

Little did I know how quickly the first response would occur.

JUST AFTER MIDNIGHT ON THE INAUGURAL day of October, the phone rang at RogerDogs. The answering machine picked up after ten rings and recorded a time stamped message from a woman who was shouting, "You've got Rett! Damn you, that's Brianna's dog! Don't you goddamned dare give him away!" The woman, who sounded three sheets to the wind, crashed down a phone on her end, and RogerDogs went back to quiet.

SIX

SATURDAY MORNING, BETTY MILLS AND I stood by the battleship of a desk in the front office as I played the midnight message back for her. Betty was dressed in a man's green and grey flannel work shirt, well-worn jeans, and her square tipped, knee high work boots. She always wore these boots, 'in case anybody's ornery'. I had once jokingly asked if she meant the dogs or the people who came to RogerDogs, thinking I was pretty funny.

Betty Mills had fixed me with a steely look and replied, "Don't matter. Keeps my shins from being nipped and lets me kick any dumbshits in the ass that need it." Betty Mills is hard to read, would she seriously boot someone in the butt? I resolved then and there to make sure it was never a Boyd butt, in any case.

After listening to the message several times, Betty Mills grunted, "Huh, bet she was calling from a bar, she sounds pretty lit and there's lots of background noise. Erase it and ignore it. She'll have to call back when she's sober enough to explain who the hell she, Rett, and Brianna are. Bet we never hear another word." With that, Betty Mills walked into the east side kennels, sparking off a round of wild barking from the dogs.

Betty Mills would have lost her bet, though.

The first day of October proved to be an exceptionally busy

Saturday for phone calls at RogerDogs, and by noon I felt I had answered at least two hundred calls from John Q. Public. "Did we want used towels?" Yes, please. "Can I drop off a stray dog?" Yes, any time before five o'clock. "Would we take a mother cat and kittens?" No, we are dogs only; Helena's animal shelter can help you. "Would RogerDogs like a donation of ten bags of Purina dog chow?" Double yes, please! Pinching the phone constantly to my ear while I tried to get some of my usual computer work done had made my ear hot and red, and put a savage crick in my neck. All in all, I had completely forgotten about our midnight mystery caller when the phone jingled merrily for the two hundred and first time of the day.

I took a swift drink of my stone-cold tea to wet my whistle, and summoned up a cheerful, "RogerDog Rescue, this is Kelly, how can I help you?"

"I called you last night, about Rett, you still have him, don't you?" croaked a subdued version of the voice we'd heard on the answering machine. Our inebriated shouter of last night now sounded wooly headed and hungover.

"Oh, hello, yes, we did have a message about a Rett who is Brianna's dog," I toned my voice down to match the caller's. Nobody hates chirpy and cheerful more than someone feeling delicate after a hard night's carousing. "We were a little unsure, though, which dog you meant."

There was a pause on the other end of the phone. "Just a second, I saw him on Petfinder last night and I don't remember what you called him. Okay, I'm looking at Petfinder now, and . . . Murphy. You've got him listed as Murphy. I'm telling you, that's my friend's dog. How did you get him? Brianna would NEVER give that dog up!"

Shee-ooot, I thought to myself. Occasionally, someone will think they recognize a particular dog in a Petfinder posting, but with almost all these putative identifications, it's actually some other, similar dog. People always believe their pooches are uniquely identifiable, but in reality, there are a lot of identical look-a-likes out there.

"I take it your friend has a Catahoula Leopard dog? They sure are a unique breed, but between the dogs themselves, a lot of them are quite similar," I gently told the woman. "It might be that Murphy isn't Brianna's dog, but just looks kind of like him."

"No! God damn it!" The voice had abandoned its previous subdued tone and was now bellowing at me like a wounded buffalo. "Listen to me! I'm looking at a picture of Rett right here in my hand. He's got two blue eyes, set in black circles like a frigging raccoon, one ear up and one ear down, and his right front leg is solid black, all the way down to his toenails, except for two white toes in the middle. The rest of him is all grey and black and stripy and splotchy, just like that picture you have on Petfinder.

Well, hold the phone, now. I hadn't taught AP Statistics for years to not realize the import of what the woman had just told me. Each of those points she had reeled off can and do show up in other Catahoula dogs. But to have *all* six characteristics present in a single dog? That raised the probability of Murphy being Rett to a near certainty.

I squinted at the phone in my hand, while thinking of the best response. I rapidly decided that this was above my pay grade and that it was time to get Betty Mills to the front and center. It can be dicey when a claim of ownership is made without actual *proof*, like a microchip number.

The unknown woman on the phone wasn't claiming that Murphy was hers, of course, but she sounded volatile to me. If a parent had called me sounding this worked up, I would have brought in the principal in a heartbeat.

"It sounds like you must speak with our director, Betty Mills," I told the woman in my best friendly and helpful voice, designed to smooth ruffled feathers. "Let me get your name and contact information first, just in case we get cut off, and I'll see if she's available."

"You bet your ass I'll talk to the boss. In person! I'm leaving Missoula now. Be there at 15:00!" The voice informed me, at high decibels, and then the call disconnected with a little bloop. So much for smoothing feathers, and I didn't have a name for Ms. Termagant who was Brianna's-friend, or even a phone number to call her back if needed. We have caller ID for the office phone, but 'unknown number' was all that it showed.

I got up to go find Betty Mills and make battle plans for the afternoon.

SEVEN

IT WASN'T UNTIL ALMOST FOUR O'CLOCK that we heard a car door slam outside of RogerDogs. By then, we had had ample time to take precautionary measures to ensure that events stayed calm and under control. Grace Oberlander and J.J. Shepherd knew to stay in the back area of the building and that no one, dogs or people was to go outside.

"Got it, Mrs. Boyd, modified lockdown, just like at school," Grace had efficiently summarized. "J.J. and I will keep our phones at the ready, just in case we need to call 911."

Betty Mills shot her a stern look and growled, "You goddamn will NOT call 911, not unless you hear shots fired!" Being well used to Betty's gruffness, Grace simply tossed her head and gave Betty an impish grin. "Okay, okay, you're the boss. No phone calls, stay inside, keep the doors locked, we're on it."

We had moved Murphy out of the office as well, anticipating that his presence could be a catalyst for nastiness. I had made fresh coffee and laid out a plate of Nabisco vanilla cream sandwich cookies, which inspired Betty Mills to snort. "You think we're having the Queen to tea or something, Kelly? Jesus!"

Like Grace, I was too used to Betty's brusque manner to really pay her any mind. My professional experience with contentious parents had taught me that an offer of refreshments is an efficient way to take the wind out of angry sails, and usher in the use of 'company manners'.

Besides, if I was in the role of Happy Hostess, it left Betty free to be the stern administrator, sort of like a good cop, bad cop ploy.

When we heard the car door slam, I took a quick look out the front office window. A tall woman in her late twenties, wearing a dark blue canvass coat, worn blue jeans and black, lace-up boots had just exited an older model, white SUV that sported more than one dent on its body. She had shoulder-length dark hair pulled back into a tight ponytail, and a face that could be described as masculine and striking, but not pretty. She looked to be either Hispanic or Native American. Her strong, black eyebrows were currently bunched together in a ferocious squint, and her wide mouth was downturned in a scowl. The woman looked seriously angry.

She stood outside the SUV, swaying slightly for a moment, as if she were catching her balance. *Drunk? Is this woman drunk?* I thought as she began to walk to the front door with a slightly lurching gait.

Betty Mills made a thoughtful, "Huh", and moved to open the front door. Betty and the woman looked each other up and down in the doorway for a moment, and then, with a short jerk of her chin, Betty said, "Army, military police. What's your branch?" Betty received a curt nod in return, and the woman replied, "Army," with no further explanation. Didn't matter. With those few words, it was established that she, along with Betty Mills, was one of the 10% of Montanans who are veterans of armed forces, establishing an immediate bond that did not include Kelly, the ex-teacher and now Happy Hostess.

"I'm Betty Mills," Betty introduced herself. "I run this show here." She flapped a hand at me and gave a slightly sardonic grin. "This here is Kelly. She's the coffee and cookie queen for the day, and she's the one who takes care of the dog in question. Come on in and sit down and get us up to speed on what's going on." Betty indicated a floral patterned, upholstered chair that, while it had seen better days, was the most comfortable seat in the office. Betty herself sat in one of the wooden chairs at the round table.

"Kelly, pour us all some coffee," she directed me. "And pass around those cookies, why don't you?" Obligingly, the Happy Hostess sprang into action as the woman sat carefully down on her chair.

"Do you want any cream or sugar in yours . . ." I asked, letting my voice trail off a little as a way of asking the woman's name.

"No, just black. I like my coffee straight up," she answered, without any name appearing.

Once Betty and the mystery woman had coffee in hand and cookies on their plates, I served myself the same and sat down on an empty chair. No one said anything for several moments as we sipped and crunched. Time elongated, stretching out like the final minutes of school before summer vacation begins.

Finally, the woman put down her coffee cup and crumpled her napkin of cookie crumbs into the nearby wastebasket.

"My name's Cici Vargas. I'm a friend of Brianna's, Brianna Norwood's." Cici paused as she opened a picture on her phone and passed it to Betty. "That's her and Rett. You can see that Rett matches up with the PetFinder picture of the dog you call Murphy, point for point. It's got to be him!"

I scooched over in my chair so that I could see the image as well. I saw a girl, younger than Cici, sitting next to a dog that, I must admit, was a dead ringer for Murphy.

The girl had shoulder-length, dark brown hair, lit with rich chestnut highlights, professionally cut into attractive layers that framed her finely boned, heart shaped face. Brianna's slightly-tipped almond eyes exactly matched her hair in color and were framed by dark, arched brows above, and high cheekbones below. Her skin was the same shade of light brown as Cici's. In the picture, Brianna looked directly at the camera with a challenging look and her cupid bow lips were curved into a slight smile that was both sultry and dangerous, somehow conveying that those lips covered teeth, teeth that could bite.

Here then, was Titania, brought to life, feral and fey. She only lacked a set of fairy wings to be off to the races, luring away delicious young men to be her playthings. *She would eat the hearts of men*, I thought, *three at least, before breakfast.*

"What do you think, Kelly?" Betty asked. "You've spent the most time with the dog. Is that him?"

"Yeah, I think Rett and Murphy have to be the same dog," I acknowledged. "If we were to calculate the probability . . ." I started to explain the theory backing up my statement, but stopped as Betty Mills gave me a harsh, stink eye.

Not now, Kelly, her look said, with enough juice left over to convey, *not ever, either.* Sigh. No one ever appreciates the mathematician in the crowd.

Betty turned to Cici. "Well, your friend can come in anytime we're open and reclaim 'Rett', if that's what she wants to do. He's run up some hefty vet bills since he's been with us, and it'd be nice if she could put some money toward that. But, push comes to shove; she can get him back for his posted adoption fee."

With a start, Cici sat upright in her chair, and swung an agitated look from Betty to me and back to Betty again.

"Rett was hurt? How?" Clearly Cici hadn't read the bio blurb posted on Petfinder about 'Murphy', which spelled out his medical travails and recovery to a happy, tripod dog.

"Well, he'd been shot sometime before he was found down in the Crazies. His left leg was too wrecked to save, that's why he had to have it amputated," Betty said to Cici, giving a pointed look at Cici's own left leg.

Cici's features closed up like a fist as she took in the news of the dog's injuries, and she snorted a hard breath out her nose. Her face turned a dark brick red as she gripped the arms of her chair, hard, and blurted out, "Something awful has happened to Brianna!"

Betty Mills and I exchanged glances. The meeting with Cici seemed to be headed south, she was looking more and more agitated, and wasn't making a lot of sense. Was she here to pick up the dog for her friend or not? If Brianna was incapacitated for some reason and needed Cici to reclaim her dog, why not say so at the first?

Betty Mills leaned toward Cici and said in her gravelly voice, "Honey, you've lost us. Why don't you start from the top and tell us why you're here instead of Brianna, fill us in on the situation. We're not in any rush. The dog's not going anywhere, and neither are we."

Cici lurched up out of her chair, startling me. She began to pace around the small office space, clearly trying to get her emotions under control. Abruptly, she pivoted in front of Betty and began to speak.

"Look, Brianna and me were buddies in Bagram, over in Afghanistan. We drove transport trucks and got to know each other pretty well. We always hung out together if we were both on base at the same time. She was a lot of fun and didn't mind getting into trouble for it. That ended for me when the truck I was driving hit an IED and I woke up in the hospital without my leg." Cici paused with a grimace and smacked her left calf with her hand, generating a hard sound, not the fist-on-flesh noise I expected. She continued with an angry glare at Betty and me. "I don't like talking about it!"

Betty and I waited silently. No talk from us, no sir.

Cici took a deep breath and moved to sit back down in her chair. "I heard from Brianna a few times when I was in the hospital, recovering, but didn't get around to replying. I figured no one would really want to keep up with me; I was busy feeling sorry for myself. Eventually, after a lot of PT, I got a new leg and a discharge, and found myself cut loose without any real plans.

"I didn't want to go back home to De Pere, where people would know me and feel sorry for me and shit. I packed up and headed west, telling myself I could enroll in college, start over, like. That's what got me to Missoula." Cici narrowed her eyes and looked sideways at Betty Mills. "I'd been here about a year and a half when out of the blue, sometime last May, my phone rings and damned if it isn't Brianna! She was stateside now, on reserve, and had wangled my phone number out of my mom." Cici paused before continuing. "Brianna's good at getting things out of people.

"She said she was headed to California, going to live in the land of sunshine and movie stars and wanted to see me on the way." Cici stopped talking again, this time looking at me.

"Say, Kelly, can a gal get a refill on coffee?" Cici asked as she sat back down in her chair.

Once again, the Happy Hostess sprang into action, pouring refills all around and dispensing more cream cookies to all. After a few sips, Cici carried on with her tale.

"Brianna showed up in Missoula with that dog, Rett, riding shotgun in her little black sporty car. Ha! It was a joke of hers, having a Beretta riding shotgun. She named him after her service arm, you know." Cici crunched up a couple of cookies and drank some more coffee.

"Brianna and Rett stayed with me a couple of days, hashing over old times and painting the town. I had a little studio apartment then, and after a few days it seemed awfully crowded with all of us wedged in there. By then, Brianna had come to like Missoula; thought she might look for work, maybe stay a while. It didn't take her long to get a job waitressing at a fancy restaurant, the Shalimar. She said the tips were astronomical, and she was flush with cash all the time. She figured to waitress for a few months, then move up to bartending and earn even more money.

"But the thing is, she never went anywhere without Rett, I mean anywhere. If we went to a bar, a restaurant, or the Farmers Market, so did Rett. All sorts of places a dog usually doesn't get to go.

"I told you she could finagle anything out of anyone, and she even took him to work with her. Old Rett would camp out in the business office while Brianna did her job, then the two of them would roll off to the next thing. She always said, 'Cici, Rett's got my six. He's my right-hand man!'

"I didn't see her and Rett super often; but a couple of times a month, we'd get together. I knew she planned to stay through the winter, at least. I never did know where she was staying; she always just met with me somewhere. But I haven't seen or heard from her since the end of August." Cici looked earnestly at both Betty Mills and me.

"When I saw Rett's picture on PetFinder, I knew something was really wrong. I tried calling her right away but her phone's dead, won't even go to voicemail. Now you tell me that Rett was found, shot, way down in the Crazy Mountains?" Cici's eyes grew hard. "There's no way that happened to Rett without Brianna being mixed up in it, too. She'd die before she'd let anyone hurt him. If he was shot, what the hell happened to her?"

EIGHT

A HEAVY SILENCE BLANKETED THE TABLE AS we sat for a moment, digesting Cici's question. In the background, the dogs sounded a chorus of barks as Grace and J.J. worked at the afternoon cleaning chores in the back of the building. For a long moment, no one moved.

Cici abruptly smacked the table with a punishing hand, causing me to jump enough to slop coffee from my cup.

"Brianna's got to be out there still. This is nuts, I need to go look for her!" She shoved her chair back and lurched to her feet, her face angry and intense. "Show me on a map where Rett was found, maybe I can get there before dark," she demanded.

Betty Mills stirred in her chair and spoke calmly to the agitated Cici. "Sit down a second, no use going off halfcocked," she said in her gravelly voice. She waited until Cici resumed her seat, still breathing in short hard bursts. "Here's what I think. From what you say about Brianna and Rett, it seems she must've been in the Crazies, too, at least to start with. But maybe Rett ran off after some animal and got lost."

Cici leaned into Betty's space and interrupted derisively, "She wouldn't have left him there, I'm telling you!"

Betty held up a commanding hand toward Cici and barked,

"I'm not done! Just listen up, will you? We're on your side, girl."

Cici sank back in her chair and muttered an apology. "Go on," she grudgingly added.

"There's a campground right at the trailhead to those falls. We can call the Forest Service office that's in charge of it; they must have people working there pretty much every day. They'll be able to tell us if Brianna's hunkered down there trying to find Rett, or maybe her car is abandoned in the parking lot because she never made it off the mountain. If that's the case, we can get a serious search party started right now, from here."

Betty Mills paused and looked us each in the eye before continuing.

"We're going to do three things, right now. Cici, you need to get face to face with the dog and make sure he's really who you think he is. I'm going to call up the Forest Service and see if they have any intel about Brianna. Kelly, you've got the schoolmarm voice that sounds so nice and official. Why don't you call up the restaurant where Brianna was working and see what you can wiggle out of them about her?"

Betty Mills pointed a finger at Cici to forestall any protests.

"I know you don't think Brianna could be in Missoula if Rett was in the Crazies, but sometimes people surprise us. If she's working, then she's not missing. We need to check that out." She pushed her chair back and stood up commandingly. "Okay, let's do it. Cici, come with me and we'll go see Rett. Kelly, get cracking on the restaurant."

Clearly, I was assigned my mission. I pulled out my phone and did a quick Google search to find the restaurant's number, and excused myself to my car, to get away from the barking.

Fifteen minutes later, I was waiting at the table, munching a final cookie, when Betty Mills re-entered the room from the back. She was by herself.

"Well, the dog is Rett, for sure. Cici opened the door to the kennel, and it was the damndest thing, Kelly. As soon as he saw her, that dog came crawling across the floor, just crying. She got herself down on the floor with him and Rett wormed his way up onto her lap, yammering to beat the band. He sounded like a toddler talking, and it went on and on. I swear he was telling her all about what happened to him and Brianna. Cici was, well, she was bawling, not to put too fine a point on it. I think seeing him without a leg hit home with her own amputation. We'll just leave her and Rett by themselves until she's ready for more human company. What did you find out from the restaurant, Kelly?"

"I got through to the manager and he was willing to tell me that she dropped out of sight early in September. He was miffed that she didn't give them any notice, just didn't come in to work on September 8ᵗʰ, when she was scheduled. Interestingly, she never even came in to collect her final wages. What about the Forest Service? Did you get ahold of them yet?"

Betty Mills sat across the round table from me and absently broke a cookie apart in her hands. She inspected the cream filling for a moment.

"Yeah, I did. Nothing to go on from them. No car parked long term at the trailhead, no woman living in the campground looking for a dog. Nobody's reported either a dog or a woman missing. I ran our situation by the gal that answered the phone, but she didn't agree that a lost dog equates with a missing owner. She says dogs get lost along the trail all the time, no big deal that Rett was found wandering on his own. She thought it was sad that he'd been shot, but it didn't surprise her. It's not exactly unusual for rural Montana.

"I also checked on the weather forecast, Kelly. You know, it's been real nice so far this fall. No snow yet, but the weather people say that's going to change after a couple of days for the Crazies, up to a foot of snow expected in the mountains. If any searching for this Brianna is going to happen, it should be soon.

"The authorities clearly aren't going to launch a search party just based on the dog. Unlike Cici, they don't believe Brianna's missing in the area, not without her car sitting around, or some other evidence she's lost out there." Betty ate the cookie and took a swig of her now-cold coffee.

"Seems to me, we should go down to the Crazies, tomorrow even, take a look around, see what we can see. We'll take Rett, too, maybe he can steer us in the right direction. If we find a backpack or anything else belonging to her, well, that would be enough to get an official search started.

"Cici's going to go for sure, there'll be no stopping her. I'm not going to let a fellow vet go on her own, especially one with mobility issues. Tomorrow's Sunday, so RogerDogs will be closed; I can get Randy to feed the dogs in the afternoon. What do you think, Kelly? You up for a wild goose chase? You could come along, with your heelers, too."

She tipped her head back and looked down her nose at me, her eyes narrowed in challenging speculation.

I stared at her, momentarily nonplussed. Had a gauntlet just thudded on the floor?

With her colorful background and gruff, commanding ways, Betty Mills is the antithesis of Kelly Boyd, retired schoolteacher. Secretly, I view her as my alter ego and have relished involvement in our shared, rescue-based exploits. We've become good friends over the last couple of years, I think. But I'd never before been invited to join in with her on a non-rescue adventure.

Was this a test of my mettle? If I declined, would I be dismissed in Betty's mind as a timid mouse of a retired lady? It seemed so, based on the look she had shot my way.

Even though it seemed like a harebrained scheme, I found myself in full agreement that yes, indeedy, Kelly Boyd wanted to be part of the action. I wasn't ready to take up residence in a rocking chair on my front porch, no, sir!

"I'm in!" I exclaimed and traded a high five with Betty across the table. After all, what could be wrong with a day spent in the Montana outdoors with two, kick-ass women, even if chances of finding a trace of the missing Brianna were slim to none?

NINE

Our impromptu search party left early Sunday morning on October 2nd, while the world was still cloaked in pre-dawn grayness, off on an expedition to the east side of the Crazy Mountains, where Rett had been picked up by hikers back in mid-September.

The Crazy Mountains are an island range set in southwest Montana, to the north of Yellowstone National Park. Their jagged, rocky peaks rise like a shout into the open blue sky and form a memorable landmark to many Montanans. No one knows for sure how they came to be named the Crazy Mountains, but most stories involve violence and insanity. The pathways into the mountains themselves are steep, twisty and full of hard to transverse cobblestones. It is not unusual for even highly experienced hunters to become disoriented and lost in their environs. Some disappear forever, leading credence to the superstitious theories that the mountain range is the domain of evil spirits.

The sun was well up in a clear, blue mid-morning sky, with only some high, scattered clouds to the west when we pulled into the trailhead to the falls along Big Timber creek. There was a light breeze blowing down off the mountains, cold enough to warrant a jacket, but the weather for the day was supposed to hold clear, and warm up maybe even to the mid-forties. The fresh scent of pines and sagebrush met us as we climbed out of the jeep and leashed up Rett. From the nearby trees a Clark's nutcracker called loudly as it flew to a new perch.

Rett needed to walk at the more sedate pace of we people, and not wear himself out tearing around off leash, as Sadie and Leo were doing. Also, if returning to the place sparked memories with him, we didn't want him to charge off on his own and lose us in the dust, taking our best chance of finding Brianna with him.

We had a general plan to walk up the trail toward the falls, and then to branch off to the north before we got too high into the trees. The notes from the people who found Rett had mentioned that they were close to the trailhead when they first saw him, but that he was in a meadow area off the path. Basically, we planned to bash around looking for clues, hoping that the dogs, Rett especially, would give us some help.

I had a few doubts as to how well this expedition would go, what with having two amputees involved. Neither Cici nor Rett had done any hiking since they had their mobility reduced; Rett especially was still making his way back physically from his surgery. The official hiking path itself posed challenges with rocks, roots and steep grade, but when we begin exploring off trail? Maybe Cici would have to park herself on a log or rock and wait for us. The whole idea that we would somehow find even a trace of Brianna seemed awfully farfetched.

But, I conceded, we had to try, for Cici's peace of mind.

Three hours later, just past noon, we were picking our way along the base of a talus slope, over a mile to the north of the actual trail. We weren't venturing up on the rockslide at all, that would clearly be more than either Cici or Rett could handle, the terrain was challenging enough for them at the base. We were all tired and cranky and in need of some food when we broke out of the pine trees into a sun-filled meadow.

"Break time, ladies," I said in my most gruff, sergeant major voice. "We need some sustenance; sandwiches, chocolate, water, and more chocolate, that's an order!"

We picked out individual seats on rocks in the warm sunshine, and Betty Mills and I dug food out of our daypacks. I had made us all lavishly thick sandwiches stuffed with roast beef and provolone cheese on crusty Panini bread. The sandwiches were accompanied by Fritos corn chips, and the whole lunch topped off with copious amounts of chocolate chip cookies. Salt, sugar, fat and protein, that's what would power us through our day. Other food groups, like cold beer, would have to wait until we got back to the jeep.

Cici's face was pinched with pain that she was trying hard not to show. Her stump must be playing up, maybe even getting blisters from her artificial leg, just like feet do with a poorly fitting boot. This meadow might be as far as we could go in our hunt for Brianna, if Cici and Rett were going to be able to make it back to the jeep. Rett was still going strong, it seemed, but without any indication that he was in Brianna search mode. In my imagination, I had seen him lift his nose as soon as we exited the jeep, and lead us into the woods, baying like a bloodhound until we found . . . a clue. Even in my head, I didn't want us to find a dead body.

As we chowed down, Sadie and Leo chased each other around through the green and gold grasses, occasionally flushing small birds into the air that Leo tried hard to catch. Maybe those were white-crowned sparrows, late in leaving for the fall migration, I mused, not bothering to put my binoculars on them to find out for sure.

Moving away from us to the far end of the meadow, the dogs found a mound of dirt that they began to investigate. They began alternately stuffing their heads into whatever burrow there was, and digging furiously to make the opening larger.

Rett, who I had let off leash when we reached the meadow, had lurched along with them, but he abruptly turned and made his way back to us, whining. He went straight to Cici, and in a replay of yesterday, threw himself down beside her, with his head on her legs, and began the odd yammering that Betty Mills had described to me.

Cici rubbed behind his ears, and crooned that he was a good boy in an attempt to sooth the dog. But instead of settling down, Rett seemed to become more and more agitated. He lumbered back up to a standing position, and began bumping repeatedly against Cici's legs, almost like a boat tied up at a pier, rocked by waves into the pilings. All the while he kept up his strange-sounding cries.

Betty Mills narrowed her dark brown eyes at Rett, and proclaimed, "You know, I think he's trying to paw at you, but can't get it done with only three legs. Why do you think he's so bent out of shape all of a sudden?"

An alarming suspicion flared in my brain and I quickly swiveled my head, looking for Sadie and Leo.

They were still across the meadow from us, enthusiastically digging near the rocks.

Why? Digging for what? They normally didn't dig, other than to make beds in the dirt. I stood up and made my way toward the dogs, a terrible suspicion growing in my mind.

Leo glanced up at me as I drew closer and shot me a doggy grin. He hunched up his back and danced around their excavation, shooting glances of gleeful naughtiness at me. This is classic Leo behavior when he has a forbidden item in his mouth such as small ball, a squeaker from a dog toy, or a bone snatched from the garbage.

There were no dog toys in the meadow, but was there a bone?

As I got closer to the dogs, I caught a whiff of decay, confirming my hunch that Leo likely had a bone from a dead *something* in his mouth. Ice-water seemed to pour down my spine as I struggled with the idea it might possibly be from Brianna.

Shit. We needed that bone back.

I abruptly changed direction and threw torn pieces of my sandwich around the area in rapid fire fashion. Sadie immediately abandoned the digging and rushed to eat as many pieces as she could before Leo got into the action.

Leo looked at me suspiciously but was unable to resist joining Sadie in a wild scramble for sandwich bits. Fortunately, he dropped his contraband item on the ground rather than swallowing it for safekeeping.

I swooped in and snatched up a small bone, hiding it behind my back as Sadie and Leo finished their sandwich search.

Things went from super-focused slo-mo to rapid and blurry after that. Betty Mills wanted to move rocks near the badger hole, 'to see what's there'. I protested, on account of not wanting to disturb crime scene evidence.

"Kelly, I know you think that bone of Leo's is a finger bone," she sparked at me with aggravation. "And maybe it is. But it might be a chicken bone from someone's lunch, and the dead smell is just from a rotten marmot or something. No one from Search and Rescue or the sheriff's office wants to come all the way out here if that's the case!"

Cici, who had wandered away from us as Betty and I continued to argue, gave a sudden hoarse cry. "Hey! Hey, Betty, Kelly! Get over here!" she shouted. "I can see some clothing!"

Cici was on top of some boulders at the edge of the talus slope, directing the beam of a small high-powered flashlight down between the rocks. She made room for us alongside her as we scrambled up to her location.

"Look down there, just through the rocks, along the light. Do you see it?"

Betty Mills gave a soft grunt. "Yeah, yeah I do. There's some red flannel showing, and I see some more bones," she said. "Do you see it, Kelly?"

I didn't, being at a different angle—but I didn't need to. The finger bone and the ever-heavier smell of decomposition were enough to convince me that a human body was present.

Betty Mills nodded sharply. "Time to call the sheriff, ladies!"

UNFORTUNATELY, BRINGING IN THE OFFICIAL INVESTIGATORS wasn't as easy as punching in 911 from our cell phones. No bars were available at our little meadow in the mountains, meaning at least one person needed to retreat back to the jeep, and maybe drive some distance toward civilization to where cell reception was once again a reality.

"Cici, you and Kelly go back to the jeep; here are the keys in case you need to go somewhere to make a call. Get the powers that be to haul ass up here, take the dogs with you, too. Kelly, you're going to have to lead the people back up here, do you have anything to mark the path, better than bread crumbs?" Betty Mills commanded us with a resurrected military police voice that brooked no argument.

Resisting the urge to salute, I assured her that I was marking a waypoint with my phone. Before she could tell me off about the evils of relying on electronics alone, I hurriedly added, "And I'll tie off flagging on trees, every so often, just so the way is crystal clear."

Cici protested that she wanted to stay onsite, but the military police overrode her.

"By the time the officials uncover whoever that is, and we don't know for sure it's Brianna, even, it's going to be long past dark and cold. Hiking out then, after the work we've done already is going to be hard enough for twoleggers. None of us is going to leave until this show gets closed out, but Cici, you can do best for Brianna to be in command of the trailhead. Kelly here knows how to organize a classroom, but she's just a civilian, and she ain't ever been in charge of something like this, with all the boots that are going to hit the ground. You take Kelly with you, and get back down to where you can call this in. Then you stay there to be in charge of incoming personnel."

I silently applauded Betty Mills' diplomacy in getting Cici to agree to return to the trailhead even as I fumed inwardly over her exact tactics. I'd like to see either one of these army women be in charge of a classroom filled with excitable teenagers. Ha! Then we'd see who was better at working with whom!

TEN

IT WAS PAST TWO O'CLOCK SUNDAY afternoon when I was finally able to contact 911 via my cellphone. Cici and Rett had both moved slowly on the way out, and phone reception didn't improve until we had driven over ten miles back toward the highway from the trailhead.

As expeditiously as possible, I informed the 911 operator that we had found a murder victim's body and needed the police. What police, I hadn't a clue, that's what the 911 person was for. It was a frustrating conversation, but in the end, it was clear that we were to wait at the trailhead parking for the first responders. I still didn't have the slightest idea who these first responders would be, but I guessed I didn't really need to know.

Cici and I fed the dogs from a stash of food in the back of Betty Mills' jeep, and powered ourselves up with granola bars that remained in our packs. Personally, I wanted a lot more than granola bars as most of my sandwich had been used as a dog lure, but that's all there was.

Then we waited. Almost an hour later, a dark gray Ford pickup rolled into the parking lot, and a single, white male, maybe in his early thirties hopped out of the cab. He was dressed for the outdoors, sporting an orange, Gortex-looking shell, a dark blue watch hat, blue jeans, and leather hiking boots that had many miles on them. We watched as he pulled a large pack out of the truck, shouldered it, and walked our way. I figured he was a solo backpacker, headed out to spend some time in the mountains, maybe to scope out hunting areas for the upcoming fall season, just as Boyd and his friends had so recently done.

However, he walked as far as the jeep and stopped, giving us and the dogs a look over. After a moment, the dark-haired man introduced himself, "Hello, I'm Jake McDonald, with the Sweetgrass Search and Rescue. I'm looking to meet up with a Kelly Boyd and Cici Vargas, would that be you?"

I was completely taken aback that our 911 call had resulted in a single SAR person. I had envisioned multiple police cars, with lights and sirens, even an ambulance for transporting Brianna's body thrown in, and a crew of maybe ten or so personnel to go into the woods and investigate the shit out the site. One glance at Cici's thunderous face told me that she, too, was not impressed with the official response.

Before I could say anything, she angrily burst out, "Where the hell are the rest of you! Didn't you hear Kelly say that there's a *murder victim* in the woods? Jesus! I know this is Montana, but it's got to be more than one person's job to show up when someone's been killed!"

Jake took a step back from the angry Cici, and drew in a deep breath. "Ma'am," he said in a calm voice, "I am but the tip of the iceberg, I assure you." Gesturing toward the logs that lined the edge of the parking area as defacto parking lot bumpers, Jake McDonald continued, "Let's take a seat for just a moment and I'll fill you in on what's happening."

Once we all had sat down on a log, Jake gave us a run down. We learned that the Crazy Mountains are surrounded by three separate counties, and that while jurisdiction for a crime would belong to the county it was physically located in, all of the county sheriff departments and search and rescue operations supported each other on callouts. By sheer bad timing, our call about finding a body had come in after two separate, earlier cries for help: two canoeists had flipped in the Yellowstone River, but only one had made it to shore, and a small child had wandered off during a family outing on the northwest side of the mountains.

"So, you see," Jake wrapped up, "we're spread really thin today. I'm here to verify that there is indeed a body, and from there, get the area tarped and secured until necessary personnel can arrive. I do have a satellite phone, so I'll be able to communicate with the Sweetgrass Sheriff from the site." He looked seriously from Cici to me. "Ladies, I don't doubt for a second that you have found a body, just as you say. But with the day we're having, you can see why we aren't pulling active searchers off the lost boater or child until we have more information to go on."

"Alright, then," I said. "Let's get going. Cici is going to stay here with the dogs. She can meet anyone else who comes in and get them directed to the clearing." Cici had reluctantly agreed to this plan during our wait in the trailhead parking lot. Neither she nor Rett were able to do more hiking. Sadie and Leo, while willing and able, were definitely not needed back at the body's location. Bad enough the one bone had spent time in Leo's mouth.

It turned out that Jake McDonald had long legs and wasn't afraid to use them. All my visions of leading him back through the woods to the little meadow evaporated like water hitting a hot frying pan, as he marched along at a pace that had me jogging to keep up in the rear. I felt like a short-legged Corgi dog, out for too brisk of a walk. I just concentrated on keeping up.

Between the GPS coordinates of Betty Mills' location, and the flagging I had tied along the way, Jake McDonald didn't need a bit of help from me, anyway. Twenty-five minutes after leaving the parking lot, we were back at the meadow, and I was panting like an overweight puppy.

Betty Mills strode across the clearing to greet us. She had become chilled while waiting for the troops to arrive, and was now bundled in her black puffy jacket and red wool stocking cap.

"You have to drive all the way to Big Timber to get a signal, Kelly?" she queried me as she faced Jake McDonald and stuck out a gloved hand in greeting. "I'm Betty Mills, glad to see you," she said, raising an eyebrow and giving him squinty eyes, making her face loudly say what her words didn't: "and where the HELL are the rest of you?" She curled her lip at him in a decided sneer that made him stiffen and flare his nostrils. He was about to reply when I jumped into the conversation, aiming to divert both parties before things got contentious. I said in a rush, "This is Jake McDonald, Sweetgrass Search and Rescue, Betty. He's the lead responder to the rest of the crew he's going to call in with his satellite phone once he sees exactly what we found." Without pausing for breath, I turned to include Jake. "So let's do the official look, Jake. The body's over here in the rocks." At that, I marched straight to the opening we had found and pointed downwards. "There, you can see her shirt, right there, if you look with the flashlight."

My words and actions successfully dampened the pissing contest that had been developing between Jake McDonald and Betty Mills. Betty gave him one last hard look before crossing to the rocks and me.

"I did a little more looking while you were gone, Kelly. You can see her hair from over here," Betty said, shining her flashlight up and under a different section of rocks.

Jake McDonald carefully looked at both the visible hair, and the patch of red flannel we had seen earlier. Jake's gray-green eyes narrowed as he looked carefully at the talus slope, and the rocks which were covering the remainder of the body.

"Can I see the hand bone you said you found?" he asked, looking between Betty Mills and myself.

I resisted a school teacher's urge to correct his 'can' to a more proper 'may', and dug the bone, encased in a Ziploc sandwich bag doing double duty as an evidence bag, out of my pack.

"Here you go. We found it in the dirt pile at the mouth of that badger hole," I said, pointing to the spot and hoping that Betty would follow my lead and not tell him the bone had spent time swishing around in Leo's mouth.

Jake took the baggy and pulled the plastic taut to get a good look at the bone inside. After peering at it from all angles, he gave a small grunt and set his pack down on the ground. Safely securing the bone in a top pouch, Jake rummaged in the main pack and pulled out a handheld gizmo that looked like a walkie-talkie from my childhood.

"Kelly and Betty, since this is, as of now, an active body recovery mission, I need to call for additional troops. I told Kelly and your friend in the parking lot that all the county search and rescues and sheriffs' departments have their hands full today with prior emergencies. I do agree that this is most likely a crime scene. That person didn't get covered up by rocks in any avalanche. There's just no innocent explanation for a body to be hidden the woods like this.

"The sheriff, Tom Landry, needs to be brought up to speed. Since there's a body involved, either Sheriff Landry or Deputy Darla Shaw will have to come to the site; they're the two coroners for the county and the body can't be moved without their say-so. A crime scene crew will come out to work the scene. Once the body is released, Search and Rescue will most likely do the physical transport down to the trailhead. From there, the body will probably go to Billings, to the State Medical Examiner's office for identification and investigation."

"I'll ask Sheriff Landry, but I don't think it'll be necessary for you to stay here. The sheriff's department will need statements, of course, but those most likely don't have to be taken onsite."

"We're not leaving until Brianna does!" Betty interrupted Jake McDonald's little speech with a brusque outburst and a poke to the front of his coat with her index finger. "Brianna's an army vet, same as Cici and me, and we don't leave a comrade behind in the field!" Now Jake received two jabs with the index finger.

Jake took a short step away from Betty Mills and held up his hands in a calming gesture as he spoke to us in a voice of amused approval, "Whoa, now, ladies, if you're up for it, you can be some real help. I need four people to man the rescue cart that we'll use to take the body out. If you two are willing, I'll need to pull less searchers off of the ongoing callouts."

Betty crossed her arms and gave Jake McDonald a ferocious glare. "Of course we're up for it, jackass, didn't you hear me? *No one gets left behind!*" she spat, and with that simple sentence committed civilian Kelly Boyd to the army mantra as well. I could already hear Boyd in my mind yelling that once again, I was letting Betty Mills involve me in a harebrained escapade. I mentally flipped my inner Boyd the bird and banished him from my thoughts.

We stood in the fading sunlight as Jake McDonald dialed up Sheriff Tom Landry of Sweetgrass County. After a lengthy conversation, punctuated with "Yes Sirs", "No Sirs", and including explanations of location and logistics with only a slight mention of unruly women, Jake signed off. He stood with his head down for a moment, looking at the toes of his brown leather boots as if there were directions written on them that needed to be deciphered before he spoke again. Betty Mills and I looked at each other in puzzlement and shuffled our own boots in growing impatience.

"Well, what's the plan, Stan?" barked Betty Mills after a long moment had passed. "Is the cavalry coming, or what?"

Jake McDonald gave himself a small shake and came out of his boot top reverie. "Sorry, just trying to corral all the moving parts in my mind."

"First things first," Jake told us in a serious tone. "Sheriff said to get ourselves and your stuff out of the clearing; he wants to treat this area as the initial crime scene. He's rounding up two of his deputies and a crime scene technician to come up here as soon as possible. Deputy Shaw will be the acting coroner on site. The aim is to get the body uncovered and transported tonight, collecting whatever evidence they can. Someone will stay with the scene overnight; a more detailed search of the area will take place tomorrow in the daylight.

"My crew will do the actual transport of the body from here to the trailhead, once all the t's are crossed and i's dotted by the coroner and the crime scene guys. The sheriff agrees that you two can help with that effort. In any event, he doesn't want you three to leave the trailhead until one of the deputies has a chance to interview you, which might not be anytime soon.

"I need to organize a couple SAR crew for body recovery, and to bring sandwiches and hot drinks to the trailhead, but then you can use the sat-phone to make calls, so no one gets worried about you back home."

Betty Mills and I cleared the area of things we had brought in with us, making sure any granola bar wrappers, etc. weren't left behind to waste the time of the crime scene techs. All three of us retreated from the clearing to a nearby wide spot along the route we had used to get here from the official USFS trail to the falls. There, Betty and I settled our butts onto a nearby downed tree and waited for our chance at the satellite phone.

ELEVEN

IT WAS LONG PAST DARK BEFORE the body of a woman, assumed to be Brianna's, was ready to be moved from the burial site. Two members of Jake's Search and Rescue team, a Jake look-alike whose name was Brad and a tall, Nordic looking woman in her mid-twenties named Jenny, had brought hot sandwiches and coffee up to the staging area, along with a litter basket and a folded up wheeled cart. With these, Jake informed us, it would be easy to move the body back to the trailhead, where an ambulance would take over.

Unlike on television, where crime scenes are processed in a few minutes, so that murders can be solved before the end of the TV hour, the minutia of details that had to be attended to in order to generate properly collected clues made for a slow process. Workers had to be suited up in Tyvek, rocks had to be swabbed down for DNA, all those swabs had to be placed in properly labelled evidence bags, and so on, ad infinitum.

There were two evidence collectors at work, both men, and one deputy, a woman, overseeing the process. They had been introduced to Betty Mills and me, but their names evaporated from my memory as soon as I heard them. My mind had hit the point of information overload for the day, and I was getting quite cold.

We weren't so far removed from the clearing that we couldn't watch them work. I silently wondered how annoyed the clue-takers would be if I asked them to uncover the body first and let us get on our way, and then go back and meticulously wipe down each and every rock. Really, would that change anything?

Betty Mills must have seen my thoughts on my face. She rose stiffly to her feet from where she had been sitting on a log, wrapped in a space blanket, and poured me a still steaming cup of coffee from a thermos.

"Hey, Kelly. You were a math teacher, so this joke's for you: What do you get when you cross a dog and a calculator? . . . A friend you can count on!"

This sparked a round of the dumb jokes people tell around a campfire, with contributions from Jake, Brad, Jenny and me, to make the time go faster. Our laughter at the last installment had just petered out when an anonymous Tyvek-covered tech approached from the clearing. My face burned with a guilty flush and I hoped we hadn't been overheard, laughing it up at the edge of a murder investigation.

The white-suited figure pulled their face mask down and announced, "We're ready to load up the body bag, and we need the basket. We'll walk her out to you when we're set."

Once the basket was handed over to the tech, Brad, Jenny and Jake turned their headlamps on and grabbed the folded-up wheeled cart that they had brought with them. They quickly and smoothly unfolded it into a cart balanced on two, in-line bicycle wheels, appended front and back with rubber grip handles for steering. I was impressed at how easily the process went; not a single frustrated curse word was needed in its assembly. I made a mental note to josh Boyd over that when I got home; no Boyd projects ever went off without imaginative and vulgar cursing as a notable component.

The sheriff's deputy, Starla? Marla? Karla?, I couldn't remember, and the two techs walked the loaded Stoke basket over to the staging area and stood back as the Search and Rescue crew attached it firmly to the cart. The woman's body, ensconced within a body bag, didn't look to be much bigger than myself. It looked lonely, inconsequential and sad, I thought, and I wanted to pat it in reassurance, but was pretty sure my hand would be sharply smacked if I tried.

The deputy informed us that an ambulance was enroute to collect the body at the trailhead; the state medical examiner would take over once the body got back to the morgue in Billings.

"A second deputy, Andy DuPries, is going to meet you," she looked at Betty Mills and me, "along with your friend at the trailhead, and get statements from you all. After that, you'll be free to leave."

The woman deputy, who had double duty as county coroner, and her crime scene techs, all stood at attention as the five of us jockeyed for position around the cart and began to move across the rough terrain toward the trailhead. Betty Mills and Jake McDonald had control of the front handles, while Brad and Jenny handled the rear two spots. As for me? Kelly was the poky little puppy tripping along in the back, yet again.

The ambulance and Deputy DuPries were waiting for us when we reached the trailhead for the last time that day. The wheeled cart made the job of moving the body out of the woods much easier than if we had been carrying the loaded litter, but it was still a difficult process getting from the clearing back to the developed Forest Service trail. Even with headlamps, bushwhacking at night over terrain filled with bushes, tree roots, rocks, and holes made for slow going for the crew. Once we regained the dirt trail leading back to the waiting cars, we cruised along like we were in the Indy-500, back up to jogging pace for me and my short legs. Was I ever going to be stiff and sore tomorrow!

Angry, raised voices suddenly ricocheted through the dark trees as we approached the final hundred yards to the trailhead.

"You're nothing but a goddamned, pencil-pushing prick, Deputy DuPries. You try to cuff me and I'll kick your ass to Kansas!"

TWELVE

WE ESCAPED FROM OUR OFFICIAL ENCOUNTER with Deputy DuPries without any of us intrepid ladies or our hounds being thrown into the clink, but it was a close call.

Deputy Andy DuPries had ruffled Cici's feathers by refusing to take information from her about Brianna, as it wasn't a known fact that the body we had found was actually hers. Uptight Andy, as we referred to him in the jeep on the way home, was a strictly linear thinker; if the Sheriff or Deputy Shaw, acting in their role of coroner, hadn't established the identity of the corpse, then it was out of line and a waste of time for him to collect information about a girl who was 'only' missing.

"Yeah, I got a little hot when the peckerhead told me that it was the coroner's job to establish identity, and that if they wanted my help, then they would ask me. Asshole! I was right *there*; maybe I could've identified her if I could've seen her.

"No, ma'am, we can't contaminate the evidence, ma'am; identification will have to wait, ma'am," Cici imitated Deputy DuPries in a high pitched, snarky voice. "That's when I dropped my pants and invited him to take a picture of my butt," Cici let out a shout of laughter. "You should've seen his face! He pursed up his lips like an old lady sucking on a lemon, and whipped his

shiny little handcuffs out and told me I was arrested for inde-
cent exposure."

Cici made round, innocent eyes at us before continuing, "I just
thought he'd like to collect some evidence himself, being so keen
and all. If the 'unidentified remains' do or don't sport a matching butt tattoo, then it's easy to make the call whether we found
Brianna or not. It could be the picture that broke the case, and I
thought Uptight Andy would be proud to supply such crucial evidence to the coroner."

Betty Mills glanced over the seat at me, her eyes lit up with a
mischievous glint, before saying, "Go on; tell us about this butt tattoo that almost got your decorated ass thrown in jail, girl."

"Well, you know, Brianna and I would let our hair down a
little when we were both on base, in Bagram. Sometimes we'd rile
up the MP's a bit with our, ahem, escapades," Cici lifted her chin
toward ex-MP Betty Mills and gave a small smirk. "One time,
after we'd spent a few days in the stockade, Brianna said to me,
'We're like those birds, Cici, that rise again when their asses get
turned to ashes. We always bounce back, better than before.' She
was right, you know, that was us to a T. We got inked with matching phoenix tattoos on our left butt cheeks the next day," Cici
finished with a guffaw.

In the next heartbeat, her face twisted in on itself, and she drew
a ragged breath filled with pain. "Only not this time, Brianna, baby,
you didn't make it back this time!" Cici plunged her head into her
hands and began to spasmodically knead her face as a high pitched,
keening cry filled the jeep.

In a big screen movie, this kind of distress from the heroine
would spark a touching scene between the strong-hearted dogs
and the girl with the wounded soul. Doggie heads would be laid on
her lap, while gentle eyes and tongues washed over her face, assuring her that they would never let her down. A paw or two might be
softly placed on her hand to be held while she cried her tears, and
powerfully poignant music would swell in the background.

In reality, Sadie and Leo acted as if Cici's wail was the death cry of a rabbit, meaning that they were missing out on a kill scene in the front seat. Unleashing sharp staccato barks, the two heelers simultaneously tried to surge through the space between the front seats. Fortunately, they jammed each other up in a rendition of Laurel and Hardy, and were unable to reach the Cici bunny. Frustrated, they fell back on the tried-and-true Sadie and Leo backup plan—bite each other. They flashed into a growling, snapping, shrieking ball of fur that was half on my lap and half in-between Betty Mills and Cici. Rett, slower to get to the party, wallowed across my lap from the other side, baying wildly in everybody's ears, just in case we needed to be alerted to the dogfight.

What a shit show!

I yanked hard on Rett's collar and sent him sprawling down into the seat-well at my feet, getting him away from the heeler duo before they had a chance to put teeth on him. Sadie and Leo fought together like this multiple times, every day, and while they sounded like furies of hell unleashed, they didn't generally bite each other hard enough to make blood flow. Add the unknown quantity of Rett to the mix, though, and all bets were off. The three dogs could easily ratchet into a full-blown, no-bites-barred dog fight, with me smack in the middle as collateral damage.

Betty jerked the jeep to a hard stop at the side of the road, as I hollered at Sadie and Leo, keeping my grip on Rett's collar and using my knees to keep him blocked into the seat-well.

Sulkily, Sadie and Leo sank back onto the back seat; Leo putting himself into time out down on the floor, facing the door in order to avoid eye contact with me.

"Kelly, you all in one piece back there?" Betty Mills looked over her shoulder at me. "Things were a little *exciting* there for a moment," she said in a tone of dry amusement.

Cici was looking back at me as well, with a look of shock on her tear-streaked face. "Jesus! Did they bite you? What the hell happened? That was like Fatal Fury for dogs!" The raucous fight had sucked the grief for her lost buddy back inside Cici as if it had never happened.

"Oh, they're just tired and had a little temper-tantrum," I casually said, not wanting to clue her in that the heelers had been on their way to her location the front seat, in full-attack mode. "Rett thought he should jump into action, but we're all settled now. No blood, no foul!"

I gave Betty Mills and Cici my best bright, confident smile. Judging from the dubious looks I got in return, I wasn't at my most convincing, but Betty Mills got the jeep back on the road, heading toward home without further discussion.

We rode along in the dark, with only the shushing of the wheels on the road for sound. I was replaying the day in my thoughts, getting my mind wrapped around the fact that we had indeed found the body of a dead woman, which to be honest, freaked me out more than a little, when the gravelly voice of Betty Mills spoke again.

"Hell, we know that body we just found is Brianna's. Why should we wait until some coroner pulls his finger out and confirms her ID with dental work or DNA with the army? It's been weeks since she was killed, and each day is just that much more on the side of *too long* without anyone trying to figure out what happened!" Betty shot looks at Cici and me, lingering long enough on me in the back seat to make me nervous for her driving. "I think that the three of us can get some answers before those imbeciles dot all the i's and cross all the t's that let them begin a proper, orderly investigation." This last bit was said in a high pitched, prissy tone as Betty Mills quoted Uptight Andy's speech to us. "Jesus, he got up my nose, the officious little prick!"

"Cici, you can stay in the bunkhouse at my place, and we can use RogerDogs as our private eye office, don't you think?" Betty cocked an eyebrow and looked at Cici and me for agreement. I wasn't sure exactly what I was agreeing to, but that didn't seem to matter at the moment—showing solidarity did. I leaned forward over the seat and, put my fist out, loudly intoning, "For Brianna!" Betty Mills and Cici stacked fists on top of mine and joined in a second round of "Brianna!" as the jeep moved through the Montana darkness toward home.

Thirteen

I T WAS A SLUGGISH TRIO THAT sat in the office of RogerDogs Monday afternoon. None of us had gotten much sleep the night before, what with arriving home past midnight, staying up to fill in our domestic partners, and difficulty sleeping once we had laid our heads down. Rett had gone to the bunkhouse with Cici instead of returning to his usual kennel at RogerDogs, with the thought that he and Cici would be good company for each other. Turned out that Rett is a bed hog when given the chance, and a restless one to boot.

"He snores, and farts, too! I tried to get him out of the bed a bunch of times, but he'd just give me a blast of his baby blues, and lay there like a big, dumb post, until I'd give up and try to get back to sleep." Cici nudged the big dog in his ribs as he napped on a braided rug by her chair. Rett popped his bluer than blue eyes open and rolled them around to look at us all, while slapping his tail against the floor in a desultory fashion.

"What a fool," Cici fondly scolded him, and Rett's tail whapped harder.

I had come to RogerDogs armed with a list of Brianna-related questions that Boyd and I had come up with over coffee that morning, and had imagined that we would spend the day focused on answering these, along with any others that cropped up. Didn't happen, though, at least not right away. I read a lot of crime mystery books and in none of them have the intrepid investigators been bogged down for hours with the nitty gritty of dealing with a full house of rescue dogs. RogerDogs that day was as busy as a Macy's Christmas sale, with dogs being adopted out and new dogs brought in, sometimes simultaneously passing in the front office. I felt dizzy by the early afternoon, as if I had spent my day locked in a fast moving, never-stopping, revolving door. Cici had been pressed into maid service, even, cleaning out vacated kennels so they could be promptly filled with a new resident. She also had the job of head laundress and chief dishwasher, cleaning the mountain of crusty food/water bowls and puppy-soiled bedding generated daily at the rescue.

Cleanliness is a Sisyphean task at RogerDogs, and today was worse than usual due to the absence of Scott Marsh. Our resident Willie Nelson look-alike had vanished for the day, leaving only a note stuck to the locked front door assuring Betty Mills he would be back Tuesday morning, sorry. Oh, the language that Betty Mills unleashed when she read that note! I was surprised the paint didn't peel off the door in wisps of smoke. I think even Cici learned some new words.

By two o'clock, the rush had mercifully dried up, the dogs had finally stopped barking, and we were able to catch our collective breath, which Betty Mills and Cici celebrated by inhaling several cigarettes each.

"Jesus, I thought I was tired out when I got up this morning." Cici took a deep drag on her current cancer stick and slowly blew smoke out from her downturned lips. "Turns out I was just fooling myself. NOW, I'm tired, for real." She squinted her eyes at Betty Mills and me, and asked dubiously, "You listen to those yammering dogs and rush your butts off like this every day?"

Betty Mills and I glanced at each other. Her flannel shirt was shredded some in the back from where a large, over-exuberant puppy had hung on with sharp teeth, and she had a skid mark of suspicious brown on her heinie. Maybe it was mud, maybe it wasn't. I was cleaner, due to my exalted position of record keeper in the front office; I had been snowed under with intake/outtake record keeping during the day and hadn't ventured into the dog areas at all. I knew without a mirror, though, that I looked like a frazzled chicken. We had been too rushed off our feet to have lunch, and from long experience, I knew an over-caffeinated, underfed Kelly wasn't a pretty sight.

"Well, girl, this was just to break you in gently to the rescue business," I said with a straight face. "Tomorrow will be a half-off sale day, and then you'll see busy." Cici's face blanched as she struggled whether to believe me or not. Betty Mills and I kept our game faces on, but soon, twitching lips and small snickers prevailed and we all three collapsed in a cathartic round of laughter.

"Half-off sale day, my butt," Cici snorted, giving me a soft punch on my shoulder. "You almost gave me a heart attack!"

An hour later, after first downing a lunch of loaded bagel sandwiches, Dot's pretzels and ice-cold fizzy Cokes, we were sitting around the RogerDog desk, hashing out a list of unanswered questions about Brianna's death, tacking on new ones from Betty Mills and Cici to the list Boyd and I had made earlier.

Where was Brianna living in Missoula? Her personal effects were bound to be full of important clues, but Cici didn't know where Brianna had gone after moving out of Cici's small place. "Hell," Cici said, "living arrangements were a touchy subject, you know. I never told her I'd moved into my car, even." Cici rubbed her jaw speculatively. "I don't think she could've been living in her car, though. It was way too small for both her and Rett, and she needed to be looking good for work, you know. Fresh and sexy is a hard look to pull off with wrinkled clothes and no shower."

Where is Brianna's car? Cici knew that she was driving a black sporty type of car, most likely a two-door coupe based on perusal of online car photos.

"The car's got New Jersey plates, and it's not in her name," Cici informed us. "Brianna got it from an old lady back East just before driving out here. The registration was good until next March, and the lady left the license plates on, so Brianna didn't feel any rush to re-register it. The police don't have any way to connect the car to Brianna, until they finally decide to listen to us."

Who had Brianna hung out with in Missoula? None of us thought it likely that her death was related to her pre-Missoula past, and a casual encounter with a murderer didn't seem to jive with both Brianna and Rett winding up in the Crazy Mountains. We all agreed she had to have gone there, willingly, with someone.

Who was treated for a dog bite in the Missoula area, back when Rett was first found? We thought it very likely that Rett would have gotten in at least one good bite while defending Brianna, before he was shot.

My imagination took hold at this point, in my mind I saw Rett grabbing the killer's arm, blood flying around every direction as they struggled, showering Brianna and covering the man's hand as he grabbed Rett's collar.

"Wait," I gasped. "Rett's collar might have the killer's blood on it! No, not that one," I said impatiently, as both Betty Mills and Cici looked at Rett sleeping at Cici's feet.

"Rett was wearing a different collar when he was first found." I jumped to my feet and began rummaging through the desk drawers. "I remember Ellie handing it to me in a white paper bag. It was stapled shut, and had 'Murphy' written on it . . . what did I do with it?" I thrashed around my office space in a mild panic before spotting the bag on the tall bookshelf that stands against the wall behind my big, gray desk. I pulled the bag down, and almost opened it before thoughts of 'chain of evidence' came to mind, thank you lessons learned from reading crime investigation paperbacks.

"We'll have to keep this sealed, to turn over to the police, so it's not like we tampered with it," I said authoritatively to Betty Mills and Cici. "But we can't give it to them yet. Until they admit the dead person is Brianna, they sure aren't going to be interested in evidence off of her dog."

"Give it to me, Kelly." Betty Mills reached out her hand for the bag. "I'll lock it in the file cabinet for safety." She used a red sharpie from my desktop stash of pens to write "October 3rd, Betty Mills" across the stapled flap as a kind of chain of evidence documentation.

We all sat and stared at the file cabinet for a few minutes, once the bag was locked up. Could it be we had evidence that would solve Brianna's murder one day after finding her body? Could it be that simple?

Reluctantly, we pulled our attention back to the list of unanswered questions.

Altogether, we had over fifteen queries concerning Brianna and her whereabouts in the time frame of her disappearance—but how to follow up on them from RogerDogs? Even going back to Missoula to investigate seemed like diving into a black hole of impossibility. What would we do there, just stump around town flashing Brianna's picture and hope to stumble onto important clues?

Our thoughts were interrupted by the Monday afternoon arrival of pink-haired Grace Oberlander and her minion, J.J, who was once again hiding inside his black hoodie. Out of the corner of my eye, I saw Cici's body tense, as if she was on the verge of exploding out of her chair.

"Good afternoon, ladies," sang Grace. J.J. muttered something of the same to his toes.

"Oh, look, there's my favorite guy! There's my Blue Blue!" Grace dropped to her knees and held out her arms to Rett, who reciprocated by plowing into her at top Rett speed, creating a pileup of wiggling, yipping dog and giggling girl on the office floor. J.J. looked mortified and tried to disappear into a corner, as a laughing Grace fended off the Catahoula dog and his lashing tongue. To my left, Cici slumped back into her chair, released from her poised-to-pounce posture that she had assumed when the kids first came into the office.

"Cici, this is our in-house nut case, Grace," Betty dryly said. "And that young man there is J.J. They come in during the afternoon to make sure we haven't screwed up entirely, and to set us straight if we have."

"Grace and J.J., this is Cici, she's the friend of Rett's owner who went out with us yesterday." Betty's face pinched some at the memory of what we had found during that outing, and the smile she had greeted Grace with drained off of her face. The same memories washed over Cici and me, shutting us down like chickens when a hawk flies overhead.

Grace, being Grace, noticed the change in our collective manner and in a flash of intuition put two and two together to come up with ten. Her dark brown eyes grew round behind the bright green frames of today's glasses, and she blurted in a rush, "Ohmygod, you found her didn't you, you found Rett's momma and she's *dead,* isn't she?" She looked at us each in turn and asked again, loudly, "*Isn't she?*"

There didn't seem to be any way to put the cat back into the bag, and I knew from long observance of teenagers that out and out denial was the most potent fuel to pour on speculation, causing a spectacular conflagration of rumor and gossip every time. I gave Grace and J.J. a rundown of Sunday's events and our unanswered questions. As I mentioned our plan to canvass likely hangouts in Missoula with Brianna's picture, I saw Grace's face fill with a teenager's look of patient pity for adults struggling to carry on in a technological world.

"Ladies, ladies, ladies." Grace sighed in mock sadness, while shooting each of us a glance that was filled with both pride and merriment. "If you would be so kind as to drop me that picture, and give us some time, we'll dig up the dirt on your friend, while you all take care of our RogerDog responsibilities. If that's okay with you, boss," she directed the last at Betty Mills with a sassy toss of her head.

"You sound pretty sure of yourself, missy," growled Betty Mills. "What makes you think you can track down her particulars, based on her picture and a name? I can run a Google search just the same as you, anyway."

"Oh, please," Grace intoned, with her eyes sparkling merrily. "Your knowledge of social media stops at Facebook, and you only know about that because I set RogerDogs up with an account when I started here. Besides," she jerked her chin in J'J's direction, "today, we're in the presence of the master. If this Brianna has an online presence, or her name or picture shows up anywhere, J.J.'s going to be all over it like white on rice. Even," she lowered her voice a little and leaned toward us conspiratorially. "Even if it's been buried or taken down."

We all looked at Black-Hoodie Boy, and to my amazement, J.J. was standing straight and tall, and for the first time since he began work at RogerDogs, looking directly at us with his hood pushed back. I had never seen his full face before. He had an impish face, with freckles and a little adolescent acne sprinkled across translucent, white skin. His eyes, so dark brown they were almost black, were framed by equally dark, peaked eyebrows. The combination of eye/hair/skin color made me think of the Celts, a people well known to be filled with blarney and guile.

J.J. turned the corners of his mouth up in a puckish smile and nodded. "I can do that, alright. Best if you don't ask how, though. Just leave it to me and Grace."

Betty Mills peered speculatively at Grace and J.J. for a long moment. "The police are going to be involved with anything pertinent that you scalawags dig up, bear that in mind, please. I don't want to be handing over any illegally gotten crap and getting bit in the butt over it. You, especially, need to keep your nose clean," she added, jutting her craggy face toward J.J.

J.J. held up his hands and his grin grew to fill his whole face. "No worries, ma'am, I can get loads of intel, all from open access search tools, even where dweebs thought they were hiding their junk. I'm not going to hack into anything that's actually secured, I promise." I wasn't sure I believed J.J., he looked way too sparkly for innocence, according to my teacher radar, but I held my peace. His words had given us plausible deniability in case of electronic malfeasance, maybe that's all we needed at the moment.

"Well, girls," Betty Mills said, "lunchtime is long gone. Let's move our butts and get the dogs done up for the afternoon. These whippersnappers can do their magic woo-woo stuff without us."

"We get Rett, though," Grace commanded as the dog stood to follow us into the kennel area. "I have to have a dog fix while I'm here, or my brain will up and shut down." Grace snapped her fingers at Rett, and he obediently flopped onto the rug at her feet. The girl popped her stocking feet up onto his back and began kneading his fur with her toes. "Ahhhh, I feel my blood pressure dropping, and my creativity soaring," she proclaimed with a sigh. "Toodle-ooo, mon amis, enjoy your janitorial duties this afternoon." She dismissed us with a royal wave.

"Umm, Grace, what about the computer?" I asked nonchalantly. "Don't you need me to get you logged in so you can use it for internet searching?" Score a tiny technological point for Kelly, I thought to myself, but then my moment of pride was shot down by J.J., of all people.

"That's okay, Mrs. Boyd," J.J. assured me. "I have a hotspot on my phone and I can tether Grace, no problem." The two kids held up their phones and waggled them for me to see. To me, it sounded like they were planning shenanigans that required a chaperone, maybe two, by god. However, I had enough sense to keep my mouth shut, and get myself out of the office before embarrassing my archaic self.

Fourteen

Betty Mills stood in the corridor along the south bank of kennels with her fists on her hips, looking in bemusement at the dogs that were greeting us from behind their chain-link doors.

"Look at all these new guys!" Betty exclaimed. "No old-timers left except for good old Kanga, Spruce, and Walleye." Kanga, a reddish-brown hound dog we believed to be a purebred Visla; Spruce, a young black Lab cross; and Walleye, a mountain of a dog who most closely resembled a haystack with legs responded to their names with vociferous demands for Betty's attention. The seventeen new dogs, not wanting to be left out, joined in the cacophony, raising the decibels in the building to a level that could cause premature deafness in humans.

"Settle down, you nut jobs!" Betty barked back at them all, while we rapidly handed out greeting treats as fast as we could to all the dogs. The command, plus the goodies did the trick, and the noise dropped to a blessedly low level.

"Look at you, Cici, you're working these dogs like a pro," Betty commented and received a genuine smile in return. I hadn't seen the young army veteran give an unguarded smile since I had met her, and realized that she almost always carried a lot of tension within, being wound up too tight for comfort most of the time.

Working with the dogs seemed to have a calming effect on her. I remembered how Rett's earlier friendly greeting of Grace and J.J. had sparked a 'stand down' response in Cici.

Huh, I thought to myself, *interesting.*

I debated whether to casually bring up my observations in conversation, or keep my mouth shut. Rocking the boat might cause it to be swamped and sunk, one side of my brain argued. My inner dialogue was interrupted by Cici's voice, however, and darn if she didn't beat me to the punch.

"You know, Betty, Kelly," Cici addressed us, while speaking directly at a large, yellow Lab as she tousled its ears. "I didn't get it, why Brianna always had Rett with her, and why she would talk about him being her spirit friend, a witisa, like in this Delaware old time story she loved to tell me. In fact, I was a little pissed with her about it, 'cause at Bagram, it was me who was close to her, and I felt like she was saying a damn dog was just as good as me.

"Being a girl in the army, especially an Indian girl, shit, you have to watch your back, you know?" Cici's gaze flickered away from the Lab toward Betty for a millisecond. "Not only is the official enemy trying to take you out, but you gotta watch out for crap from your own side. Lots of rude shit from guys on those scores. And on top of that, being posted overseas to where the enemy is trying to take you out, and almost does?" She paused again and hit her artificial leg against the kennel door with a hollow clang. "Well, that just upped the ante.

"I have PTSD and a brain injury, according to the army. But I always thought *they* were nuts to think I had a mental health problem. So *what* if I'm 'on guard', bad shit happens and you need to be ready for it, is my thinking. I did have to agree to see a counselor after my last run-in with Missoula's finest, though, and he's been trying to tell me differently, that I need to stabilize." She took a deep breath in, and slowly let it out.

"But since I've had Rett with me, 24/7, I've felt myself *relax*, and it was so weird, it was hard to put a name to the feeling. When those two kids came into the office just now, as soon as I saw how Rett greeted them, it was like a switch got flicked off, you know? It didn't matter that I didn't know them from a hole in the ground. If Rett judged them as safe, so could I.

"I think this is the kind of shit my counselor has been yammering about. He's been telling me about a group in Spokane called Service Dog ParTners that gets service dogs for vets to help them with PTSD and other stuff and trying to get me interested. The whole idea got me checking into dogs that need rescue, thinking how one might be mine someday, if I did join the program. That's why I was looking at Petfinder in the first place, when I saw Rett the other day. You know, maybe the idea has legs after all, no pun intended." Cici gave a harsh laugh at her own joke.

"The counselor, Sean, isn't a bad guy. He helped me get my paperwork together for disability pay." Cici made a hard snort through her nose. "I guess all of those letters assigned to a vet can bring in some good, instead of just bad. He tries hard to get me not to feel *diminished* by them, like I'm not supposed to feel *diminished* by being a cripple, or *diminished* by taking money for asking to be labeled GOD DAMNED DISABLED!" Cici's voice had started to rise with the first *diminished* and by the end had risen to a shout, accompanied by bits of spittle flying into the air.

I was pretty sure we were seeing some of the alphabet soup in play, PTSD from a TBI caused by an IED that lead to Cici being an amp-UT, would be my guess. But it seemed prudent to keep my thoughts to myself, and pretend I wasn't actually present. Shakespeare was on the money when he wrote *seeing too much sadness hath congealed your blood and melancholy is the nurse of frenzy.* I didn't say that out loud either.

Cici's face was a dark red, and contorted into an angry looking snarl. The dogs, agitated by her shouting, were all on their feet, barking wildly once again.

Betty Mills just calmly kept cleaning in a kennel, not reacting in the least to the angry woman, the loud dogs or invisible ex-teacher.

Eventually the dogs quieted down as Cici rubbed the back of her neck and glared at her feet in silence.

"Shit," she said finally. "I need a smoke."

Smoking inside RogerDogs is a no-no; Betty and Cici departed to the outdoors to coat their lungs with nicotine and tar, while I stayed behind. After we were once again all inside cleaning kennels, Cici picked up her conversation.

"If we're right, Brianna's never coming back for Rett. She doesn't have any family at all that are going to claim him; Rett and me were the closest things to family that she had. I want Rett, Betty, it's like him and me belong together, with Brianna in common and that we're both down a leg." Cici turned away from the kennel she was cleaning to face Betty full on. "Let me adopt him, Betty. Please. He can be my service dog, and we'll get hooked up with one of those vet and dog groups to do the training together." Cici's face, usually locked in on itself, was open in an almost naked plea. I once again tried my best to be invisible, not moving an inch, breathing with tiny shallow breaths, and making my mind fill with white noise to keep my brainwaves from causing a disturbance.

I couldn't see Betty Mills from my frozen statue position, but I imagined that she was standing tall with a stern but thoughtful look on her face. Certainly her words backed up this image as she slowly replied, "Cici, I think you and Rett are good for each other; I'd like to see him with you, absolutely. I don't know squat about any groups matching dogs and vets, except what you've mentioned about that SDPT bunch. I don't know how you'd get yourself and Rett into a program like that.

"I do know that Rett can't go home with you from RogerDogs until you've got a home to take him to. Living in your Mobile Hotel isn't going to cut it." Betty Mills finished with a note of somber finality in her voice.

I tried to become even more invisible than before, wondering how Cici would react to this mix of approval and shut down of her

Rett-Cici dream. Would she flare up and invoke butt kissing a la her encounter with Uptight Andy? Maybe snatch up the pooper scooper that leaned against the kennels at her side and try to get a few licks in?

Instead, Cici gave my shoulder a small push as she burst into laughter. "Sheee-it! Kelly, you look like a scared little bunny. What's the matter? You think I'm going get kinetic or something?"

Betty Mills was laughing, too, and I sheepishly joined them. So much for the Kelly Boyd brand of subtlety. We all three did a little shake-off, and continued with the afternoon chores of cleanup, exercise, and getting to know the new dogs.

As we worked, Cici took back up the subject of pre-adoption requirements.

"I know I need a steady place to live, that's what the Spokane people said. I need to keep myself out of bars and below the notice of the Missoula police, to boot. Rett can't go home with someone who's going to be out hooting and hollering until all hours, or maybe not coming home at all, on account of spending the night in the hoosegow." Cici tossed these comments over her shoulder with a nonchalant sangfroid.

Cici's words made me realize how little we knew about her. Clearly, she had already built up a storied past in Missoula. Would a police check of her background turn up arrests for the violence that often goes hand in hand with drunken rampages? What exactly was behind the fact that Brianna had stopped living with Cici, and had not shared the location of her new residence with her putative friend?

The door to the office suddenly banged open with a loud crash, causing every dog in residence to sound off at the top of their fool heads. Grace stuck her head into the corridor, grinning unrepentantly. She rolled her hand at us in a circular, come-here motion, while holding the door open with her hip. Betty, Cici and I glanced at each other questioningly as we put down our cleaning gear and walked back up to the office. Grace and J.J. only had been snooping on the internet for less than an hour. How much could they have uncovered?

Turns out that a master, unleashed onto the information super-highway, can do a lot within an hour. Maybe if we gave him two whole hours, J.J. could find Jimmy Hoffa, Amelia Erhart and D.B. Cooper to boot.

We now knew where Brianna had been living, since she had posted a picture of herself and her new roommates on Facebook. Using their faces as the basis for more searching led to a name, and the name to an address via utilities records.

Brianna herself used the Facebook moniker Newt2MT and had used a red newt as her official page picture, but the wealth of Brianna selfies posted on the site clearly established her ownership.

She did indeed drive a black coupe with New Jersey plates; we now knew the license plate number of the car.

Besides spending her time working at Shalimar's, hiking up the Rattlesnake canyon, and going to the dog park, all with Rett at her side of course, Brianna apparently had become very active with the group TrapNoMore Montana. It appeared from her comments, pictures and replies that Brianna had even participated in a few workshops organized by them. Along with the Humane Society, TrapNoMore holds free seminars to teach the public about the danger trapping poses to dogs, and how to free a pet that inadvertently runs afoul of a trap or a snare.

I had attended such a workshop when we lived in Billings and had been traumatized at the idea of Sadie or Leo as collateral damage in a trapper's killing device. To this day, I carry wire cutters for snares and a homemade gizmo, built from a tie-down strap and two heavy duty carabiners that, god willing, would allow me to release a deadly Conibear trap before it suffocated a trapped dog.

As the recitation of facts slowed to a halt, Betty Mills focused on Grace and said, "There's more, isn't there, girly. You look like a cat that's got into the cream. Go on, spill it," she encouraged with a crook of her finger.

Grace sat up straight in her wood chair, pushed her bright green glasses up her nose and beamed at J.J. "You show them, J.J., you're the one who unearthed this little titbit."

The boy tipped his chin down, shyly, but a pleased smile played across his face and he motioned us over to see what he had on his phone's screen.

Little titbit, my foot!

J.J. had unearthed a bombshell. Brianna was involved with eco-terrorists!

Fifteen

A S WE WERE BUSY COMPUTER SLEUTHING at RogerDogs, a man named Matt Morgan was working in his garage in the southwest end of Missoula. Matt was in a foul mood that Monday afternoon. Trapping season was fast approaching, and he was spending some time getting his sets oiled and ready. He breathed heavily as he hoisted a heavy, double handful of coyote leg traps down from his attic space and dropped them with a clatter on his waist-high, wooden work bench.

Usually, working with his traps was an enjoyable project for Matt, but at the moment, he was consumed with roiling feelings of dark outrage. Trapping meant a lot of things to Matt, it was a part of his Montana, blue collar roots, and the money from it was a welcome addition to his cash flow. But living near liberal, left-wing Missoula, as he did, put Matt in close proximity to activists who wanted nothing more than to shut down this way of life.

"Goddamn bunch of bunny-hugging, granola eaters," he muttered to himself, running a large hand through his close cropped blonde hair in a gesture of exasperation and frustration. He was a member of the Montana FurTrappers Association and had just read an email from them warning members to expect more physical interference with trap and snare sets this season. Apparently, there were rumors of an underground opposition group in the Missoula area, one that meant to model their efforts on Earth First ecoterrorism activities, feeling that the more mainstream protest groups such as TrapNoMore Montana weren't getting results fast enough.

The email urged members to be vigilant of their traps and to report any illegal interference to the Montana Fish, Wildlife, and Parks department, but to stay away from direct confrontation with the perpetrators.

"Like hell," Matt muttered to himself. "Like *HELL*! I'm not going to just stand by . . ." Snorting, Matt set a large pot of water onto a hot plate on his work bench; boiling his traps would be the first step in prepping them for the season.

Waiting for the water to boil, he thought back on his confrontations earlier in the September with the small woman and her weird looking dog. He had first seen her in Missoula, with a bunch of long haired idiots protesting at the FWP office when he had gone to get his trapping license for the year. He hadn't been able to resist flapping the permit at the group when he exited the building and supposed he had picked her up as a stalker from that encounter.

She had next shown up at his workplace. He was at his job in the Fur Emporium and there she was again, all up in his face, shrieking about her little animal friends. Here, Matt paused in his recollections, and his mouth twisted in a sinister, downturned grimace while his light blue eyes briefly darkened in a murky glower as he rubbed his clean-shaven chin hard.

"Yeah, that's right, *bitch*, couldn't leave well enough alone, could you? Wasn't enough to show up at my work, you thought you could come at me at home! Caught you in my garage and taught you a lesson, didn't I? Now you won't be bothering *anyone* anymore, will you?"

Matt stood rigid and still for a moment breathing hard through his mouth as he replayed the memories over again in his mind.

Finally, with a deep breath, he straightened up and shook himself like a dog coming out of water.

Whistling now, Matt began placing traps into the pot of boiling water. Trapping season started in a month, and he would be ready on day one.

No worries.

Sixteen

"**B**E SURE YOU TELL HER ABOUT the elf named Alf," Boyd said, tongue in cheek, as he leaned over my head to look out the window. It was Tuesday morning, two days after we found Brianna, and we were standing at an east-facing picture window in our sunny breakfast nook, watching Deputy Darla Shaw make her way to our deck steps from her county sheriff's vehicle.

"Hush, Boyd." I grinned and gave him a friendly pinch on his upper arm. "Get a load of that car, don't officers drive regular police cars anymore? It seems *sneaky* to be decked out in SUVs like ordinary people. Except for all the fancy grill work on the front end, there's nothing to clue you in that that's a police car."

"You're right, Kelly. The big brown and yellow 'County Sheriff' signs on the sides are just meaningless," Boyd dead panned, earning himself another pinch on his arm.

"You can't see the words until you're right up on it; I'm talking about driving down the road and being able to recognize a police car from miles away, like it used to be. This one's under the radar until it's too late!" I exclaimed dramatically.

Boyd's face crinkled up in laugh lines as he tried to keep from guffawing out loud at the idea that Kelly Boyd, the most law abiding driver on the road, was concerned over incognito police vehicles.

He never lets me drive when we're on a trip together because he claims I drive like someone's grandmother.

"Have you *ever* been pulled over, Kelly? What do you care what a police car looks like?" chuckled Boyd in amusement.

"It just gives me the willies to drive up on a police car and not realize it until you're *right there*," I said. "It just startles me, somehow. Now, hush! Here she is."

The day had started with an early phone call that interrupted our morning routine. Boyd caught the call as he was in the kitchen getting the coffee ready while I was in the master bath, finishing with a shower. I heard Boyd's telephone voice as I was getting dressed, and tried to guess who was on the other end of the line. It didn't sound as if he was talking with Betty Mills, or with a guy friend either. Maybe a sales rep for chainsaws? They wouldn't call so early, though, no use pissing off your potential client by being a chirpy, early bird.

"Sheriff's office is sending a deputy out here to talk with you, Kelly. They'll be here in a couple of hours," Boyd informed me nonchalantly when I joined him in the kitchen after letting the heelers out into the yard for their morning frisk about. His easy tone was at odds with the 'gotcha' gleam that showed in his dark brown eyes. Boyd had been both impressed with the amount of information that we amateur detectives had dug up about Brianna, and alarmed that we didn't intend to share with the police until they were ready to admit that Brianna was dead, gone, and murdered to boot.

"Damn it, Kelly, if that girl was mixed up with fire setting eco-terrorists, you need to let the police know, now! That's regardless of whether she is or isn't the body you found!" Boyd had almost shouted at me last night.

That was the bombshell information that the master internet sleuth, J.J., had discovered. He and his tricky internet ways had managed to unearth a photo that showed a bonfire conflagration of flames shooting fifteen feet or more into the air. At the edge of the light, a dark figure could be seen stood looking at the flames with her face partially visible. It was Brianna. J.J. and Grace had linked the bonfire picture to news coverage of an early August fire near Spokane that had torched the Rendezvous Emporium, a business dedicated to buying and selling wild caught furs, and trapping supplies. Two known eco-terrorist groups, the Eco-Liberation Front (ELF) and the Animals Live Free (ALF) had claimed responsibility for the fire. Brianna had apparently upped the ante from her non-violent anti-trapping activities with TrapNoMore.

Now, with the sheriff's office coming to call, Boyd obviously intended to ensure that all our beans were spilled. Despite feeling disgruntled that Boyd was getting his bossy way, and so soon, I also felt pleased that I would be able to hand over our knowledge and let the sheriff's office get busy doing their job.

As the deputy exited the white SUV, I was pleased to see the officer who had been in charge at the Crazies' crime scene, rather than the antagonistic Deputy DuPries. She had been professionally calm, cool and collected and could no doubt find her way out of a paper bag, unlike Uptight Andy. I even managed to remember her name now, Deputy Darla Shaw.

Deputy Shaw, seen in the daylight and no longer covered from head to foot with her white, Tyvek crime scene suit, was a woman whose physical attributes reminded you that Montana, along with the Dakotas and Minnesota is a stronghold of Scandinavian settlers. She wasn't as tall as Boyd, but towered a good eight inches over me. Deputy Darla Shaw possessed the white-blonde hair, high cheekbones and light blue eyes that would let her pass as a native in her pick of Denmark, Sweden, or Norway.

I opened the door for Ms. Scandinavia as she reached the top of the redwood deck stairs and greeted her with a cheery, "Good morning!"

I made introductions between Boyd and Deputy Darla Shaw as smoothly as if I hadn't forgotten her name during the body recovery, and we all three settled at the round table in our terra-cotta colored breakfast nook, armed with fully leaded coffee and further fortified with thick slices of an Entenmann's crumb cake.

Sadie and Leo were penned up in their kennel in the mudroom for safekeeping. We didn't trust Sadie; she was likely to unilaterally decide that it was time for the deputy to leave, and deliver well placed nips to encourage Deputy Shaw to the door. Oops, bad manners, don't you think, to let your dog bite the nice police officer?

"That was tasty, Kelly, thank you. Breakfast seems a long time ago, and I forgot to fill up my travel cup before hitting the road. Gotta have my daily caffeine or the world just isn't right," Deputy Shaw said as she set her fork down on her now-empty plate and took a final sip of coffee.

She pulled a notebook and pen from a sharp looking black messenger bag that I instantly coveted. I leaned a little closer and squinted my eyes at the bag's label. If my bifocaled eyes were correct, it sported an emblem from the Red Oxx luggage company of our hometown, Billings.

Hmmm, I thought, *that would be a dandy Christmas present for . . . me!* and made a surreptitious note on my own pad of paper, so I wouldn't forget to let Boyd know, later. Boyd noticed me noticing and gave me a husband smirk for being fashion distracted in the face of an official investigation. I narrowed my eyes back, daring him to say anything about it to Deputy Shaw.

"Kelly and Boyd, I'd like to thank you for agreeing to meet with me this morning," Deputy Shaw intoned in an official manner. "I would like to start by apologizing for the rough patch you all had with Deputy DuPries the other night." A twinkle appeared in Darla's eye, and her voice took on undertones of merriment as she continued. "I understand he took a little offence at the manner in which Ms. Vargas showed him some identification evidence?"

We all took a moment to smile; I had told Boyd all about Cici's near arrest over the bare butt tattoo disclosure. He was sorry to have missed it.

Clearing her throat, Darla continued. "Andy's a good police-man, but he's new to the job and sometimes finds himself in a little over his head. Reality doesn't always quite line up with the hand-book, and he gets flustered and pulls the knee jerk, arrest 'em card. He'll trust his own judgment more after he gets time and experi-ence under his belt.

"Nope," she continued, with her mouth twitching into a full out smile. "There's nothing in the handbook about proper procedures to collect evidence found on a lady's bare ass!"

Deputy Shaw became abruptly sober as she spoke again. "Cici's tattoo was important, we were able to see enough of a match on the body to tentatively identify the remains as Brianna Norwood. Knowing that Ms. Norwood was an Army veteran, we sent in den-tal X-rays and DNA samples for identification with Army records. The DNA will take a few more days, but based on the X-rays, we know for sure that the body you all found is indeed Brianna Norwood's."

We sat in silent homage to a young lady who was dead too early. None of us had known Brianna in person, but the loss of anyone in their prime sits heavy on the heart. *Death lies on her like untimely frost*, I breathed to myself. *Revenge should have no bounds.* I was mixing and matching my Shakespeare, but I felt the Bard would agree it fit the moment, and not frown at me unduly harsh.

Boyd, seated across the table from Darla, sat up a little straighter in his white wooden chair and placed a comforting hand on mine, giving me a little squeeze of encouragement. I squeezed back, ban-ishing Shakespeare and melancholy for another time.

"Do you know how Brianna died, Deputy?" Boyd inquired, fix-ing his Boss man face on her and leaning forward. In response, Deputy Shaw's face became even more sober and she too sat upright at attention to deliver her news.

"We do. Brianna was shot with a .22-caliber weapon, the same as her dog, only Brianna was shot in the head. I'm sorry. Your friend was murdered, no two ways about it."

The comforting hand on mine now squeezed a little harder. "Tell her what you know, Kellen!" it commanded. Mine gave a hearty pinch in reply, "Shut up and back off, Boyd, you're not the boss of me!" Thirty-two years of marriage lets you develop an amazing repertoire of nonverbal communication, I must say.

Deputy Shaw didn't notice our silent skirmish as she dug out a small tape recorder from her messenger bag and sat it on the table near her notebook. She looked at Boyd and me and said, "Now that we know for sure the body is Brianna's, I'd like to hear everything that you know about her, her disappearance, and how you came to find her body." She held up a hand to stave off any comments from Boyd or me.

"I know. Deputy DuPries refused to listen to this when you tried to tell him about Brianna, on-site. But please, for Brianna's sake, don't let ruffled feathers get in the way of helping us out now. Any scrap of information you have is important, and I want to hear about it. I'm interviewing you, Ms. Mills and Ms. Vargas separately today, not to try to catch anyone out, but because different viewpoints see different details, and we need all of them.

"I'd like to record the rest of this interview," Deputy Shaw went on. "Boyd, if you think of anything while Kelly is talking, I'm going to ask you to jot it down rather than speaking up. I think your questions are important, but let's deal with them at the end." She passed a notebook and pen across the table to Boyd and gave him a look that managed to be friendly but stern at the same time.

"Are you ready, Kelly?" I nodded and she depressed the Record button on the machine.

"This is Deputy Darla Shaw, interviewing Kellen Boyd on October 4th at 10:37 a.m. Mrs. Boyd, this interview is being recorded with your permission. Mrs. Boyd, please, in your own words, tell me what you know of Brianna Norwood and how you came to find her body on October 2nd."

I took a deep breath, and began at the beginning, with the discovery of Rett wandering lost in the Crazy Mountains. I hoped she had extra batteries and cassette tapes because I wanted to tell her the whole story, suspicions and conjectures and all. Whoever wanted to hear the truth and nothing *but* the truth wasn't interested in finding answers, in my book.

The only information I held back was the fact that our internet sleuthing had been accomplished at the hands of Grace Oberlander and J.J. Sheperd, rather than ourselves. We all had agreed that this tiny fact was not germane to official inquiries. I felt some guilt that we had involved minors in a murder investigation in the first place, and was determined that they be kept clear of further entanglement.

"Don't forget about the dog collar at RogerDogs," I reminded Deputy Shaw as she was packing up her things. She was on her way to the rescue where she would meet with both Betty Mills and Cici for their official interviews.

"It's locked in the office file cabinet," I continued. "Betty will have the key. It's in a white paper bag, stapled shut, with 'Murphy' written on the outside, since that's what we were calling Rett, then. Nobody's opened that bag since the vet tech put Murphy's collar in it, right before he had his leg surgery." I was pointedly reminding her about the collar and its potential as critical evidence. It hadn't seemed to spark as much investigative fervor during my interview as I thought it deserved. My nose would be seriously out of joint if the collar was left to languish at RogerDogs.

"Will do, Kelly," Deputy Shaw assured me. "Only don't hold your breath waiting for the results, though. Our office is turning all of the DNA evidence over to the state medical examiner office, and even for a murder, it's going to be a week or more before we get any feedback."

A week or more! I fumed internally, *that's too long!*

"Why aren't there any portable DNA analyzers that can run the samples in the here and now?" I groused. "You've gone that way for fingerprint analyses, haven't you? Run the prints while you've got suspects sitting on the sofa, and Hey Presto! Slap on the cuffs if you've got your man!"

I tried to keep peevish dismay out of my voice, but could tell from Boyd's face I hadn't quite succeeded. He took a step closer to me and put a calming hand on my back, as if Sadie wasn't the only bitch in the house who couldn't be trusted not to bite.

"Absolutely, that would be fantastic, but we don't have such a thing, Kelly," Deputy Shaw calmly replied. "Maybe in the not too distant future, but at the moment, the medical examiner's office is the only way to go. It's frustrating, I know."

She took a step of her own closer to me and her features settled into a expressionless deadpan, her eyes suddenly flat and hard like the eyes on a day old dead fish. When she spoke again, her voice had taken on the stilted tones of someone reciting a canned speech.

"There will be multiple law offices investigating Ms. Norwood's death, including the Missoula police and possibly the FBI, if the connection to ALF and ELF pans out. You may always contact the sheriff's office with questions or information; we are the office in charge, but I'm sure that you don't want to get involved further with Ms. Norwood's murder, murder's a nasty business. A word to the wise, Mrs. Boyd; it appears that the victim and her friend, Ms. Vargas, are out-of-state Indian vagrants with checkered pasts, they and their friends in Missoula won't be the kind of people you're used to associating with. In cases like these, its usually some drinking buddy that turns out to be the killer, Ms. Vargas herself might be responsible.

"Really, Mrs. Boyd, you and Mrs. Mills should send Ms. Vargas back to Missoula and let law enforcement do their jobs," Deputy Shaw now spoke in a condescending, pompous tone that raised my hackles as much as her words themselves.

"Somehow, I think Mrs. Mills might be more likely to want to color outside of the lines, Kelly and I'm trusting you to help rein her in," Deputy Shaw finished with a once again friendly smile.

"Deal?" she said, reaching out to shake my hand.

Nonplussed by her rapid flipflops in attitude, I mumbled an affirmative reply, operating on autopilot as I tamped down my angry confusion caused by her derogatory slam at Cici and Brianna and their putative Missoula connections. What was she trying to imply? That Brianna brought her murder on herself by being from out of state and brown? And she was throwing shade at my fellow musketeer for the same reasons, almost out and out accusing her of being a shiftless, drunken murderer? Oh, baby, if Deputy Shaw waved that flag in front of Betty Mills, Betty would get her back up and charge in like an angry bull. There would be no turning her aside from continued sleuthing then!

SEVENTEEN

"Look, Rett, it's Kelly Boyd, in the flesh. Wonder where she's been the last couple of days?" Cici Vargas greeted me as I stepped out of my trusty, blue Subaru in the RogerDog Rescue parking lot on October 7th. It was Friday now; four days had passed since we found Brianna's body. Cici was dressed for the colder day in a fuzzy, dark blue fleece jacket worn over tan Carhartt work pants. A sporty red stocking hat pulled low over her ears covered most of her dark brown hair. The day itself was gray and cloudy, with a promise of snow in the air. A sharp wind was playing around the parking lot but it failed to deter Cici from a cigarette break.

Rett bobbled over to me, his tail whipping the air into a hurricane, eager to greet his Kelly. He forgot his manners and popped up on his hind legs so that his tongue could lick my face as enthusiastically as his tail was thrashing the air.

"Aghhhh!" I gurgled, fending off the tripod's affectionate attack. "Get down, you big lug!" Rett obediently sat at my feet, but continued licking whatever part of me he could reach, as I gave his ears a thorough rub down.

The three of us abandoned the parking lot for the warmer RogerDog office. I poured myself a cup of coffee and took my seat behind the gray, metal behemoth of a desk. Cici leaned her hip against the back of a wooden chair and took a sip of her own coffee, while Rett settled down on the rug at her feet.

"Well? We haven't seen hide nor hair of you for a few days. I thought maybe the Deputy had packed you off to jail or something." Cici lifted her coffee cup at me in a questioning manner.

"Ha, ha, nothing as glamorous as incarceration," I dryly replied. "After talking with the deputy, Boyd and I went down to Billings with the dogs for a few days in the bright lights and big city. We moved up here from Billings; it's nice to go back sometimes and have dinner with old friends. What's new at RogerDogs since I've been gone?"

Boyd had suggested the trip to Billings, just after Deputy Shaw left our house last Tuesday morning. He pitched the trip as a pre-holiday shopping expedition, which should have alerted me to deviousness on his part. Boyd hates to shop.

We hadn't traveled more than ten miles away from home before I found he had other ideas than shopping on his mind. Instead, he wanted to physically separate me from RogerDogs for several days, and to use the drive-time and forced proximity of the pickup cab to ensure I was a captive audience for what he wanted to say.

Boyd had shot a quick side glance at me riding in the passenger seat of the truck and cleared his throat to make sure I was listening before speaking in a nonchalant tone.

"So, Kelly, you're going to keep yourself clear of that whole Brianna – Cici mess, right? Sounds like they're both a couple of shady characters who blew into town and got mixed up in street crime in Missoula. It's too bad what happened to her, but it's over and done with for you and Betty Mills, right?

"I'm assuming that Cici will have cleared out by the time we're back from Billings, but if not, I think it would be a good idea for you to take some days off from RogerDogs, Kelly, just to let things settle down to normal."

Boyd stopped talking as I gave a strangled cry of outrage over his pompous little speech. He turned his face toward me and his eyebrows twitched together and his mustache bristled as he clocked the look on my face. I'm a pretty even-tempered lady, if I do say so myself, but when I do lose my cool, it pays to run for the woods. And I was hot, let me tell you. Steam was pouring out from my ears.

"You look here, mister!" I said sharply, razors in my voice. "Neither you nor the decorative Deputy Darla has so much as met either Cici or Brianna in person, so you don't know what you're talking about! Anything that woman had to say bad about them probably came backhand from that asshole Deputy DuPries, I bet. I've spent enough time with Cici to like and respect her. Boyd, I'm surprised at you being so quick to pass judgement, especially based on such obviously prejudiced source!"

"Well, okay, point taken, I don't know them," retorted Boyd. "But neither do you, Kelly, not really. This whole murder thing, that doesn't have anything to do with RogerDog Rescue. Now that the dog has been claimed, Cici can go back to Missoula with him and that's that. It's not anything else to do with you and Betty." Boyd made a dismissing slice through the air with his hand to underscore his words.

"Shows what you know, Daniel Boyd! Cici, Betty and I are a team, like the three musketeers! It sounded to me like the sheriff's department isn't going to try very hard to catch Brianna's killer, what with their half-assed idea that Cici is guilty. Brianna was a beautiful young woman with her life ahead of her. She was devoted to Rett, and had a good paying job in Missoula, Boyd, she wasn't some skanky homeless drunk Indian like the deputy was portraying. So, yeah, Boyd. I actually do think some investigating on our part might be a good thing!" I wasn't quite shouting at Boyd, but it was pretty close.

At that, we drove on in stony silence with Boyd hunched over the steering wheel like a large angry bear and me turned away from him as far as I could manage in the passenger seat, arms and legs crossed in silent fury. Over an hour passed, and I gradually cooled down and regained my temper.

We were almost to Billings when I decided to take advantage of fact that Boyd, too, was a captive audience in the pickup. There were some serious things I wanted to say to him that had been on my back burner for a long time now and by god, he was going to hear them. I took a deep breath and turned toward my husband of over thirty years.

"Boyd, I want you to listen to me. You may not have realized, but I really had a hard time with retirement, and moving away from Billings, where all our friends were, to go live in the country for the first time in my life. At first I felt pretty lost without my identity as Mrs. Boyd the Math Teacher. But it turned out to be a blessing, because, guess what, I have a lot more to me than being a math teacher, and the move gave me a blank slate to work with in figuring who Kelly Boyd, ex-teacher would be for the future. I don't have to worry about a school board sitting in judgement over what I do or don't do anymore, Boyd.

"I love working at RogerDogs with Betty, it's given me a chance to spread my wings and fly in a new direction and I'd don't plan to quit anytime soon," I said firmly. "Retirement also didn't make me stupid. I'm quite able to pick my own friends, mister."

Boyd shot me a look from under his bunched eyebrows and grunted in reply but didn't say anything more on the subject.

The argument followed us through the evening like a small dark cloud, but you don't make it through thirty plus years of marriage without being able to compartmentalize disagreements and put them on hold, maybe indefinitely. I'd said my piece and the conversational ball was in Boyd's court. It was up to him if he wanted to carry on with further discussion, or leave it lay like a dead dog.

It was almost 11:00 when we settled into the king-size bed of our Billings' Airbnb and turned out the light. I was just drifting off to sleep when Boyd's voice rumbled through the dark.

"So, you're a musketeer, huh?"

Was there a slight, teasing lilt to his voice? I certainly thought so.

"That's what I said, mister, and don't you forget it," I replied in a tone that wasn't altogether unfriendly, giving his side a small prod with my fingertips.

"Well, ma'am," Boyd continued in a warm, buttery tone. "It just so happens that I've got a nice sword available if you need to practice your 'en garde's.'"

I smothered a laugh as I rolled closer and snuggled up to him.

"Is that so? What class of sword are we talking about, hmm? A rapier? A broadsword? 'Cause I'm not interested in any tiny, little dirk, buddy." He laughed and pulled me closer.

No more words were spoken that night, yet détente was achieved as we silently agreed to disagree. The small dark cloud was sent packing, leaving us free to have an enjoyable stay in Billings after all.

But this was too much information to share at the office. Loose lips sink ships and marriages, both.

Cici gave me a slightly puzzled look, as if she could tell there was something I wasn't saying about the trip to Billings, but then shrugged her shoulders and went on.

"Not a heck of a lot new here. You know how it is, dogs come and dogs go, nothing exciting to report except for the runaway Chihuahua . . ." Cici laughed and filled me in on how a teacup Chihuahua named Diva had escaped upon arrival at RogerDogs and lived in the building like a little mouse, creeping out of hiding only at night to eat food left out by Betty Mills.

"We weren't even sure it was her that was eating the food, could've been Diva got outside and froze to death or got eaten up by a critter, and a real rodent was cleaning up the dog crunchies. Then Betty had the idea of putting the food down in that kennel on the corner where you have the camera set up. Sure enough, here comes that little bit of a dog, creeping into the room after midnight, then scurrying away when the food was finished."

"How did you catch Diva, then? She's not still on the loose, is she?"

"Of course we got her back." Cici huffed at me in mock aggravation, "No itty-bitty Chihuahua is going to outwit Cici Vargas and Betty Mills! I wanted to put down sticky paper like you do for mice, but Betty ix-nayed that idea. She insisted that we use a live trap and brought one up from her and Randy's place. Worked like a charm, we had little Diva back in her digs this morning. You should see her, Kelly, she's like one of those pocket dogs that movie stars carry around in purses, she's so small."

I rubbed my chin, as if in deep thought. "Maybe Betty should adopt her then, you know, do the whole fancy purse and designer dog routine as an advertisement for RogerDogs?"

We both dissolved in a laughing fit at the idea of no-nonsense Betty Mills, dressed in her no-nonsense work clothes, but accessorized with a stylish pink, Louis Vuitton purse containing a tiny Chihuahua just peeking out from its depths.

"What the hell are you two har-de-harring about?" demanded the woman herself as she abruptly opened the door from the kennel area, nearly whumping Rett on his backside. "Don't you know we got enough shit in the back without you adding to the pile in here?" Betty's rough voice sounded like she was in the middle of a bout of pissiness, but her brown eyes were dancing merrily. She took a few steps into the office and looked me over.

"Hmm," she said seriously. "You don't look like jailhouse food made you lose weight while you were inside. What do they feed you in there, anyway, Kelly?"

Betty Mills' serious expression dissolved into an out and out grin, "Good to see you back, girl. You're just in time, too, ain't she, Cici?"

Betty and Cici looked at each other with conspiratorial smiles and I swallowed past a sudden knot in my throat.

With a sense of foreboding mixed with equal parts of anticipation, I sat down, leaned back in my office chair, and asked, "In time for what, pray tell? Not anything to do with investigating about Brianna, is it?"

"Don't sound so *suspicious*, Kelly," Betty Mills replied with a droll smile. "My goodness. I'm sure we all promised like good girls that we wouldn't do any such thing."

Betty Mills looked at me with rounded, innocent eyes. "But Cici here is going to be taking Rett as her personal dog, you know, just as soon as she squares away housing in Missoula. It would be *irresponsible* of her to take on a dog and not know how to rescue him from a trap, don't you agree, Kelly? Rett's already down one leg, he can't afford to lose another one." Betty paused and her eyes opened even wider. Maybe she was channeling her inner Bambi.

"There's a workshop in Missoula this coming Wednesday, October 12th, all about keeping dogs safe from traps, and how to rescue them, that's five days from now. It's a joint thing, put on by TrapNoMore Montana. Cici and Rett should go, for sure. It's her clear responsibility as a dog owner-to-be," Betty said solemnly.

"Not our fault if the workshop people recognize Rett and want to talk about Brianna with us," chipped in Cici, with an innocent look of her own to match Betty's. Twin Bambis, the two of them.

"And, that nice Deputy Darla called yesterday and told Cici that she was free to get Brianna's stuff from where she was living; the Missoula police have gone through it all. Cici needs to find Brianna's army discharge paperwork to get her buried in a national cemetery. So you two have official permission to poke around her house," Betty tacked on, in perfect tag team style.

I opened my mouth to voice agreement with their plan but before I got a word out, Cici broke in with a harsh laugh.

"You're gonna spout some white bread crap about 'leaving the investigation to the professionals' aren't you, Ms. Schoolteacher?"

I shot her a surprised look at her combative tone, as startled as if she had whapped me in the face with a wet towel. Cici stared back, giving me a look of mixed scorn and pity, her lip lifted in an angry sneer.

"Sure, Kelly, if it was someone like *you* who was found under the rocks, there'd be a grand investigation, one that all the good citizens could approve of. But for people like Brianna and me? A couple of itinerant, out of state Indian ladies with checkered histories with the law, who maybe killed each other when drunk? Shit, nothing's going to happen unless we're pushing things along. I've been in Montana long enough, even before Deputy Shaw's visit to know that's how it works here, even if Brianna and I are back-east Indians instead of from some Montana tribe. Or do I need to paint a red hand across my mouth to make it picture clear for you?"

I sat silent at the table, remembering with chagrin how I had at first felt on board with the blond-haired, blue-eyed Deputy Shaw, until her implications about Cici's and Brianna's backgrounds had ruffled my feathers. If she had kept her mouth shut during our meeting, I would've felt sure that Brianna's murder investigation was in good hands, and easily promised to steer clear of any further investigation.

Cici was right about Montana's dismal reputation in general when it comes to the investigation of missing and murdered indigenous women. The state, under pressure to do better, has recently formed a MMIW task force to look into the matter, and images of Native women with red-paint handmarks across their mouths abound in the news and on billboards. The topic is in the news enough you would have to be living under a rock to be unaware of the issue.

From the other side of my desk, Betty Mills gave me a slow nod. "I think we need to keep looking into things, Kelly. Not doing anything out of line, but who's to say how hard the official investigation will be pushed? Except maybe to pin Cici here as the killer!" She smirked at me before continuing. "That was my take away from our Deputy Shaw. Whoo-ee, Kelly, you should have heard her giving Cici the third degree!"

"Wait, Deputy Shaw interviewed the two of you together?" I asked. "That doesn't seem like a good police procedure."

"'Course not! We used the office for the interviews but before she arrived, I'd employed my cutting edge technological skills and swapped the nanny-cam equipment around, so I could sit in that back kennel and listen in on Cici and the deputy," Betty paused and gave me a sly wink, her eyes dancing with merriment.

"Betty! You didn't!" I grinned at her in frank admiration. "That was inspired!"

"Yep, I got to hear all Deputy Shaw spouting nonsense six ways to Sunday, trying to get Cici to say she had killed Brianna. Doesn't seem to me that her office is going to try to catch the real killer anytime soon."

"Look ladies, before my meeting with Deputy Shaw, I wouldn't have thought being Indian mattered a hoot in hell, I mean this is murder we're talking about! And, okay, maybe that's 'white bread' of me.

"But Deputy Shaw gave me a taste of what you're talking about, with the slant that a proper white lady like me would want to stay clear of getting mixed up with the likes of Cici and Brianna. Ha! I'm not backing off! We're the three musketeers!"

"Good," Betty exclaimed. "That's settled. I've got to stay here at RogerDogs and run the show, but you two of you can slide on up to Missoula for a couple days, catch this workshop, collect Brianna's things and investigate the shit out of things, can't you?"

"I'm in for anything that's not blatantly illegal, dangerous or needs me to sign anything!" I announced, and we did a round of high fives for the musketeers.

THE WORKSHOP PUT ON BY TRAPNOMORE Montana wasn't for several days, yet. Looking at the weather prediction for the upcoming week I saw that Missoula was expecting its first snowstorm of the season to arrive on October 12th, the day of the workshop, dump snow for the day and then clear out on the thirteenth, with weather conditions reverting back to sunny, with daytime temperatures above freezing.

Travelling safely in Montana during the late fall, winter and spring means paying attention to the weather and staying close to home if storms are predicted. Weather maps these days are miraculously accurate, making them a valuable tool rather than a joke, as was the case in the pre-internet days of my youth.

"We should drive to Missoula on Tuesday, October 11, the day before the workshop, Cici, the roads will be clear and dry then. Once we're there, we'll be set, even if it's a bad storm, we'll be able to negotiate Missoula traffic okay. I vote we plan to stay a couple of days, that'll give us plenty of time to get stuff done, and for the roads to clear back up," I said as I showed Cici and Betty Mills the ten day weather forecast on my phone.

Betty Mills made a coughing noise into her hand that sounded remarkably like, "Chick-en."

I stood up from behind my battleship of a desk, put my hands on my hips and narrowed my eyes at her.

"You got something caught in your throat, Betty? Or do you have something to say? Speak up, we didn't hear you."

"Naw, you're good. Nothing wrong with spending some days in Missoula, it'll give you two more time to look into things."

Betty turned to Cici with a twinkle in her eye that told me she wasn't done teasing me yet.

"Kelly here has a snowflake allergy, Cici. It's a wonder she manages to live in Montana during the winter at all. Yessir, those little white things landing on her car can send her straight into shock; it's a terrible sight to see. You have to be ready to grab the wheel and take over if she's driving."

Betty Mills leaned in toward Cici and spoke in a confidential whisper.

"Boyd doesn't let her drive if they're both in the car you know, on account of her fits."

I pretended to throw my desk-top eraser at Betty Mills, but refrained from actually releasing it into the air. I could claim that as an ex-teacher, I was too adult to indulge in such behavior, but that would be a lie. Instead, long experience has shown me that I have the throwing skills of a two year old, and that Betty would be 100% safe from my missile, if I were to actually launch it. It was potential embarrassment that stayed my hand, not maturity.

"Don't you two have actual work to do today?" I griped. "Away with you!" I made a swooshing gesture at them with both my hands.

Betty Mills exited the office, back to doggie chores of some sort. Cici, though, cocked her head at me and rolled her hand in a come-with-me gesture.

"Walk around and meet the new dogs, why don't you, Kelly? Before you get hunkered in and stuck behind the computer for the day."

This actually was a good idea. I was in charge of writing up the PetFinder bios for our posted dogs which requires a certain familiarity with the animals' temperaments and pre-RogerDog histories. If I didn't have pictures and at least some interaction with the dogs, I couldn't do my job properly.

"Sure thing," I replied, grabbing my iPad for notes and photos. "Lead on, McDuff, show me the fair Diva and her cohorts."

"We'll start with the little gal we put in the Quiet Room," Cici said, reaching for the door that led to Rett's old digs, our isolation room at RogerDogs. "This one was tied up to the front door when we got here yesterday, no note, no nothing. Poor thing was awfully cold, and too upset to eat anything all day yesterday. We put her in the Quiet Room with a bunch of shredded newspaper on the floor, and extra bedding to huddle up in. Hopefully, she's settled down some."

The door to the room swung open, and Cici stepped inside, murmuring "Hey, girl, how's my little Rascal today?"

She stopped so suddenly I plowed right into her back. As I stepped off to Cici's side, I could see what had made Cici jerk to a stop. A medium sized, short haired dog, liver colored with pretty, tan highlights threw us a scared look as she shuffled in a slow circle, straining hard as if to poop, but not producing any product. Rascal's eyes showed rims of white at the edges of her irises. This is called *whale eye* in dogs, and it's a sign of a distressed, frightened dog.

"That doesn't look right," Cici said. "Rascal looks like she's in pain, doesn't she, Kelly?" Rascal took a short breather, but then went right back to her constipated hunch, still producing nothing out her back end.

"Shit," I said. "She might have a blockage in her gut, that's really bad."

Dogs eat the weirdest things, sometimes. Dr. Rex once told me about a pit-bull that was brought in because of continuous vomiting and complete stoppage of poo production. Dr. Rex wound up doing exploratory surgery and found the dog had consumed an entire braided rug while the owner was at work.

"The guy said, 'I wondered where that had gone!' when I showed him the unraveled rug after his dog's surgery," Dr. Rex told me in an unbelieving tone of voice. "The guy was a bachelor! It was just him and the dog, living in the house. What did he think happened to the rug? Tiny elves came down the chimney and stole it away?"

Fortunately, the dog did come through his surgery okay, but as the rug had unwound and stretched all through its intestines, the poor guy would certainly have died without intervention. That story made me fear for Leo, who ate crap that could be bad for him any chance he got.

We stood in silence, anxiously watching Rascal; then Cici spoke up with some relief in her voice.

"Looks like she got *some* shit out of her system, anyhow. Look out to your right, Kelly; you about stepped in a big pile."

I glanced down to my side, and indeed, there was a heaped up mound of black almost touching my shoe. *Feces that black might mean internal bleeding*, I thought worriedly. Just as I completed that thought, the pile wiggled and stretched before my disbelieving eyes.

"That's not poop!" I gasped. "That's a puppy!"

"The hell you say!" Cici started my way as I bent down and snatched up the newborn puppy.

"Stop! Look out! There might be more, don't step on them!" I screeched in panic. Cici froze and looked wildly around the floor and its thick covering of shredded newspaper. Oops, so much for being calm and competent in the face of a dilemma.

"Ahem, I mean, look around carefully and see if there are more puppies," I said, modulating my voice down from a shriek.

The bitch had cleaned the membrane off of the puppy I held in my hands, and had apparently eaten the afterbirth as well. The little guy was breathing all right, squirming and crying, but was still wet. Renewed labor had interrupted the dam and left the black puppy on his way to becoming chilled. I rolled him in the bottom edge of my favorite, green check flannel shirt and began rubbing him dry.

Cici was moving slowly about the room, looking in the shredded paper for any other newborns. She had almost completed a full circuit of the area when she gave a shout and snatched a white colored lump up from her feet.

"Ohmygod, Kelly, I found one! It's inside of plastic!"

It wasn't plastic, of course. Puppies are born inside a clear membrane sac that must be removed in order for them to breathe. Usually the mother dog takes care of that by roughly licking the newborn, but sometimes, especially with first time mothers, human intervention is needed.

"Quick! Use your shirt and wipe that stuff off! Get its head down lower, rub it with your shirt. Wipe its mouth and nose! That's it! Keep rubbing!"

Here, Cici's army training came in handy, bless her. Instead of becoming befuddled and flustered by my shouted directions, she flashed into action and followed my rapid fire commands to a 'T'. By the time I crossed over to her, watching carefully where I stepped, in case other little bundles were hiding in the bedding, the white puppy's skin had pinked up, including its little tiny tongue, and it began to add its shrill cries to those of its sibling.

"Whoa, now. Whoa, now," Cici breathed reverently. "That's, that's really something!

"Look at this little pumpkin, Kelly! Ohmygod, I saved a puppy!"

Cici's voice was filled with soft wonderment, and unless I was mistaken, there were tears shining in her eyes.

"You did great!" I congratulated her. "Keep the little guy wrapped in your shirt, so he stays warm. I'm going to get Betty; we need to set up a whelping box and get some heat lamps in here. Looks like Rascal's planning on producing at least one more puppy, too."

We looked back at the scared little mother dog who had been temporarily forgotten during the discovery of the puppies. She had laid down and was stretched on her side, with her unfocused eyes staring ahead in rigid fixation. A quick glance at her back end showed that a little tiny nose was just peeking out of the birth canal.

"Betty!" I bellowed from the open door. "All hands on deck, delivery in process! Run for it!"

Betty can move pretty fast when she's motivated, and she made it to us just in time to see the third puppy, another black bundle, come into the world.

"What the hell?" Betty demanded, looking at Cici and me, each with a puppy wrapped in our shirts and at the brand-new mother, Rascal, who was busy providing care to her third puppy.

"That dog's just a puppy herself! No way did I think she was pregnant when we found her yesterday. Goddamn! What if she'd had those puppies when no one was here? Could've lost them all!"

Betty Mills inspected the puppies that Cici and I were cuddling.

"These look in the pink," Betty Mills pronounced. "Did you have to do anything for them?"

Cici recounted how we had found the puppies laying in the shredded paper, and how the white one had been gray and lifeless looking when she had picked it up.

"But Kelly knew what to do! I did just what she said, and it worked," Cici recounted in a modest way, but her face shone with pride over her role in the puppy's survival.

Betty's face was soft as she looked down at Rascal and the third puppy, which was now squirming across the bitch's belly, blindly looking for its first meal.

"You two did just right." Betty said quietly. "Let's put your puppies down with the other one and make sure Momma lets them all get a good drink of warm milk."

Rascal sniffed the black and white puppies as we put them down at her side and began to lick them firmly, all over. The black one squalled and made to move away but she pinned him down with a paw until he had been sufficiently washed. In a few minutes, all of the puppies had their fill and were fast asleep in a heap with Rascal curled protectively around them.

"Is she done popping out puppies?" Cici asked. "I always thought dogs had, like, six or seven at a time."

"We'll have to keep an eye on her," Betty grunted as she stood back up from the mother dog's side. "It may be she's done with just the three, that wouldn't surprise me with her being so young herself, but she could start straining again, too. If six hours go by without any more excitement, I think we can call it at a litter of three."

Betty looked side-eyed at Cici and me as we stood with our eyes glued on the little family, still brimming with exhilaration over the surprise birth and our role in its success.

"Seems to me, you two need to get busy in the naming department. The white one's a little girl and the black ones are split, one each," Betty informed us with a grin. "I call dibs on the black pup that was born after I got here, her name is Beetle. She sure scurried around like one when she was looking for a teat to latch onto."

"The white one's Zephyr," proclaimed Cici. "On account of her being a gentle breather and all."

I hurriedly masked my surprise that zephyr was a word in Cici's vocabulary. Feeling ashamed of myself, I dropped my face down as if focusing on the last unnamed puppy, hiding the fact that my face was potentially red with embarrassment.

Sheesh, was I turning into a literary snob, post-retirement? I have long been a Shakespeare aficionado and have often caught flak for being a math teacher with a large, non-technical vocabulary, and it pisses me off every time. Now it seemed I would have to watch my butt to make sure I didn't slide into snootiness of my own.

"Squid," I said at last. "He's black as ink, and I almost squished him when I stepped into the room. That makes him a Squid."

"Squid?" said Boyd incredulously, his face crinkled up in disbelief. "Those two army women let you call him that?"

Boyd and I were standing in the kitchen, concocting an enormous batch of Boyd's signature chili. The predicted change in weather had sparked us into making our annual supply of hearty chili. Once properly simmered, we'd eat some for dinner, and put the rest up in the freezer, ready to be reheated during the upcoming snowy months.

I was acting as sous chef for the operation, chopping mounds of onions, garlic, cilantro and green peppers, while Chef Boyd browned up the chorizo, judiciously adding spices as he taste-tested his work.

"What does being in the Army have to do with not naming a dog Squid?" I paused my chopping to dab at my streaming eyes with a paper towel. Wearing eyeglasses gives me a little protection from onion fumes in the air, but the sheer amount I was processing tonight had overwhelmed that line of defense.

"Because Navy recruits are Squids. You're a Joe if you're in the Army," Boyd explained patiently. Turning to take the cutting board full of chopped onion from me, he went on. "You should've named him Joe, that's what I'm saying."

"Hey, it was my pick, and I picked Squid, mister. Besides, Joe would be out because Joe's a person's name. None of RogerDogs have people names; it's a thing Betty Mills has a bugaboo about.

Dogs that come in with a person's name get renamed, for their stint with us." I paused as I pushed the diced peppers and minced garlic into Boyd's frying pan.

"Of course, adopters can change the dog's name to whatever they want once they get the dog home, so Squid may not stay Squid forever."

Boyd was quiet for a few minutes as he stirred the meat mixture occasionally, just enough to keep it from burning. In past chili making operations, we have *always* burnt the meat, and were determined not to repeat history this time.

Sitting on a high stool at the granite topped kitchen island, I breathed in the heady smell of the commingling spices. Too bad you couldn't bottle the smell to market; we'd be millionaires for sure.

I was starting to open up the cans of kidney beans and crushed tomatoes that would be the next additions to the chili, when Boyd cleared his throat and said in a low, serious voice, "I want to talk with you about going to Missoula with Cici."

Startled at his change in tone, I stopped with the can opener and turned to face him. Boyd's face matched his tone; there was no more Boyd banter or jocularity in play now.

"I realize I was off base when I went along with Deputy Shaw's malignment of Cici. I'm all for you going along to help her out with 'next of kin' duties for Brianna. We both know how overwhelming that can be, you kind of need someone along to help out, or you sink like a stone and wind up having to redo stuff three or four times.

"But I'm worried that you two are going to wander off topic if you hear any interesting information about Brianna while you're up there, and then you might accidently step into something dangerous. I want you to promise me that you won't do *anything* to investigate 'leads' that you might stumble onto. Someone killed that girl, and they don't want to be found out—not by the police and certainly not by you and Cici. If Brianna was really involved in eco-terrorism, those aren't people you want to make nervous."

Boyd took a deep breath. "I'm not trying to be the boss of you, Kellen Boyd, I just want to know you'll keep yourself safe."

Were Boyd's eyes glistening? They looked suspiciously shiny, maybe from the onion fumes, but maybe not.

"Oh, honey," I said, moving to the stove to give my handsome husband a hug around his manly-man, aproned middle. "We'll be okay. We've got some official stuff to do for closing out Brianna's affairs, and that means we'll have some conversations with her friends and co-workers. Of *course*, we'll be looking for intel while we're doing that, but we're not planning to do any stakeouts or chase anybody down a dark alley or anything. If we turn up information that we think needs to be checked into, we'll back off and call the sheriff's office and let them handle it. They might have some preconceived prejudices, but I think they'll do right if we dig up good information; if not, you and I and Betty can put pressure on them. Look, I'll even put Deputy Shaw's number on speed dial before we go." And at that moment, it all seemed like a perfect plan for safe sleuthing.

We stood there for a moment, enjoying the closeness. Is there anything sexier than a good-looking man cooking in your kitchen? I was on the verge of suggesting a 'nap' as soon as we got the chili on simmer, it seemed to me that there were some new sheets on the bed that hadn't been properly tested for consumer satisfaction as of yet, when the smell of scorched food hit my nostrils.

"Shit!" yelled Boyd, breaking the embrace and the mood as he began to scrape frantically at the frying pan. "Goddammit, Kelly! We burnt the damn chili, *again!*"

Oops.

Eighteen

As we drove along the two-lane highway from Helena to Missoula on Tuesday morning, October 11th, nine days after finding Brianna's body, the weather stuck to the predicted forecast. Temperatures hovered just above freezing, and isolated snowflakes swirled their way to earth, descending from low lying, ragged clouds.

But the roads were clear with no ice in sight, and, contrary to Betty's description of my snowflake phobia, the few pieces of white stuff landing on the car did not invoke hysterics on my part. *So there, Betty Mills*, I thought, and gave a little humph to myself. *I'm perfectly capable of driving in a snowstorm even if I prefer not to.*

"Did you say something, Kelly?" Cici turned away from the view out her window and looked at me curiously. Whoops, I must've been a little louder with my defiance than I had intended. Embarrassing! Retired math teacher now talks to herself. What's next? Claiming that my dogs can talk to me, just like real boys and girls? *That way madness lies; let me shun that,* I thought, mentally crossing my fingers and invoking Kings X.

"No, no, I just had a frog in my throat for a second," I said, leaning forward and fiddling with the heater controls as a distraction.

Fortunately, Cici changed the subject.

"Hey, Kelly. I've been meaning to ask, why did Betty name the place RogerDog Rescue?"

"Well, funny you ask. When I first started, Betty claimed it was only because the name 'Betty's Barkers' was taken already. Really though, it's a nod to the military, like saying Roger to the dogs that need us. But I didn't hear that side of the story until I'd known Betty for almost a year."

A working heater was the reason that we were driving my trusty, blue Subaru rather than her more spacious SUV. Randy, Betty Mills' husband, had ordered parts that were needed to fix Cici's vehicle, but they weren't in yet. I was wearing a heavy, solid green, flannel shirt layered over a long sleeved t-shirt that proclaimed "There are only 10 kinds of people in the world, those who understand binary numbers and those who don't". I think this is one of the funniest jokes ever, but it makes Boyd roll his eyes every time I wear it.

Cici, on the other hand was wearing a short-sleeved, black t-shirt with no overlayer. I glanced at her and waved a hand at the heater. "Feel free to turn up the temp, if you want," I said.

Cici grunted in reply and went back to looking out her window.

Only Cici, I and Rett were making the trip to Missoula, so the smaller car wasn't an issue. There was still plenty of room for the three of us and our limited luggage, with extra room for any of Brianna's things that might need to be hauled around. Deputy Darla Shaw had contacted Cici and informed her that the Missoula police were finished looking over Brianna's things at her rented room. Cici was free to remove any and all items at her leisure, but the deputy had also mentioned that the roommates wanted Brianna's stuff packed up and gone ASAP. Deputy Shaw had also given us a heads up that a news release about Brianna's death would be in the papers soon.

"Did you see the article about Brianna, yet?" Cici asked me with a stab at nonchalance, keeping her eyes fixed on the view out her window.

"Wasn't much of an article," I snorted. Boyd had found the October 10th item in Helena's Independent Record, the Billings Gazette, the Bozeman Daily Chronicle and the Missoulian several days earlier and showed it to me. Boyd is a news junky and keeps online subscriptions to these newspapers, plus the Wall Street Journal; he devotes his early morning hours to 'keeping up' as he puts it. The sheriff's office had cast a wide, if shallow, net by posting it in each of the newspapers for these four western Montana cities.

"It was just a bitty thing." I continued. "It was a press release from the Sweetgrass Sheriff's Office, not a full article written by a journalist. And it was a 'just the facts, ma'am' piece. Stated that a week ago a woman's body had been discovered in the Crazy Mountains by backcountry hikers. Body identified as Brianna Norwood, who was believed to have been living in Missoula, foul play is suspected, authorities are looking for her car, please contact if you have any information, blah,blah,blah. That was it! Nothing about Rett being with her and being shot, too. In fact, the picture that was posted was from that one you gave the police of her and Rett, but it was cropped down to just a head shot of Brianna. I guess I was hoping for banner headlines or something, this just seemed so . . . piddly!" I whacked the steering wheel, feeling affronted for Brianna, all over again.

Cici thoughtfully rubbed her upper lip and slowly said, "I don't know that it's a bad thing, Kelly. If we talk to people who knew Brianna, but maybe don't realize she's dead, they might be easier to *talk* to, you know, not spooked about knowing a murdered person, or super-pious about her, just because she's dead. Brianna wasn't an angel, that girl *lived* to color outside of the lines. We need to hear people dish out the dirt about her, not tell us in hushed tones about some 'Saint Brianna' who never existed."

I glanced briefly toward Cici, curiosity about her and Brianna's backgrounds overcoming my inclination to mind my own business.

"Cici, you mentioned something about a Delaware dog story that Brianna told you. Is that the tribe she belonged to, and you as well? And if that's a 'white-bread' silly question, just say so and we'll pretend I didn't ask."

Cici grunted and turned away from me to stare out of her own window for a while, long enough for me to decide that silence was her answer. Then with a pained smile on her face, she turned back toward me.

"Well, I guess I should apologize for calling you 'white bread' the other day. I sure as hell don't like it when I get called crap." She held up a hand to forestall any response from me. "Just shut up and listen, okay?

"Brianna and me are Indian because its stamped across our faces and written in the color of our skin and hair but neither one of us is an 'official' Indian, as in properly written down in some enrollment leger. So to some people we don't count as Indian at all, you know.

"Now, my mom's one hundred percent Indian, some a mix of Ojibwe and Cree but her folks drifted from Canada to Milwaukee in the 1950's, and stayed there as illegal immigrants. All the time she was growing up the topic of family history was hush-hush. They told her that talking about their background would get them sent away, and then Social Services would get her. She doesn't know much about her family background, really, and sure doesn't want to talk about it."

A look of embarrassment and chagrin spread over Cici's face as she paused.

"It's silly, because my mom was born in in the United States, and so were my sister and me. But she really believes we'll all be deported back to Canada if word gets out about my grandparents being northern wetbacks.

"My Indian grandparents both died before I was born. My dad's white like you, Kelly and Mom always wanted us to fit in with his family. Ha! As if. My white grandparents were pretty pissed he married an Indian and never wanted anything to do with us.

"Mom and Dad moved to De Pere for work in the paper mills after they got married. That's where I was born and raised, and by the time I managed to graduate from high school, I couldn't wait to join the army and get out of town.

"Anyway, I never looked into background stuff about my grandparents, it just wasn't up for discussion in our family.

"But Brianna, shit, she hungered for anything about her 'Indigenous heritage' as she put it. She was orphaned in Philadelphia as a toddler when her mom died of an overdose, and she grew up in a bunch of foster homes, with nothing to call her own except the 'Native American' on her birth certificate. She said she *could* be Delaware, and I guess that's true. But that wasn't anything she had any proof of beyond being Indian and being born back East. She knew a bunch of stories and legends and took a lot of pride in being good in the outdoors, saying it was because of her blood. She couldn't understand at all why I wasn't really into being Ojibwe/Cree. I always blew her off when she wanted to talk about being Indian and now I wish I hadn't. We could've had a lot of fun digging into it all, Kelly. Shit."

With that, Cici turned and stared again out her window. This time she didn't turn back.

It's less than a two hour drive from Helena to Missoula, and Boyd and I like to stay in Zootown, as Missoula is affectionately known, whenever we want some 'big city' time. Missoula, with a population under a hundred thousand, is a far cry from an actual big city, of course. But with its funky, college town vibe, and gorgeous natural surroundings, Missoula is a great place to spend a few days away, enjoying townie entertainments. Even simple activities such as grabbing a cup of coffee at a downtown café take on a special glow when done in Missoula.

Boyd and I are frequent flyers at a few, choice Airbnb's in town where the owners have come to know us and our dogs, and welcome us as repeat customers whenever we are in town. I had made reservations with our favorite rental, a two bedroom cottage located just to the north of the University golf course. The cottage has an enclosed backyard for Rett, and a full, well-stocked kitchen for the human guests. The little bungalow is within walking distance to the University, downtown, a neighborhood Greek restaurant and, most significantly, the house where Brianna had so recently rented a room.

Cici and I had timed our trip to arrive in Missoula just after the Tuesday lunch rush at Brianna's workplace, the Shalimar. Ostensibly we were there to collect Brianna's last work check from the manager, but in reality, we were hoping to find answers about the girl, to dig up the dirt, as Cici had so succinctly put it.

Tomorrow, we would venture to Brianna's house to see what, if any, information could be gleaned from her left behind things and from her ex-roommates, who would hopefully be loquacious in regard of their memories of Brianna. Although, from what Deputy Darla Shaw had told us, both roommates, Jori Haupsted and Lila Sanderson, were reticent to speak about her.

Poor girls. I imagined that every word spoken to the Missoula police brought the horror-show of murder closer to their own doorstep. Too much information would let the foulness slide inside, invited as it were, never to leave again nor allow itself to be driven away.

This would explain, I mused, why the girls are in a hurry to move Brianna's things out of the house. With her possessions gone, her presence could be banished to a thing of the past, not to be mentioned in the future.

Maybe the relief of seeing Cici and I packing up Brianna's things and ridding the house of her shadow would open up the spigots and information would flow more freely. Facts, gossip and hearsay, any titbit would be welcomed by us and our sympathetic ears. Once the door shut behind us, I doubted we would have a second chance to speak with Jori and Lila.

Nineteen

Tuesday morning, as Cici and I were enroute to Missoula, Matt Morgan hurriedly swung his pickup into the crowded parking lot of the Fur Trade Emporium, and cursed as he was forced to slam his brakes to avoid rear-ending a Prius as it backed out of a parking spot. He was late for work today, and hoped his boss, Big Earl Taggert, wouldn't notice. Matt had been late several times in the last few weeks, and Taggert's patience with him was growing thin.

Matt hustled inside, heading directly for the back of the shop where the trapping supplies and firearms were kept. Matt's experience as a bonafide hunter and trapper was the reason Big Earl had hired him; Matt had zero sales experience to bring to the table.

Speaking with a real woodsman who had hands-on familiarity with the items sold at the store was a draw for customers who admittedly could buy the same items online or at Walmart for cheaper. Matt had the veracity that people wanted in their salesperson; customers liked to talk with him about his time in the woods. This allowed them to feel like they were part of a loose brotherhood of hunters/trappers/woodsmen and gave a special shine to the shopping experience at the Fur Trade Emporium. It made Matt gag.

Working with customers who didn't know squat about being in the woods, or worse, were in his face with anti-trapping, anti-hunting propaganda didn't come easily to Matt. It was hard to keep his face from showing the derision that lurked underneath his outwardly friendly, customer-service smile. There were days when he fantasized about punching the daylights out of the next person who offered up their ignorant drivel and storming off the job—but knew he needed the job for its steady money and for the employee discount for his personal trapping supplies.

Matt had an even more insidious need for a positive relationship with his boss; Big Earl had the connections that allowed Matt to garner profit from forbidden furs. There are laws governing what animals can be *legally* trapped in Montana, but the non-target animals in the woods don't know that they aren't supposed to step into a baited trap or snare, do they?

If a protected animal is caught, say a lynx or wolverine or swift fox, what's a guy supposed to do? Just let the animal go to waste? Big Earl could handle the sale of the pelt for him, for a large cut of the money of course, but hey, better than a poke in the eye with a stick, Matt thought.

Matt made it to his counter without being spotted by his boss or other Fur Emporium employees, and hurriedly opened his register, stuffing his coat and gloves under the counter, so that he could pretend to have been at his post all along. Once everything was ship-shape, Matt gave a sigh of relief, and rolled his shoulders to release built-up tension, promising himself that he would come to work twenty minutes early from now on, no more close calls with Big Earl Taggert, no sir. That he had made this exact promise to himself the last couple of times he had been late didn't register in Matt's mind.

Matt's relief was short-lived, though. He was kneeling on the shop's wood laminate flooring, designed to look like the pine boards of a cabin but without the upkeep of actual wood, putting out some new stock on a low shelf when a pair of size fourteen logging boots came into view. The oversized boots were attached to an oversized man who would now be looking down on Matt from his height of six five, if his view wasn't blocked by his XXXL gut.

Big Earl Taggert had arrived.

"Good morning, Matt," rumbled Big Earl as he peered down at the back of his employee's head. Big Earl's eyes were black and glittery, what could be seen of them beneath his jutting eyebrows. Big Earl had wild, curly black hair that he wore down to his shoulders, long enough to seamlessly blend with his heavy black beard. All in all, he gave the appearance of an enormously fat, black bear. He could look genial and teddy-bear like for customers, but Matt knew that Big Earl, like a real bear, was always dangerous and always to be treated with caution.

Wondering furiously if his late appearance had been noted after all, Matt felt a cold sweat break out across his shoulders and neck. *Easy now*, he told himself, *just take it easy, let him say if there's a problem, maybe he's just here to shoot the shit.*

"Morning, boss," Matt answered, as he finished placing boxes of Conibear traps and Canadian snap nooses onto the shelf. Matt stood up and gestured toward the shelf. "Looks like we sold quite a few of these since I was in last." He nervously ran a hand through his close-cropped, military-styled blonde hair.

"Yeah, yeah, business was pretty hot the last couple of days, everyone's getting jacked up for the start of trapping season," Big Earl replied. He swung his corpulent body onto one of the unsuspecting stools that sat in front of Matt's counter, and stared at Matt in a cool, speculative manner that made Matt sweat harder.

"Say, Matt, you remember talking to me about going down to the Crazy Mountains to scout around for *special* tracks?" Matt was so relieved that Big Earl wasn't talking about his late arrival at work, it took him a moment to process what his boss was asking about.

"Uhh, yeah, right," Matt stuttered out, digging in his memory for specifics of this earlier conversation with Big Earl. "Yeah, there was a rumor about skunk bears down there, and I was going to check it out." Matt grew more confident of the conversation as he went on in a pious tone, rounding his bright blue eyes in a show of innocence. "I wouldn't want to look at setting a trap line there, myself, if there really are wolverines around. Those are special, protected animals, you know."

"Well, did you actually go?" Big Earl asked, shifting into a more comfortable position on the overloaded stool. The stool wobbled some, but rallied under pressure and staid upright and in one piece.

"No, not yet," Matt answered cautiously, wondering at the speculative look on Big Earl's face. "Between working here and doing some fix-up on my roof, I haven't taken the time. Why? Have you heard any more scuttlebutt on sightings? Did someone actually find one of those buggers?"

"Not found a wolverine, no." Big Earl pulled a newspaper out from under his arm and flipped it onto the counter. It was folded open to the Local-State section, and he pointed to a small article near the bottom of the page. "Seems a young woman was found dead down there by hikers. Didn't know if one of the hikers was you." Big Earl peered closely at Matt with his beetle eyes, and paused.

"She looks familiar, too. Any chance she's one of the rabble rousers who read you the riot act in here about a month ago? The article says she was from Missoula."

Matt stared at the picture of Brianna Norwood and was filled with the cold horror of recognition. *Oh, god, it was her.* The bitch had not only turned up again, but Big Earl was standing there letting him know she was linked to Matt!

Brianna and four others had come into The Fur Emporium over a month ago, posing as legitimate customers. Matt still burned with anger and humiliation as he remembered how taken he had been with Brianna and her questions about the traps, snares and lures that were for sale. For once, his smile had been genuine, even as he recognized her ignorance about the products.

Then, on a signal from a skinny, ineffectual looking man with scraggly hair bunched in a pony tail and a pitiful soul patch perched his weak chin, she had begun to scream in Matt's face about killing, animal suffering, blood on his hands that would never wash off, you name it. As she screamed and customers looked on with open mouths, the other members of her group began spraying fake blood onto everything in sight. It had been a nightmare. The police had been called, but Brianna and her cohorts had fled from the building before they arrived.

Matt thought furiously as he pretended to read the article. Big Earl may have seen the ugly altercation between Brianna and himself in the store, but she had left the store afterwards, on her own power, with the rest of her do-gooder, tree hugging friends while he, Matt, had stayed and spent the rest of the afternoon helping to clean up the damage. Big Earl would've seen that as well.

As for later, when Matt had caught that very same girl, on her own this time, trespassing in Matt's own garage, there had been no one to see what happened next. The girl had been too busy wrecking his personal supplies to notice Matt step into the garage and quietly shut the door behind him. No, no one but Brianna and himself had been on hand to witness the outcome of their after-midnight encounter.

Or had someone?

Was someone just now reaching for the phone to call the police, as they stared at the picture of Brianna Norwood in the paper?

TWENTY

"JESUS GOD, KELLY," INTONED CICI IN an all-too-audible voice. "Look at the prices on this menu! Who in their right mind would pay this kind of money for food? Maybe in New York, okay, but this is Mizz-*oooo*-la, which is in Mawn-*tan*-a, last I checked." She peered at me over the top of the menu in her hands in outraged disbelief.

I stepped in close to Cici and hissed at her, "Shut up, Cici. Piss these guys off and they're not going to share anything with us except the shortest way to the door." I gave her my best schoolteacher frown to boot. Chastened, Cici lowered her voice to an almost inaudible mutter as she continued perusing the menu.

We were cooling our heels in the opulent waiting area of the Shalimar while a beautiful, college-age hostess, dressed to the nines, went to see if the manager had time to meet with us.

What would it be like to go to work in the morning dressed for the Oscars? I wondered silently, and tried to imagine myself decked out in a similar sleeveless, backless, slinky gold lamé dress, while perching on her glittering, five-inch stilettos. In my imagination, I took two steps and fell off the shoes to earth again; bad things happened to the dress on the way down.

Nope, not for Kelly, not for all the tea in China. I was in my comfort zone, dressed in one of my schoolteacher outfits: a navy blue, long sleeve, V-neck sweater that was pulled over a pair of soft grey slacks, and accessorized with a russet and gold, floral patterned infinity scarf. The scarf even matched my suede ankle boots. Shazam!

Cici herself was outfitted today in a more professional look than usual. At my insistence, she had traded her men's flannel shirt for a dark green polo shirt embroidered with 'RogerDog Rescue' on the left front pocket. Almost a year ago, I had convinced Betty Mills to order some official shirts for us to wear at local Adopt-a-Pet fairs. There were spares on hand at RogerDogs and it had been simple enough to grab one for Cici before we hit the road.

Rett turned his head to me as I took a seat on the sumptuous bench that the Shalimar thoughtfully provided so customers could take a load off while waiting for a table. Upholstered in deeply padded, burgundy leather and tastefully bedazzled with glass diamonds, the bench was as opulent as a throne and sitting on it made me feel as if I were a queen. I guess if people feel like royalty, they don't mind the sky-high prices.

Rett, of course, had to stay seated on the floor, poor puppy. We had brought him to the Shalimar with us in the hope that his presence would be visual proof that we were legitimate representatives of Brianna. If Cici was right, Brianna had been allowed to bring Rett to work with her; he would've spent his time in the manager's office while she sashayed through her shift. Blue-eyed Rett, who had tragically lost a limb in defense of his mistress, would stare imploringly at the as of yet, unknown manager, triggering waves of sympathy and loss from the man. The manager would become a willing font of inside information about Brianna and her relationship with co-workers and customers, holding nothing back.

That was our hope, anyway.

Ten minutes later, we followed Ms. Gold Lamé down a thickly carpeted hall that was dimly lit by expensive-looking wall sconces. We halted in front of an imposing, solid cherrywood door that proclaimed 'Office' in authoritative black letters scrolled across a frosted pane of glass. The glass was backlit from within, and after a quick knock from the hostess, a deep voice informed us we should enter.

Cici and I shared a nervous glance, it was show time!

I twisted the ornate gold handle on the door and began to push it open, planning to enter first, with Cici and Rett coming in after. Rett, however, hadn't gotten that memo; he boisterously charged past me as soon as the door cracked open. His sudden move caught Cici by surprise, and the leash sailed out of her hands before she had a chance to rein him in. His fifty-plus pound body contacted me mid-thigh and I found myself batted to the side as neatly and efficiently as if Rett was a hip-checking hockey player. Sign him up for the Oilers!

Embarrassingly, gravity took over on my part, and I wound up planting my butt on the hall carpet with an 'Oof' loud enough to be heard in Edmonton. So much for professional poise.

I was scrambling up to regain my feet and dust off my dignity when I heard a hoarse cry from in the office.

"Bree . . . Bree! Get in here, girl, goddammit, where have you been?"

Cici and I opened the door fully, and stepped just inside the office. A wide, solid man in his late forties or early fifties, with a round, open face was sitting in a high-backed wood and leather office chair turned to face the door. He was folded over, petting whatever part of an over-excited Rett he could get his hands on, as the dog whirled in tight circles, rolled on the ground, and attempted to jump into his lap in a non-stop cycle of frenzy. Need I mention that Rett's tongue and tail were flashing around at hyper-speed?

The man looked expectantly past Cici and me from underneath a shock of straight brown hair that fell across his forehead, and frowned a little when no further person came into the room. He gave Rett a final, friendly swat on his rump, and pointed to a large, denim dog bed that was nice enough for people.

"Place, Rett," he said in a firm, authoritative voice. Rett's round blue eyes look imploringly at the man, but the pointing finger did not waver. With a deep sigh, Rett bobbled to the dog bed and flopped down on his side.

The manager rose from his chair and stood looking at Cici and me with an impassive face. "Introductions, then, shall we?" he said in a flat voice, devoid of emotion. "I'm Darrell Forsun, the head manager here at the Shalimar. Clearly you have some connection to Brianna Norwood, or you wouldn't be here with her dog." Mr. Forsun stood staring at us with hard, suspicious eyes. After a moment that was a mini-eternity, he stepped back toward his executive desk.

"Please. Forgive my manners. Come and sit down." He gestured at two wing-backed chairs in front of his desk. Once we were all seated, us in the wing-backs and him in his leather throne, Darrell steepled his large hands under his chin and looked at us expectantly.

"Mr. Forsun, I'm Kelly Boyd, I'm a retired math teacher who volunteers with RogerDog Rescue, outside of Helena and this is Cici Vargas, from here in Missoula. Mr. Forsun," I rushed on in a nervous twitter before Cici could get a word in. "Have the police been in to visit with you about Brianna?"

"No." Darrell Forsun sat upright in his chair, a look of wary suspicion forming on his face as he looked back and forth between Cici, me, and Rett, who was sprawled indolently on his luxury bed. "I haven't heard from anyone about Brianna or from Brianna herself since she stopped coming into work, back in late August, early September. Why are the police involved? Speak up, ladies! I want to know what's going on, *now*, if you please!"

"Mr. Forsun," I began, scrambling to organize my thoughts. This man hadn't been interviewed by the police? He didn't even know Brianna was dead? From the sound of his voice calling to 'Bree', he had maybe been more than just an employer. Should Cici and I grab Rett and flee, leaving the police to get their asses in gear and take care of police stuff before we muddied the waters?

"She's dead, *Darrell*." Cici's harsh voice broke through my mental scrambling. "Some asshole shot her in the head and stuffed her under a bunch of rocks for the bears to find. Jesus god, don't you read the fricking newspaper?" Cici's face was clenched into a knot and her narrowed eyes glared ferociously at Darrell whose own face was now stretched with shock and disbelief, his mouth hanging open wide enough to catch a whole flock of birds, never mind flies.

Well, there's no unsaying that, I thought. *Full speed ahead then, and damn the torpedoes.*

Mr. Darrell Forsun spun his chair away from us and gave us his back for what seemed like a full hour, but couldn't have been for more than a minute or two. When he turned back to us, his eyes were deeply bloodshot, and shiny with unshed tears. Most color had drained from his face, but it had returned to its previous impassive mask.

"Please, as succinctly as possible; tell me what the hell is going on?"

IT TOOK A WHILE TO FILL Darrell Forsun in on what we knew. Somehow, neither of us felt we should hold back any details about Brianna's murder. Darrell's obvious shock and emotional response to the news, coupled with Rett's joyful reunion with the man, seemed to give him an unsaid pass from suspicion. I was beside myself with disbelief that the Missoula police had not been to interview him, though. Was it possible that they were doing a shoddy job of looking into Brianna's death? I could feel my promise to Boyd further wavering in the turbulence of doubts.

"Technically, Cici and I are here just to pick up her final check," I wound up at last. "But we were hoping to hear if you or other employees had noticed anything, well, out of the ordinary, involving Brianna before she disappeared. Of course, we thought the police had already been here and covered that ground, too."

Darrell shifted in his chair, rocking it backwards before speaking. He looked hard at Cici and said, "You knew, Brianna, right?

Really knew her, not just a casual, get together for a drink now and then type of friend? She talked about an army buddy she had here in town that she was pretty tight with, I'm assuming that's you?"

Cici grunted in affirmation.

"Okay, then you know Brianna was on a different plane, shall we say, than other young ladies. When she was working it was like having a lit firecracker in the room. She drew attention from everyone, like moths to a flame. Some waitresses resented her; she always brought in the most in tips, even if she worked fewer tables.

"But the men? Holy Hell, it was something to watch them sit up and take notice when she sashayed into the dining room. They all but strutted around like roosters, puffing out their feathers, vying for her attention."

"How did Brianna react to all that? Did she fan flames, or just take it in stride?" I asked, mentally picturing Marilyn Monroe as a Shalimar waitress, all sexy innocence as she drove men to distraction and women into scandalized, red-hot jealousy.

"It depended. Brianna was hard but fair with the other waitresses. She'd do her job and do it well, and would help the others out if they were getting rushed off their feet. But she didn't take shit from them either.

"We had one new girl who was giving all the others attitude and pulling crap stunts to mess with their work. I would've given her the boot, but Brianna caught her in the parking lot after closing, first. Can't really say what happened, but no one had any trouble with that girl afterwards. And the other waitresses left Brianna alone, too."

Making a mental note that jealousy and spite from co-workers might be relevant to Brianna's death, I moved on and asked Darrell about male customers.

"Were there any who seemed to hang around when she was on shift? Any who seemed, I don't know, *off*?"

"Men hung around that girl like bees on a honeypot, Kelly. She had a regular following who would come in when she was working and either get a table or hold down the bar. She was quite a draw, I'll tell you," Darrell closed his eyes in thought and stroked his clean-shaven chin.

"She had a tight working relationship with one of our bartenders, Adrian. They both liked to work together on the late shift, until closing. He'd be the one to ask if there were any problem customers. Bonus for you, he's actually working the day shift today, if you want to talk to him."

Darrell stood up smoothly from his chair in a move that silently conveyed that our interview with him was at an end, time to go ladies. Calling Rett off his bed, we got to our feet as well. Darrell ruffled Rett's ears for a moment at the door and his face softened as he looked at the crazy-quilt dog.

"When you're done speaking with Adrian, tell him to carry the dog bed down to your car. It's Rett's and he may as well get the use out of it," Darrell Forsun stopped speaking abruptly, and put a hand out toward Rett's leash.

"Rett does have a safe home now?" he asked with some urgency. "He's not at risk for being put down because he's homeless?" His eyes, suddenly as hard as stone, flicked from me to Cici and back again.

"I won't have it," he said in a low, fierce voice. "I was very fond of Brianna. She would spend a short time visiting with me after her shifts when she came to the office to collect Rett. That dog meant everything to her, and I won't see him put down." As he finished speaking, Darrell Forsun stood at his full height, with his chest expanded combatively at us, and I suddenly felt like the very small woman that I am. Brianna had been taller, younger, and a fit Army veteran with mad combat skills, but if she had gotten on the wrong side of a physical altercation with this man, there was no doubt who would have won. Maybe we shouldn't be so quick to give him a pass from suspicion!

"Ah, cool your jets, big guy," Cici casually replied, obviously not rattled in the least by Mr. Big. "Rett's with me now, and he's got RogerDogs to back me up if needed. He's made in the shade, for life." She placed her hand onto Rett's head and the dog adoringly swiveled his eyes to look at Cici, while dropping into a perfect sit-at-attention, eager to take direction from her.

Mr. Big shrunk back down to a normal sized Darrell Forsun at her words. "Well, good, I'm glad to hear that. Don't forget the bed when you leave. Also the business office will have Brianna's last payment ready for you as well." He leaned forward to shake hands first with Cici and then with me. With a final, "Ladies," Darrell Forsun turned back into his office and shut the heavy wood door, leaving us on our own to track down Adrian the bartender.

Twenty-One

Cici led the way through the Shalimar dining room on our walk to the bar, which turned out to be located near the front of the restaurant, off to the right of the dining room as you came through the main entrance. The room, with its walls of padded, dark green leather, its black marble-top bar, and its pewter gray, circular stools sporting sleek, cushioned backs, oozed a hushed, masculine ambience. Powerful people would meet here to broker back door deals, I thought. It was the antithesis of a typical Montana cowboy bar.

"This place looks different in the daylight," Cici observed as we approached the empty bar. "I've never seen it so bright looking and, well, empty. Course I haven't seen it at all, for a while." Cici gave me a look of wry chagrin. "If you remember, I'm on the banned guest list here."

"Well, if you promise to behave, I'll let you slide for the moment," an amused voice spoke from behind us.

We turned quickly to see a thin, smaller man, maybe five eight and a hundred thirty pounds, wearing a white shirt, black vest and black string tie which proclaimed him to be the bartender. He was crossing the room toward the bar and us, carrying a tray laden with a stacked pyramid of bar glasses.

Yet again, Rett rushed to greet an old friend, but fortunately for the glassware, Cici kept a tight hold on his leash this time. Rett had to settle for bouncing up and down while trying to strangle himself with his collar.

With a cry of "Rett! Buddy!" the bartender swiftly deposited the tray of glasses on a nearby table and stepped within reach of the excited dog. Rett responded by shooting straight up in the air, while pulling his legs in so that he became a hairy cannonball with a head attached. The cannonball was snatched tight to the man's chest at the height of the leap in a move that had clearly been practiced many times before. Two sets of bright blue, impossibly round eyes laughed into each other. If the man were to apply black eye makeup, he and Rett could step out as a matched pair.

Giving Rett a final squeeze, the bartender lowered the dog down to the ground, noticing his lack of a left front leg as the dog stood. "Hey, what's happened here? Brianna's turned up dead, and Rett's missing a leg? The paper didn't say nothing about this." The man gave us a quizzical look, and curled his fingers at us as he said, "Fill me in, ladies, give Adrian the goods.

"I know you," he proclaimed, pointing at Cici. "You're Brianna's friend who isn't allowed here anymore, at least to drink. I was working *that* night, you know." Adrian's eyes twinkled as he looked Cici over. "I met you, too, at the Midsummer Night bonfire down at the river this last summer. But I don't know if you would remember me from either occasion . . ." Adrian's whole face was filled with merriment now.

I put my own pair of blue eyes on Cici and my eyebrows shot upward questioningly. Cici knew Adrian and hadn't mentioned it?

"Yeah, well, it's not like I knew your name, or anything," Cici replied. "I didn't even know you worked here with her.

"We met at the bonfire party, in the dark, down at the river," Cici clarified for me. "It was a wild night, and, ahem, it might be that *some* people got shit-faced and walked home on their lips . . .

and possibly don't remember who they met, real well." Cici gave a small cough into her hand and cut her eyes at me.

"Just in case, my name's Cici Vargas, and I'm pleased to meet you officially, Adrian." She leaned forward and shook Adrian's hand.

"We just got done conversing with Mr. Darrell," Cici went on. "He gave us the green light to come talk with you about Brianna. He didn't know that Brianna was dead, but you do, right? I guess you read the newspaper better than him. Just curious, though, have you talked with any police about Brianna? We thought they would've been by, but apparently not to talk with the manager."

Adrian's eyes grew even rounder, if that were possible, and a look of caution appeared on his friendly face. He looked around the empty seating area in a furtive manner, before picking up his abandoned tray of glassware and walking to the black marble topped bar. Not looking at us, he reached over the bar to pull out a white bar cloth and began to polish the glasses. One glass, two glasses, and then three were buffed to a professional shine before he jerked his chin at us over his shoulder.

"I need to work while we talk. Why don't you come over here so we don't have to yell?" Adrian kept his focus off of us as we shimmied up to the bar on his right side, giving us only brief side eye looks as he spoke.

"Somebody's ass is going to be grass," he said quietly. "An employee turning up dead? Mr. Forsun should've been told about that almost before it happened, and his bosses down in Vegas about two seconds later." Adrian stopped talking and made significant eye contact with Cici and me.

"You hear what I'm saying about *bosses in Vegas*? Local police give the restaurant the white glove treatment; it's not surprising that they haven't interviewed staff, at least at during their working hours. But for Mr. Forsun not to have even been told about it? Could be some ugliness over that, and I don't want to be caught up in it, you know?"

With a shake of his head and shrug of his shoulders, Adrian seemed to set his apprehension aside. "What do you want to talk with me about? Are you looking for someone to take Rett now that Brianna's gone?" He nudged the dog in the ribs with the toe of his shoe, a move that was greeted by the dog with a playful grab of his foot, and a mock growl.

"No, sir! Rett's taken!" Cici barked at Adrian, and then somewhat sheepishly continued in a milder tone. "I mean, I'm adopting him, he's going to be, like, a service dog for me."

"We heard about Brianna's dustup with her coworker from Mr. Forsun, and wondered if there had been any trouble with other staff, or with customers, or if anyone just seemed overly interested in Brianna, in a creepy or scary way," I said.

Adrian moved back behind the bar, and began to put the polished drinkware away. As he worked, he told us, "The thing is, we're not supposed to get involved with clientele here, it's worth your job to start dating either customers or co-workers. And this is the top gig in town for restaurant work. No way would you let it go for a casual pick-up, you know?"

Adrian put down the glass he was holding and leaned closer to us, telling us in a furtive undertone, "Bartenders at the Shalimar get ten percent of the bar tab. Most places offer five percent, at the most. And we don't have to split our tips with any of the other workers.

"Waitresses do good, too, even though they have to split out tips to the bussers and hostesses. A waitress will easily take home a couple hundred a night in tips. That's a lot of money compared to most jobs in Missoula. And everything is paid in cash here, wages included." Adrian cocked an eyebrow at us, checking that we realized the import of the cash payments. Cash money, of course, is easier to fudge with the taxman, which can represent a significant hike in value on the dollar.

"Brianna, well, she did even better than that," Adrian stopped talking momentarily. A hangdog, half-ashamed look crossed his face and he intensively scrubbed at the glass in his hand as if he could wipe away his memory. "She talked me into giving her a cut on my bar bill percentage; in return for her working hard to increase drink sales. She swore I'd earn more money working as a team, even if my percentage was less."

Adrian looked sideways at us from under his eyebrows, his mouth downturned as if he expected us to laugh at him. I was willing to bet he hadn't really understood how a smaller percentage could indeed mean more money, just as long as it was taken from a larger base. A truth learned from the math classroom: lots of people don't ever understand percentages. Hasn't stopped the world from turning, though.

"So there's no way Brianna would've risked getting kicked off the job for 'fraternizing', as management puts it. She was all about making customers happy so they'd spend a lot of time and money in here, but treated everyone with the same sassy, flirty-ness.

"You know that song about boots that walk on you?" Adrian had moved on to folding cloth napkins into fancy origami shapes, but paused to look at us, checking for recognition of the song. We both nodded.

"That was like Brianna's theme song when she was working. She was just *audacious* with how she interacted with customers, and they ate it up. It was always clear that she was hands-off, though. The Shalimar isn't the kind of place where you handle the waitresses, no, sir.

"Most of the people coming in are high end: bankers, lawyers, out of town high rollers, yada, yada. Not friends or acquaintances of the workers here. It's a little *toney* here for regular people, if you get my drift.

"There was one guy that Brianna knew though, a skinny little guy with greasy long hair that he always wore in a ponytail and the dinkiest goatee on his chin, who would come in every so often and hang out, making moon eyes at her," Adrian narrowed his eyes, and folded more slowly as he replayed his memories in his head.

"She'd get all pissy when she saw him, and make snarky comments about him following her around. She didn't like it at all that he would come in here, but there wasn't any way to make him leave as long as he behaved himself, and drank enough to pay for his spot at the bar."

"Did she ever say why she didn't like him? Or where she knew him from in the first place?" I asked. Since we had walked into the restaurant, we had heard about a dust-up with a coworker, discovered that the workplace and its manager might be linked to the Vegas mob, and now there was a potential stalker thrown into the mix. What a den of vipers the Shalimar was turning out to be! I planned to burn up the phone lines to Deputy Shaw as soon as we were clear of this place.

"The first time I remember him showing up, she made some remark to me that he followed her around like a dog; she'd met him at some meeting that was all about animal rights. I told her that it would be easy to get him warned off from the Shalimar, kinda like happened to Cici, here," Adrian smirked at her before continuing. "Brianna didn't go for it though. She just shrugged and said it wasn't the end of the world if he came in. He apparently 'knew people', people she was trying to get hooked up with, and he was her 'in'. It made him useful enough to her that she was willing to put up with him hanging around."

I flashed back to the picture of Brianna at the arson fire in Washington that had been claimed by several groups as a planned act of destruction. Had this person been her link to those violent, eco-terrorist groups?

"Did she say anything more about the 'people' she wanted to meet? Or about this guy being able to hook her up? Was it something to do with animal rights if that's where she met him in the first place?"

"I can't say, Kelly, I asked her about it one time that the guy was here; Brianna just laughed and said something like if she told me, she'd have to kill me afterwards. I thought she was just blowing

smoke, telling me to mind my own business. But now that she's
dead, not just dead but actually *murdered*, I don't know. What if she
was into some serious shit and wound up dead because of it?"

Fifteen minutes later, we were back in the Subaru with Rett's
plush dog sofa in the back and a handful of cash that was Brianna's
last payment from the Shalimar. The Shalimar was a beautiful,
high-end restaurant to the innocent eye, but I felt like we had seen
an ugly underbelly of the place that left me feeling lightly coated in
slime, even seated in the car, driving away. No, there would be no
future dining at the Shalimar for Kelly!

I piloted the car to my favorite Missoula grocery store, the
Orange Street Food Farm and sent Cici inside with a list while I
dialed up Deputy Darla Shaw for a catch-up session. Other grocery
stores might have cheaper prices, but for a foody, the Orange Street
grocery is the place to go. They stock items that aren't available to
Montanans elsewhere in the state; a stay in Missoula isn't complete
for Boyd and me without a visit to the store.

I made several attempts to track Deputy Shaw down via telephone. Calling her office led me down the electronic pathway to
her voicemail. Insufficient! I wanted to speak to the woman herself,
but even her cell phone went unanswered. I was forced to leave
my name, number and reason for calling, just like any ordinary
citizen, rather than one calling with red-hot tips to a murder investigation. Grrrr.

Stymied for the moment, I hopped out of the Subaru and went
to find Cici and make myself useful with the grocery shopping.

TWENTY-TWO

Deputy Darla Shaw swung herself out of the county sheriff's white SUV and shut the door hard, making a satisfying 'whump' to punctuate her own growly mood. It was almost two o'clock in the afternoon and Darla hadn't had the chance to eat since her long ago breakfast bagel and coffee, consumed before coming on duty at six in the morning. Usually she had tide-over snacks stashed in the SUV: almonds, granola bars, and dried fruit, all sorts of goodies to keep a working woman on the move, but yesterday, she had switched vehicles with her co-worker, Deputy DuPries, so he could take her regular ride to Billings for scheduled maintenance. Her snack stash didn't make the switch, unfortunately, and was now on its way to Billings with Deputy DuPries.

Asshole's probably eating it all, too, Darla grumbled to herself.

It had been a busy day full of nothing for Deputy Darla Shaw. She had gone on three callouts that had each been resolved before she reached the scene. Not in a single one of them had anyone thought to cancel her appearance before she showed up. It had grated on her to outwardly remain an amiable, supportive professional while inwardly wanting to shout at the irresponsible so and so's.

She knew she should be glad that the Wilkinson's toddler had only been sitting in a cupboard eating cereal, rather than wandering away from the house, but would it have hurt to let the sheriff's office know the tot had been found *before* she had driven almost fifty miles to their house?

Ditto for the elderly bachelor farmer who had parked his car on the wrong side of the barn when returning home the night before, drunk as a skunk she suspected. In the morning, when he didn't see the car parked in its usual spot, he called it in as stolen, before discovering it when he fed the horses. Nope, no phone call to cancel that alert, either.

The third callout had been a domestic violence report; supposedly the man of the house had broken his wife's nose and threatened to shoot her before he drove off to work. When Deputy Darla Shaw had arrived, the wife claimed that it was all a misunderstanding. Her explanation now was that their *pit-bull* had broken her nose by flinging his head into her face with puppy exuberance; the husband had threatened to shoot the dog, not her. She had been terribly upset at the time, but now felt her husband didn't really mean it, no intervention by the county's finest was required, have a nice day, officer.

Deputy Shaw strode into the office building that housed the county sheriff's department, stopping to say hello to the receptionist, Maudy Becker. Maudy was a stern faced, older woman who wore her determinedly red hair in a beehive of permanently waved curls. She peered commandingly over the tops of her half-frame tortoiseshell readers at all incomers to the office and was their gate-keeper; no one was allowed to breech her control point to access the sheriff or deputies without the go ahead from Maudy Becker. Darla had mentally summed her up as a bitch-on-wheels when the two had first met, but she had come to grudgingly admire and rely on Maudy's ability to keep the public at bay unless a deputy desired to speak with them. Cerberus himself couldn't do as well as Maudy Becker.

"Good afternoon, Maudy, how's the day shaping up here? Anything new I should know about?"

Maudy sniffed derisively. "Nothing for your concern. That ignorant doofus, Mr. Sietzer, was back in with a fresh complaint, but I convinced him that arresting his neighbor because the neighbor's dog sired a litter of puppies from his own precious pooch, well, that's just not under the Sheriff's purview."

Deputy Darla Shaw laughed out loud at this news. Mr. Sietzer was a regular at their office, wanting the attention that came along with making a complaint, she supposed. Unauthorized doggie sex was a new one, though. Darla briefly wondered if that was even a thing you could run through the civil court, but shook off the thought. Not her monkey, not her circus. She had real duties to attend to.

Darla walked into the deputies' bullpen, pulled out her comfortable office chair from her regulation metal desk and sat down with a sigh. The other deputies made do with standard issue, hard back chairs, but Darla had early on brought in her own, personal, ergonomic office chair that could recline and was height adjustable. She figured that as the only woman deputy, she was going to be different no matter what, so she may as well embrace the fact and be comfortable at work.

Darla gazed fondly at the picture of her husband, Eric, posed with his red roan quarter horse, which stood in pride of place on the back corner of her desk. She and Eric were two ranch kids who got married right out of high school, expecting to continue with ranch life and raise themselves a packet of children along the way.

The plan had been to work on big spreads as managers until they could buy their own operation, same as their parents had done—but, to their dismay, those kinds of positions were scarce on the ground and land prices were soaring beyond their reach. Eric and Darla had struggled along for the first year out of high school before the high dollar wages of the Stillwater Mine in the

Beartooth Mountains had lured her Eric to the underground life, bringing platinum and palladium to the world instead of calves and lambs.

They moved to Big Timber where he could catch the mine's shuttle bus to work, and Darla found herself knocking around Big Timber, at loose ends while Eric was gone on his long shifts.

She had been cleaning houses in the area for wealthy out-of-state clients, as much for something to keep her busy as for the money, when she had noticed an advertisement in the newspaper announcing openings with the sheriff's department for deputy sheriffs. Intrigued, she had put her name in the hat and gone through a selection process that included physical fitness and firearms testing. Darla had turned out to be the top candidate, owing to her dad's insistence that in this life, an independent girl needed be an expert in three things: how drive a stick shift in any vehicle, change a tire in under ten minutes, and shoot the 'eye out of a squirrel' with both hand guns and rifles.

Her dad had now passed away from a heart attack, but he had been tickled pink when his little girl became a deputy sheriff; he had bragged on her at his local watering hole until the day he died. She was sure he now spent a lot of time perched on a cloud, looking down at her, telling all the nearby angels about her latest exploits. It was a nice thought to carry through the day, anyway, although, at the moment, she suspected he was unhappy about her repeating anti-Indian rhetoric from the bullpen while interviewing the ladies who found the dead body in the Crazies.

Darla winced in memory of her out-of-character behavior. Even-keeled Sheriff Landry had been out of the office that day, and the second in command, one B.T. McManus, a dyed-in-the-wool redneck originally from Texas, had whipped all of them into an anti-Indian blame fest during the daily morning meeting. In a moment of weakness, she had lapped it up with a spoon, eager to keep up with the good old boy bluster while being young, and very much a woman, and then gone on to belch it out on the three women as she interviewed them. Ouch, she thought, and tamped the shameful memory back down as she focused on her husband's picture.

Darla and Eric still planned on getting property 'one day' and salted away as much of their earnings toward that goal as they could manage. Kids were on hold for the duration as well, but they were young and had time to make a family happen. In the meantime, she would be Deputy Darla Shaw, ready to ride into action on behalf of Sweetgrass County residents.

She fired up her computer, and while she was waiting for it to awaken from its slumber, looked through her pink phone messages that Maudy had left in a neat stack on her desk. Mom had called, probably wanting to know if she and Eric could come to a family dinner; Kelly Boyd had called, asking to speak to Deputy Shaw at her earliest convenience. She had to think for a minute about who Kelly Boyd was, the name was familiar but didn't ring a bell right off.

The Medical Examiner's Office had called, asking for a callback. *Oh, yes, please,* Darla thought, *let it be the results from the dog collar DNA check.* Hands down, this was the call she was returning first.

"Medical Examiner's Office, this is Penny speaking, how may I direct your call?"

"Penny, this is Deputy Darla Shaw with the Sweetgrass County sheriff's office. I'm returning the call of," she paused and squinted at the message slip written by Maudy, "a Dr. Greene, I believe. Would you connect me, please?"

After a series of clicks and some truly bad elevator music, a high pitched, nasal voice came on the line that instantly put Darla in mind of a heavily pimpled teenage boy, instead of an adult male.

"Yes, this is Dr. Greene." No inquiry as to how he could be of help was appended to this guy's greeting.

Darla repeated who she was and why she was calling.

"Oh, yes. Did you happen to read my email? I sent it after I called and left the call back message."

"Uhhm, no, I'm just pulling up my email for the day, now. Let me look at it quick while I have you on the line." Darla didn't want the good doctor to escape from the phone in case she had questions about the message. A speedy read through the body of the email showed her that the blood on the dog collar was human and was not Brianna Norwood's.

"So, have you sent the profile to CODIS yet, or is that in my bailiwick?" Deputy Darla Shaw inquired. The Combined DNA Index System, CODIS, would tell them if the blood found on the dog's collar matched any known criminals in the USA. If there was a match, they might be lucky and get a quick closure to the girl's murder.

"I went ahead and sent it in already," Dr. Greene replied. "That's in my email, too."

Well, excuse me, Darla thought, *guess I didn't read your every golden word.*

"Any results yet?" She tried to keep her voice cool and collected, to avoid sounding like someone hopping up and down with eagerness and impatience, as her inner Darla was doing at this very moment.

"No, but it should be soon, at least by later afternoon. I'll shoot you an email as soon as I know. Time is of the essence in a murder investigation, Deputy," the nasal voice of Dr. Greene informed her piously.

"True that," she replied, making a face at the phone in her hand. Who did this 'time is the essence' jerk think he was? "Am I cc'd with the CODIS request so I get the results same time as you?" she asked him sweetly.

"Uhmm, no, I'll have to notify you by separate communication," Dr. Greene muttered in a somewhat chagrined tone.

Ha! She had thought so. This Dr. Greene wanted to hog the glory of an investigatory hit, rather than facilitating the notification process.

"Please give me an update by four-thirty this afternoon, regardless. I would like your cell phone number; too, in case I need to reach you and you're away from the landline." This last bit was given with a note of steel in Deputy Darla Shaw's voice that sent notice to Dr. Greene that it wasn't exactly a request.

Take that, Dr. Officious Prick, Darla thought as she concluded the phone call and hung up.

She would wait to call Kelly Boyd back. Most likely the woman just wanted a personal update on the Brianna Norwood investigation. Deputy Darla Shaw had genuinely liked the three women who had found Brianna's body, but it always astounded her how much civilians wanted to be kept abreast of ongoing investigations. Everyone, down to people she met while walking her dog or grocery shopping, wanted to know all the details. It took a lot of effort to refrain from telling them all to bugger off and mind their own business. Her job wasn't dependent on winning reelection, but her boss's job was. *Don't foul your own nest,* she told herself constantly.

With a sigh, Deputy Darla Shaw put the rest of her call-back slips to the side of her desk, and pulled up a copy of the department's pre-formatted incident report form. She wanted to complete the paperwork for the morning's callouts while the details were fresh in her mind, hopefully clearing her desk of the dull documentation before the CODIS report came back.

Yes, returning Kelly Boyd's phone call could definitely wait until the CODIS report was in hand.

TWENTY-THREE

DINNER HOUR HAD COME AND GONE with no word back from Deputy Darla Shaw. It was starting to feel as if, in truth, no one was actively investigating Brianna's killing, and I for one, was deeply annoyed. Cici didn't say anything directly to me, but I could feel anger building up inside her like molten lava inside of a volcano, getting ready to spew out over the world at large. Rett, too, seemed to clue in on her manner and wouldn't leave her side, instead leaning into her legs and nudging her hand occasionally.

I very much wanted to call Boyd and have a venting session, but Cici had me a little worried as I watched her sit on the sofa, staring into space with a face that looked more stone like as the minutes went by. Me kvetching out loud to Boyd where she could hear might be like throwing gasoline on a smoldering fire. Instead, I sent him a quick text, just to check in, promising him a longer phone call tomorrow, when Cici was at her job interview.

Action is better than sitting and stewing, I have always thought. Maybe a walk around the neighborhood would dissipate some of the negative energy, for the both of us.

"Cici, let's leash up Rett and get some fresh air before we hunker in for the night," I suggested, aiming my voice at upbeat, but beneath the level of annoyingly perky. "Rett's got to have a crack at being outside, no matter what."

Rett lurched to his feet at the sound of his name, outside, and leash. He launched himself into an orgy of ridiculous behavior, whirling in tight circles at Cici's feet and emitting high pitched yips as if he were a tiny puppy, all the while rolling his bright blue eyes around at us like marbles. The dog and his silliness sparked a laughing response from Cici, and just like that, the volcano vanished.

"All right, all right, you goofy goose," Cici said. "Let's get bundled up and see what's what in the neighborhood."

Winter darkness had brought out the stars over Missoula when we hit the streets for our evening walk, but the temperature was still above freezing. We'd walked several blocks, stopping frequently to let Rett investigate bushes and lamp posts, when Cici spoke up.

"Say, Kelly. Brianna was living in a house near here, right? What say we see if anyone's home? If so, we can get a heads up on how much stuff she still has there, make arrangements to come back and haul whatever away."

I couldn't see any downside to trying. As Cici said, the house was in the same neighborhood as our Airbnb, it would be easy to walk by the place. If no one was home, no big loss. We could always telephone later, if we struck out.

"Sounds good to me, nothing ventured, nothing gained," I replied, pulling out my phone and using Google Maps for directions to the house in question. "Looks like we just need to go two blocks over, and half a block to the east."

WE WERE IN LUCK, BOTH OF Brianna's ex-roommates, Jori Haupsted and Lila Sanderson, were spending Tuesday night at home and were in when we knocked on the door. The girls lived in a red, single story, older model home with wood siding, on a tree lined street near the golf course. The neighborhood was a mix of owner-occupied houses and ones that were rented out to groups of college students, but there was no evidence of partying or other college shenanigans at the moment. Most houses had some lights visible behind curtains, but no other people were out on the street.

It was full dark when we arrived at the house, and snow had begun to fall steadily, the flakes looking like white moths circling the streetlights. It was a black and white and gray colorless Montana night, soon to be whiter with the oncoming storm. I was very thankful we had driven up to Missoula when we had. I mean, really, why drive on snowy roads if you don't have to? Hopefully tree limbs that were still covered in fall leaves wouldn't get weighed down to the point of breaking. Widespread power outages would result, if the branches pulled down power lines.

We rang the doorbell, and after a short wait, the porchlight clicked on.

A tinny voice from overhead alerted us to the existence of a doorbell camera that allowed those inside to give strangers on the porch a once over without having to open the door. With a murdered roommate, this seemed like an excellent idea. We pulled off our stocking caps and helpfully smiled at the camera, wanting to put the house occupants at ease.

"Hello? Can I help you?" said the doubtful, tinny voice. Why, I lamented to myself, why are girls taught to be so accommodating and polite? We were utter strangers; her roommate had been recently killed. Surely it was 'alright' to demand we identify ourselves immediately or the police would be called, at the very least. If she was my daughter, I would want her to be pointing a shotgun at us, while she ascertained our bonafides.

Once again, Rett's presence was the wedge that literally opened the door for us. As the shortest person, I had been standing in front of Cici and Rett, but Rett now moved to my side at the sound of the intercom, where he could be seen on the camera feed. Good thing for me the door had been locked. The sound of the deadbolt clacking open gave me just enough time to step back and avoid being smacked in the face as the door was flung open so hard it rebounded.

"Ohmygodyou'vegotRett!" a young female voice cried, blurring the words together into a single falsetto shriek. A long haired, blonde girl flew out the door, landing on her knees by the dog and swooping his head up into a double armed hug as she squealed, "RettieRettieRettie! Ohmygod!" The young woman was wearing a blue crop top underneath an open, long sleeve yellow shirt, and, of all things, a bright red pair of shorts. Her apparel was a direct challenge to the lack of color in the outdoors. I felt like summer had just punched me in the eye.

Surprisingly, Rett sat without moving, as still as if he were a gigantic stuffed toy. Given his exuberance during his reunions with Darrell Forsun and Adrian, I expected more of the same now, especially with the giddiness on display from his current admirer. Perhaps he was loath to encourage her to greater displays of girlish frenzy. Some time ago, Boyd and I had seen musical that featured sorority girls whose role was to screech, "Ohmygod! Ohmygod! OHMYGOD!" in shrill, microphone assisted voices and this girl would have fit right in with them, no microphone needed. I was deeply thankful that Rett wasn't sending her into the stratosphere with an overly enthusiastic greeting.

"Lila, Jesus, shut the front door will you?" a deeper toned voice shouted from within the house. "Some of us care how high the heating bill is, you know?"

The blonde girl scrambled to her feet on the front porch, releasing Rett from her anaconda squeeze. "Ohmygod, sorrrry!" she called back inside. "You must be Brianna's friends? The police said that someone would come and collect her things? Is that what you're here for?"

"Lila, for chrissakes! Bring them inside and *shut the damn door!*"

"Oh, yeah, for sure, come inside." Lila swooped a hand toward the inside of the house and added primly, "We can't afford to heat the outside, now can we?" She added a little giggle on the end of that declaration. Cici was staring at her in open disbelief.

Apparently little Miss Lila didn't line up with her expectations for a roommate of Brianna's.

"Where are her pompoms, Kelly? Don't she seem like she'd have a pair welded to her butt or something?" Cici suggested in my ear as we followed Lila inside, and at last, got the front door closed. I made a shushing gesture with my hand. Probably Lila was impervious to mild insults, but still, honey catches more flies than vinegar.

"Jori, come and meet Brianna's friends, they've come to collect her things," sang out Lila.

A tall girl, in her early twenties, came into the living room where we stood. She had the kind of round face that people describe as moon-faced, and little brown button eyes that looked at us watchfully. Her light brown, crinkly hair was just past her shoulders in length and worn loose. She pulled it up into a high pony and secured it with a band from around her wrist as she looked at us.

"Hi, I'm Kelly Boyd," I supplied into the void left when Lila stopped talking, probably because she really didn't have the slightest idea who we were. "This is Cici Vargas, Brianna's friend. You must be Lila Sanderson?" I gestured at the blonde girl. "And you're Jori Haupsted?" I asked the tall girl.

"Yeah, that's me. Sorry I yelled about the door, Lila sometimes just wanders off and leaves it open for bugs to come in and the heat to go out."

We stood in awkward silence in a small living room that was filled with normal college furniture: nothing matched, everything looked pre-owned and worse for wear. The coffee table only had three legs, a stack of books did support duty at its far corner. Everyone stared at everyone else and waited for someone to take charge, while Rett whined and pulled at his leash, wanting to search the house for Brianna, I supposed.

"Maybe we could see Brianna's room?" I suggested. "I don't think we could take much away with us tonight, but we can get an idea of what's there, maybe make a start on packing up, if you have garbage bags we can use?"

"Yeah, sure, that would be good." Jori moved to lead us down a hall. "Lila and I put all of Brianna's stuff from around the house in there, so there's not anything left in the bathroom or anywhere. Lila, get the box of garbage bags from under the sink, will you?

"This is my room, Lila's is across the hall, that door's the bathroom, and this is where Brianna slept." Jori opened the final door to what must have been intended to be a storage space. There were no windows and no closet in the room, the space was barely long enough to house the twin mattress that lay along one wall. Across the room, clothes hung in the open, supported by a tension rod that was parallel to the mattress. Milk crates held some shoes, charging cords, books and general bathroom stuff: curling iron, makeup bag, hairbrush, and shampoo bottles. Some carved stone animals sat on a small shelf. These were the only nod toward decoration in the room.

Evidence of Rett's occupancy was given by the wads of dog hair that lurked along the walls, especially in the corners. Clearly he had shared the bed with Brianna, based on the solidly fur-felted comforter. I was mildly grossed out by the amount of dog hair in the room. *This is why Sadie and Leo sleep in the mudroom*, I thought to myself. *Ewww.*

"It's not a big space," Jori said defensively. "We gave her a good deal on the rent, though. Mostly we wanted a third person to split the utilities with, is why we let it out at all." Jori looked at her feet and shuffled them slightly before continuing. "The landlords don't actually know that Brianna was living here, as far as I know. I don't know how the police knew to come here."

I kept my mouth closed, and hoped Cici would as well.

"What did the police take with them?" Cici asked. "I don't see her phone or her iPad here, just the charging cords." She looked at me. "Brianna had a used iPad along with her phone, she didn't use a bigger computer. I think her phone was most likely with her, but the tablet? She didn't carry that around with her so much."

Jori squinched her eyes almost shut and her mouth formed a hard scowl as she replied, "You think the police told us anything? It was a pair of thick-necked storm troopers who came here; they about banged the door down, knocking on it. They told us that Brianna was dead, and that they were here as part of a murder investigation. Made us sit down in the kitchen while they went through her room, and then took 'statements' from us about Brianna They asked a bunch of questions like who her friends were, did she do illegal activities, blah, blah, blah."

Lila interrupted from the hallway, where she stood with the box of garbage bags. "We didn't know anything about her, really. I mean, she and Rett slept here, and it was really nice she could drive us to the grocery store, because Jori and I don't have cars, but she never had anyone come to the house. Most days we never even saw her!"

Lila continued indignantly. "Those policemen kept asking us about who she knew that was in Free the Animals or something, and whether we were part of it. I finally called my dad and told him we were being badgered by police. My dad's a criminal lawyer in Boise; he had me give those guys my phone and told them we weren't going to say one more word to them unless a lawyer was present.

"Then they went away. They did carry some stuff out; I bet her iPad is with them," Lila finished.

"Did the police say anything about her car? It's not parked here, is it?" I looked at both Jori and Lily for confirmation.

"No, no one mentioned her car. I haven't seen it since she's been gone," Jori replied. "Have you, Lila?" Lila shook her head vehemently, whipping her long blonde hair into contrails around her head.

"It's been gone since Brianna didn't come here anymore," Lila said, making round imploring eyes at Cici and me. "I feel so bad

that we didn't realize that she was *missing* and call the police ourselves when she must have been laying out there, *dead*. But she
never told us in advance if she was going to be gone or not, sometimes she was gone for over a week, even. So we didn't *know*!" Lila's
eyes filled with tears, and she began to cry. She thrust the box of
garbage bags at us and whirled into the bathroom, banging the
door shut behind her.

"Drama queen," muttered Jori. "You'd think she and Brianna
were BFF's the way she's carrying on. Phhh, they probably didn't
say more than ten words to each other since Brianna moved in."

Huh. I had noticed that despite Lila's effusive greeting of Rett,
which he had politely tolerated but otherwise ignored, Lila hadn't
seemed to notice that his leg count had been reduced since she
last saw him. Now Jori, too, was saying that Lila didn't interact
with Brianna. So how had Brianna wound up living in here in the
first place?

"Jori, how did Brianna come to rent the room here? Not through
Lila, huh?"

"I met her at a wildlife film festival that the Department of
Forestry was hosting last May. I'm a Wildlife Biology major, and
I was taking tickets and stuff to help with the festival; she and I
got to talking at the reception party, afterwards. You know, just
a low-level get-together to eat cookies, drink punch, schmooze
with the filmmakers sort of thing. She was really interested in the
films, how they got made, what was the background of the people
doing it. She said she wanted to have a career that was centered
around wild animals, and I filled her in on the program that's at
UM. It's the best place to get a Wildlife Biology degree, and not
just in Montana, either.

"Anyway, she also said how she was looking for a place to live,
since she had decided to stay in Missoula. I liked her, so I told her
about the Tiny Room, that's what Lila and I call it, and said she and
Rett could live there. Rett was with her at the festival, he's a cool
dog, huh?"

"Didn't you need to check with Lila first?"

"No, my name's on the lease here. Both Lila and Brianna are subletting from me. I don't think the landlords really know about them, but as long as we're not bothering anyone . . ." Jori's voice trailed away as she gave me a mischievous wink.

The three of us began to work at packing up Brianna's few things. Clothes went into garbage bags after the pockets were checked. All her clothes would go to Goodwill; Jori volunteered to be in charge of dropping them off. Any paperwork that had been left behind by the detectives was bundled into a canvas tote bag that we found under some shoes; we would read through the papers at a later date, before discarding anything as junk.

Rett was enjoying himself cavorting on the bed, burrowing underneath the comforter and peeking back out at us. I had a cat once who liked to do that, and gave him some playful swats on his hidden butt. Just like my old cat, he whirled around under the covers and tried to bite me through the comforter.

"Oh, look out for the Bed Monster!" I laughed, swatting him some more, while Jori looked on with amusement.

"Come on, Kelly, quit farting around with the dog and lend a hand." Cici gave me mock grief, her grin belying her gruff tone of voice. "Why don't you find something to wrap up those little carved animals, I'd like to keep them."

Jori spoke up, "I'll take these bags of clothes out to the garage, and grab a handful of newspapers from the recycling stack while I'm out there. Those'll be good to use. I'll see if there's a small box, too."

Cici and I listened to the sound of Jori's footsteps receding down the hall as we sat back in silent, mutual agreement that a break was called for. Cici looked at the now empty milk crates and shook her head.

"Not much more than a pot to piss in, is it?" Cici said slowly. "And I'm not much better; all my shit fits in my Mobile Hotel. You know what they say, Kelly, about freedom equals having nothing?

It doesn't seem really wild and free anymore, just . . . inconsequential. Damn."

She rubbed the back of her neck hard for a moment, then turned and poked the Bed Monster, inspiring fresh body surges and fake snaps from under the blanket.

"This job interview tomorrow could be the start of a fresh page for Rett and me. Got to tell you, Kelly, I'm more nervous about it than I ever was driving one of my transport trucks." Cici whacked her prosthetic leg. "And look how that turned out. Got my fingers crossed for a better outcome from this job!"

Betty Mills had arranged for Cici to interview on Wednesday, October 12th, at an animal rescue group in Missoula, called Zootown Zoo. Rescue groups around Montana all get to know one another; Betty and Jana Toski had started their organizations about the same time and had mutual respect for each other. Betty Mills and some of the Montana rescues don't see eye to eye; they probably dislike her as much as she disdains them, but she and Jana rub along okay. Betty had even told us to ask Jana if she still liked mules from Moscow as much as she used to; the small, wicked grin on Betty's face at the time told me there was a story behind this reference, and that she didn't mean four legged creatures, either. Apparently Betty and Jana were sometimes drinking buddies as well as rescue warriors.

"You'll do great, Cici," I said, knowledgeably. "Remember, it's not just you interviewing, it's you and Rett as a package deal. You both know your way around RogerDogs, this place just has other types of animals deal with. We've pre-tested Rett out on cats and horses and you know he did great. As for you," I pointed a finger her direction. "Shoveling shit is shoveling shit, it doesn't matter so much what kind of butt it came out from." I arranged my face into a wide-eyed picture of solemnness before continuing. "Ms. Vargas, I have complete faith in your ability to rise to Head Shitwoman by Christmas."

Cici got a good laugh out of my foolery, thank goodness. There were times, like at the Airbnb earlier in the evening, when Cici goes off in her head and her outward façade fractures, like an image on TV pixelating into blocks of color, rather than presenting a cohesive picture. I assumed that these were moments when her PTSD was gaining the upper hand, and it was gratifying to be able to head off an episode by getting a laugh from her. To his credit, Rett seemed to sense when these spells of 'whatever' were building in Cici; he would lean on her, nudge her with his nose and paw at her to regain her attention and making excellent use of his big, blue eyes when she finally made eye contact with him.

I've read articles about dogs and their use of eyes to communicate with humans. Apparently some breeds of dogs are more adept with this non-verbal technique than others, with snub-nosed dogs like boxers and French bulldogs at the top. Researchers have found that these breeds have a more highly developed center area of the retina, allowing them to focus better on a single object, like a face, compared to a sight hound that has more development in the outer edges of the eye.

Rett didn't have a short, flat face, but, man, did he know how to work a person over with his googly blue eyes.

Footsteps in the hall alerted us to the return of Jori, bringing the promised newspapers. She handed us a stack and nodded at the front-page headline and photo of the issue on the top of the stack.

"Look at those baby wolverines with their mama," Jori said. "They were born down at the zoo in Billings. Brianna would've gone nuts to see this. I bet she'd have been in Billings by the next day and she'd've camped out there until she got to see them, live."

Jori got a speculative look on her face as she continued to stare at the picture. "You know," she said slowly. "I think that might've been the last conversation I had with Brianna, talking about wolverines."

"But, this newspaper didn't come out until September 24th, and she was already dead by then," I pointed out, not sure what Jori was saying. Was she confused about the dates?

"I don't mean these wolverines in particular," Jori replied impatiently, not saying 'dumbass' out loud, but it was written clearly on her features. Chastened, I kept my mouth shut and waited for her to go on with her thought.

"I was working at the kitchen table one night, pulling an allnighter to write a paper on how wintertime, back-woods activities can be disruptive and detrimental to species like lynx and wolverines. Just a single person snowshoeing through their territory can make them move on. It's called 'functional habitat loss' and it's a big deal for those animals.

"Anyway, Brianna came in from her job up at the Shalimar and saw my reference stuff about wolverines. She was all excited and told me that she was going to go out in the woods and see some. I kind of scoffed, because they're really elusive. I told her she'd have to be crazy lucky to see one in the wild, ever.

"She got a funny expression on her face, secretive and sly, but laughing, too, like she was enjoying an insider joke. She shook her head at me and said, 'Well, good thing I have a crazy guide, then!' She looked super pleased with herself, but that was the end of the conversation. I was too pressed for time sit around talking, you know?"

Jori shook her own head, sadly. "I don't think I ever saw her again. She was always in and out of the house, sometimes gone for days at a time. I'd forgotten about the wolverine conversation, though."

"Do you know what the date was, Jori?" I asked urgently. "What date was the paper due? I don't think anyone knows exactly when Brianna actually disappeared, this could help pinpoint that information."

Jori looked startled at the idea, and quickly left to go to her bedroom to retrieve the due date from her computer.

Cici leaned toward me, with fire in her eyes. "Kelly, this is big. This 'guide' to the wolverines, I bet Brianna wasn't saying he was loco crazy, I think she meant he was a guide to the Crazy mountains! This bozo is the one who took her down there and killed her!"

TWENTY-FOUR

Cici's Wednesday interview at Zootown Zoo was scheduled for ten o'clock, sharp. It was our plan to walk into the reception area a good ten minutes early, calm, cool, and collected. Because of the snowfall the night before, and the potential for treacherous city streets, we actually left the Airbnb by eight-thirty.

We made it to Zootown Zoo an hour later, without a single fender-bender, although we did slide through one intersection. Success!

The rescue was on acreage just outside of Missoula to the southwest, and had been started as a horse rescue by Jana Toski some ten years earlier. Soon after taking in her first rescue horses, Bilbo the donkey needed a home, and joined the herd. Bilbo was followed by three other donkeys, ranging in size from miniature Mediterraneans, less than three feet at the withers, to a single Mammoth Jack named Goliath, who was the size of a small horse. Next came the miniature pig who, like many of his kind, failed to stop growing at his human's idea of 'miniature'. People also began asking her to take in cats and dogs. Jana found that she relished running an all-animal rescue, and Zootown Zoo was born. She even had a Bactrian camel for a short while, while his owner found property in the area.

"And snakes! Shit, Kelly, her website says she sometimes has *snakes*! I'm not going to take care of anything that slithers, I *hate* those goddamn things!" Cici exploded when she was studying up on Zootown Zoo via Google. After her outburst, I gave her a level look with some starch in it.

"Look, you're going in for an interview, okay? Snakes may not even come up. If they do, put a positive spin on it; tell Jana you aren't used to snakes, but you're *willing to try*. Same as you did with horses—you weren't used to them, but you were willing to learn." Betty Mills had mentioned that Cici was skittish, i.e. scared shitless, around Randy's horses at first, but after several days of working side by side with Betty or Randy, had learned to competently feed, and muck out the three Mills' horses on her own.

"Yeah, maybe. Whoo, Kelly, I thought Betty's horses would bite me, kick me and stomp me flat. I never would've gone near them except they were so calm with Rett, you know? I figured since they didn't kill him straight out, maybe I'd be okay, too."

"Well, there you go. The snakes aren't going to kill Rett either."

Ten minutes before ten o'clock, Cici, Rett and I presented ourselves in the reception area for Zootown Zoo. I stopped just inside the door, taking in the attractive area rug with geometric patterns done in faded jewel tones that covered the open floor space, and the comfortable-looking, green velvet, wing back chairs that flanked a stylish, blue-stained wood desk. All this opulence was topped off with the presence of a chirpy co-ed receptionist who sported fingernails decorated with nail art. I simultaneously felt both envious of Zootown Zoo, and defensive of good old RogerDogs. This operation clearly operated on a higher dollar scale than our somewhat scruffy, make-do rescue. You could see that in an instant.

Jana, alerted to our arrival by the bubbly young receptionist, was quite a change from the Betty Mills model as well. Jana had ash blonde hair pulled into a smooth chignon at the back of her neck. With her large, gray-green eyes and high cheekbones set in a long, firm jawed face, she was a dead ringer for the actress who plays Penny Knatchbull, in *The Crown*. Jana was quite tall, at least five nine, and dressed in a soft, roll-collar, brown sweater and artfully distressed jeans. If it weren't for the fact that she was wearing rubber boots splashed with what looked like authentic shit, I wouldn't have believed that she was a hands-on owner/operator of an animal rescue.

Cici was outfitted in a clean, RogerDog polo shirt, and jeans that did not have any holes in them yet. I had made her scrub all bits of poo off of her work boots for first impressions, but those boots were ready to wade into work. Her hair was gathered into a pony tail, nothing fancy, but neat, and as always, no makeup was on her face. Cici was not and never would be, a femme fatal, but that's not necessary for a hands-on, shit shoveling animal worker, is it?

I myself wore my favorite, cerulean blue oversize sweater layered on top of a RogerDog polo shirt of my own, and a dressy pair of silver-gray, stretchy jeans. No shit of any kind lurked on my sweet little gray ankle boots, and they, by god, were going to stay that way. I was here strictly as a verbal reference for Cici, if needed.

We introduced ourselves around, with Rett making a solid impression by sitting up on his haunches and extending his remaining front paw to Jana for a shake. We had never seen Rett do this before, but leave it to Rett to have interview manners ready to roll.

"Cici, let's walk around and view the operations here at the Zoo. I'll introduce you and Rett to the animals and we can talk about what you'd do for us. We can look in at the little apartment, too."

If Cici were offered the job, she would have access to a small, onsite studio apartment where she and Rett could live. As an employed person with a steady wage, and reliable housing, Cici and Rett would then be eligible to apply for admittance to the Spokane S.D.P.T. program for veterans. Through their program, Rett could become a certified service dog for Cici and help her control her PTSD, and maybe learn to help brace her if her balance faltered. This all was a long way from the version of Cici who drank too much, fought too much, and lived in her car. I had my fingers, and toes, crossed for her.

I would come back to pick Cici up at noon, giving me two free hours to track down Deputy Darla Shaw by telephone and fill her in on the information that had come our way.

DEPUTY DARLA SHAW WAS IN THE middle of restoring her favorite work vehicle to its ready-to-roll-with-Darla state when her cell phone buzzed in her uniform pocket. As she had suspected, her co-deputy had emptied the vehicle of her stash of snacks, and annoyingly left behind a pile of trash. At least there wasn't gum stuck to the ashtray, nor had the ashtray been used for any actual ashes.

Darla deeply appreciated the fact that none of sheriff's office employees smoked. Cigarette stink on clothing bothers everyone but the smoker, and was one of her personal pet peeves that had to be set aside when dealing with the public. Now if there were only some way to convince Andy DuPries to grow up and graduate from the using the malodorous deodorant spray favored by teenage males. As the only female deputy, maybe she was the only one bothered by it? She wasn't going to let on that she noticed *anything* personal about Andy DuPries, however. His buddy boy co-workers or Sheriff Landry himself could have that joy.

Deputy Darla Shaw glanced at the cellphone screen and groaned as she saw the incoming call was from Kelly Boyd, whose calls from the day before were still unreturned. Darla had put off calling the woman back until the medical examiner had relayed the DNA CODIS results, and the malingering dipshit had kept her waiting until this morning, despite her pointed request to be contacted by close of business the day before. She was sure Dr. Green had deliberately 'forgotten' to contact her as a petty power play on his part, most likely hoping to provoke an outburst from her that he could then dismissively treat as noise from a hysterical woman.

Disappointingly, CODIS hadn't turned up any matches to the DNA from the dog collar. Unless they got lucky and matching DNA was collected in the future from the person for some reason, the clue of the bloody dog collar was not going to identify their murderer.

The only other physical evidence from the crime scene, a partial fingerprint on a brass casing found in the meadow, didn't match with any known miscreants, either. Also, there was the question of whether the casing was even linked to the crime. People in Montana do like to shoot their guns; any number of people could have done so in the meadow, prior to Brianna's murder.

Brianna and her movements that led to her and Rett's presence in the Crazy Mountains remained a mystery. When did she travel there, and with whom? Where was her phone and why was the phone company taking so long to send her phone records? Dammit, this was a murder investigation! Where was her car? Surely if the vehicle with its distinctive New Jersey plates was parked in the open, either in Missoula or Montana at large, it would've been reported by now.

Had the murderer driven it away from the scene and ditched it somewhere far away? Maybe leaving it with the keys inside in a high car theft area? She had heard that cars stolen in some cities, like Portland, Oregon, could be run through a chop shop within two hours, finishing up as burned-out relics on the city streets. With thousands of cars stolen a year, it would be unlikely that law enforcement would ever know if Brianna's car had joined the dystopian junk heaps of a big city.

Darla sat back in the driver's seat of the SUV and closed her eyes with a sigh of resignation. Truth be told, she was reluctant to speak with Mrs. Boyd after she, Darla, had made such a horse's ass out of herself during the interview of the retired teacher. Had she really gone so far as to intimate that Cici herself might be responsible for Brianna's death? Well, the less said about that the better.

She could, however, envision Kelly Boyd calling Maudy in the next moment, prompting yet another little pink callback slip to land on Darla's desk. No, better to man up and call the woman back now. At least she could deal with the call in the privacy of the sheriff's vehicle instead of the open deputies' room which would be filled with big ears at this time of day. She would try to re-establish herself during the call, without issuing an out and out apology. Sharing the DNA results from the dog collar would be her olive branch, Darla thought. Reaching reluctantly for her phone, Deputy Darla punched the callback icon next to the record of Kelly Boyd's recent incoming call.

THE CELLPHONE IN MY HAND GAVE an angry buzz, reminiscent of an agitated rattlesnake, startling me into dropping it as fast as if it really was a squirming serpent. The phone, apparently enjoying its new reptilian role, slithered immediately into the narrow space between the driver's seat and the console as it continued to buzz with an incoming call. Crap, crap, crap and a half! I jammed my hand into the narrow space, banging my knuckles hard against the console, and just managed to get my fingertips on the phone with enough purchase to retrieve it.

"Hello? This is Kelly." I held the iPhone to my ear, praying that I had answered the call correctly, and in time. My iPhone was pretty new to me; I never knew whether to swipe (in what direction?) or tap, (single or double?). Maybe I should try sending up smoke signals in lieu of answering the damn thing. Might be more reliable.

"Good morning, Kelly," a cool female voice said in my ear. "This is Deputy Darla Shaw, returning your phone calls from yesterday and again this morning." Oooo, Deputy Shaw did not sound thrilled that I had attempted to contact her, no not at all.

"I do apologize for the repeated calls, Deputy Shaw. I didn't mean to be a nuisance." I had learned long ago that a quick upfront apology was very effective in taking the wind out of the sails of aggravated parents, and hoped it would be equally effective with annoyed officers of the law.

"No, no, it's alright," Deputy Shaw spoke in a mollified tone. "It was busy yesterday and I was waiting on DNA results from the dog's collar before I called you back."

I sucked my breath in at that bit of news and held it, waiting with high hopes for a super solve CSI type result. I must have made an audible gasp; Deputy Darla's voice softened as she continued. "There's no match for the DNA we got from the blood on the collar, I'm sorry."

"But, but, but," I stuttered. "The blood is definitely from some *unknown person*, right, it's not Brianna's or the dog's, is it? The DNA is from who killed her, we just don't know who?" I was sick from disappointment, and wanted to kick something, hard.

"That's right, it's still important information, but as far as the DNA goes, we're in a waiting game. Could be the perpetrator gets picked up next week for some infraction that gets their DNA run through the system. We can only hope." She didn't mention the possibility that the dirt bag could live the rest of his life without getting a DNA check, but we were both thinking it.

"What about other evidence? Was anything found onsite?"

Deputy Shaw's voice now rebounded to officious brusqueness. "Kelly, I'm really not at liberty to discuss an ongoing case. I probably shouldn't have even told you about the DNA results. Now, was there anything else? I need to get rolling with my day."

"Well, yes, actually there is. Cici and I are in Missoula, wrapping up some of Brianna's business, and we came across information that we don't think the Missoula police have. I thought I should tell you directly? Do you have time right now, or we could schedule a call back?" Now it was my turn to feel annoyed. Damn it, the sheriff's office wouldn't have even found Brianna's body if it weren't for Cici, Betty Mills, Rett and myself. *And Leo*, whispered my mind, making my stomach lurch with the memory. Talking with us was different than discussing the case with John

Q. Public, and I didn't appreciate getting the bum's rush from Deputy Darla Shaw!

I was gratified when Deputy Shaw paused in her hurry to get off the phone.

"Go ahead. I've got time to listen right now." Her voice contained the same wariness that I hear from Boyd when he imagines that I'm going to cause his blood pressure to spike, but knows no graceful way to not hear me out. I pushed right past her unspoken trepidation and filled her in on our findings.

I lined out the salient points from our time at the Shalimar and Brianna's house-share, making sure she knew that the Missoula police had not interviewed either Darrell Forsun, who maybe belonged to the Las Vegas mob; or the bartender Adrian, who had a description of a potential Brianna stalker. From the roommate, Jori, there was the tip about wolverines, the crazy/Crazy guide and the 'last seen date' of September 5th, verified by the due date of Jori's assignment.

Feeling encouraged by the silence on Deputy Shaw's end, I happily forged ahead with a summary of Rett's behavior toward the different people we had met. He had so clearly demonstrated that neither Darrell Forsun or Adrian had been the shooter, and had confirmed that both roommates were very hands-off and distant with Brianna during her time at the house.

Suddenly, Deputy Shaw wasn't so silent anymore.

"I don't believe what I'm hearing from you, Mrs. Boyd!" Deputy Shaw exploded in my ear. "You've been poking around asking questions in a murder investigation, before these people have been interviewed by the police? And you're nutty enough to think the dog can say whether someone's involved in Brianna's murder or not? I thought I made it plain when I spoke with you and your husband that you are to keep out of police business!" Her voice was rife with incredulousness, and she didn't sound one whit impressed with the clues we had found.

This conversation was clearly going downhill. Feeling grateful that the more volatile Cici wasn't in the car listening and perhaps responding in her own colorful manner, I took a deep breath before answering the highly irate deputy.

"Deputy Shaw, we didn't talk to these people with the intention of interfering. We went to the Shalimar to pick up Brianna's last paycheck, and the house where she lived to clean out her things. I believe you, yourself left a message with Cici that it was okay to do that," I added tartly. "We had no way of knowing ahead of time that nobody official had talked with the Shalimar employees, and we certainly didn't 'pump' anyone for information. They were upset over Brianna's death and happy to see Rett; we simply listened to what they had to say. I certainly hope the sheriff's office doesn't intend to disregard this information just because you don't like the manner in which it was collected. Or because it doesn't fit with some preconceived idea on your part of who's the guilty!" I knew I sounded stiff and angry as I replied, but the deputy had once again ruffled my feathers in a major way.

What? Did she think Rett wouldn't reliably recognize the person who shot him and his beloved mistress, the person he had more than likely bitten hard enough to make bleed all over his collar? If she thought a dog would greet such a person with joyous abandon, she didn't know shit and I for one was very disappointed in her.

The rest of our conversation was curt and brief. Nobody was happy with anybody. By the time we had pushed our respective disconnect buttons there wasn't much bonhomie left between the two of us. I, for one, longed for the days of *real* telephones that could be hung up with a satisfying bash at the end of an angry conversation. The puny, little *bloop* of a disconnecting cellphone just doesn't suffice.

I sat in the front seat of my Subaru, with weak sunshine coming through the windshield, replaying the conversation in my head and adding in lots of choice bits that I hadn't thought to say at the time, none of which were particularly nice, but very pleasurable to imagine. Finally, in order to help calm myself before Cici and Rett finished their interview, I opened the Kindle app on my phone and worked at reading my current book, *Ava's Man*. It took me four tries to read a page and have any idea what it said, but by the time noon rolled around, and the car door popped open to let in a jubilant Cici and Rett, I was far away, in the Deep South, living in a time gone by but brought richly to life by the author.

TWENTY-FIVE

IT WAS TOO COLD AND SNOWY to utilize the wonderful outdoor patio at Locally Sauced, my hands-down favorite barbeque restaurant in Missoula, but we went there anyway, for a celebratory lunch after Cici's successful Zootown Zoo interview. It was past the lunch rush when we arrived, and we were able to score a seat where Rett could join us under the table. We were honest and didn't claim he was a service dog or anything; it certainly wasn't our fault that Rett behaved so well that the servers just *assumed* he was.

Cici could hardly stop talking about the interview and upcoming job long enough to put food in her mouth and chew. There had been no snakes involved, Rett solidly ignored the livestock while Cici demonstrated her horse-handling and goat-wrangling skills learned at Betty and Randy Mills' place. The two of them were introduced to the donkeys and potbellied pigs as well. Again the interactions went smoothly.

"You should have seen Rett with the pigs, Kelly, he didn't know what to do with himself! He froze like a statue when he saw them; you could almost see his brain whirling around in little circles trying to figure out what they were. And then they started ambling our way, grunting and whuffling with each step, right up to where they could all touch noses."

"What did he do then?" I asked with a grin on my face.

"Well, his eyes were rolling around in his head like blue marbles, but Rett, he didn't move a hair. The pigs kept sniffing him over and grunting, friendly like, it seemed to me. Rett must have decided they were friendly, too. All of a sudden he just relaxed and did his lop-sided bow at them, like he wanted to invite them to a romp. I hadn't been too sure about the oinkers myself, but you know, they were like big fat friendly dogs more than anything. I scratched one behind the ears and on the butt, and he fell over on his side, boom! Just lay there, grunting for more! Their hair is weird, Kelly, it's really wiry and tough, but otherwise it was like giving a big dog a good scratch.

"So the pigs and us will get along good." Cici smiled jubilantly.

"I'm going to be working in the back, just with animals and the other animal workers. All the upfront stuff like dealing with the public gets done by dressed up office workers, thank the good Lord. I get the heebie jeebies dealing with strangers and their stupid questions, and now I don't got to.

"Me and Rett will work six days a week, early morning and again in the afternoon-evening, and we'll live in a little studio at the back of one of the buildings. It's part of the job that we're on-site during the night, from midnight on, too, unless we've arranged being gone in advance."

Cici stopped talking for a moment, and looked at me with a crafty expression on her angular face.

"Don't think I don't know that the hours are set up to make sure I don't really have time to go out hootin' and hollerin'. I get it. But, you know, Kelly, that's all good." She reached down and ruffled Rett's ears; good boy Rett whapped his tail against the wood flooring but stayed in his 'down'. "Me and Rett, we don't need to do that kind of stuff, do we boy?"

Call me a coward, but I couldn't bring myself to tell Cici about my verbal dustup with Deputy Darla Shaw. What good would it have done? Instead we finished up our excellent lunch of pork ribs with meat so tender it could be pulled off the bones with our lips alone. We had split a full rack, which allowed us to indulge, but kept us from eating until we passed out at the table, in emulation of the flopping potbellied pigs at Zootown. Snow was coming down steadily now, in fat, feathery clumps, the promised storm showing up exactly as predicted by radar. We exited the restaurant past the back patio that extended toward the Clark Fork River, adjacent to the site of the summer farmer's market, and agreed that we would return when the grass was green for a reprisal.

"I'm gonna get my own rack next time, though," Cici asserted. "And I'm going to eat until I pop. Whoo-ee, that was good food!"

SNAP!

With horrifying power, the large Conibear trap triggered onto the neck of the beautiful Border collie. The collie's head was twisted to the left, enough for the round, helpless eyes to be seen, begging for release. A man's deep voice boomed nearby.

"You have three minutes to get that trap open or the dog will asphyxiate and die; work steady, work smart." A chunky woman in her thirties stepped up to the realistic stuffed animal held in a demo trap and worked the leash she held around the spring pin on one side of the heavy-duty trap. By making several passes around the pin to create a mechanical advantage, the frowzy haired woman was able to squeeze the spring closed. But, by herself, she wasn't able to secure it in place with a metal clip attachment of the trap. The clip had become stuck inside the closing spring, and it took the aid of Mr. Towbert, the TrapNoMore representative putting on the demonstration, to get it back in place. Four minutes had gone by, and only one side of the trap had been released and secured.

We were in downtown Missoula at a Wednesday evening public education seminar put on by TrapNoMore Montana. I had attended a similar one last year in Helena, and I still have frequent nightmares over the idea of Sadie and Leo running afoul of trappers' snares or Conibear traps. Maybe it's a more humane way to trap wildlife, to have the animals die quickly in those devices, rather than lingering for days in a traditional leg-trap, but the fact is a trapped pet will die very quickly as well. If a dog steps in an old-fashioned leg trap, there'll be damage but they can be saved. These seminars are meant to educate dog owners on how to keep pets out of traps and snares, and how to save them if the worst happens and they get caught. Behind this educational overlay, though, is an anti-trapping agenda that aims to have trapping outlawed in Montana, at some point in the not-too-distant future.

Mr. Towbert, a large man with a chest-length, tangled beard that showed more gray than brown, stepped back from the stuffed dog in the trap to address the small group of people attending the seminar.

"If you can get even one side open within the three minutes, your dog has a chance, if the trap didn't kill them outright by snapping their neck, that is. You'll hear a gasp from the dog when the first side opens up and they are able to breathe a little bit. Remember to get a leash back on the dog before opening up the other side of the trap! Dogs are beyond terrified when they're caught in a device, and will run off when released, if given a chance. You don't need to lose your dog just after saving it from a trap." Mr. Towbert laid out four more Conibear traps, already sprung and mercifully empty, and invited us all to come forward and practice our leash release technique on the deadly contraptions.

As other members of the audience shuffled forward to test out their newly learned trap release skills, Cici, Rett and I gravitated to the far side of the room where a young woman with gold-rimmed glasses was setting up a table display of TrapNoMore brochures. Behind her on the wall were poster size photos of dogs that had been casualties of Montana trapping or hunting. One poor dog had been killed right in Missoula proper by an illegally set trap at the Clark Fork River, not far from where we had lunch. Another poster showed two husky-cross dogs had been mistaken for wolves and shot by over-eager hunters. Horrifyingly, one photo showed a proud woman hunter holding up what clearly is the pelt of a dog, not a wolf, after she had shot and skinned it.

The young woman looked up as we approached her table and focused on Rett's lurching, three-legged gait.

"Oh my god, did he lose his leg in a trap?" she asked in a hushed, solemn tone. She seemed so reverential at the idea of Rett being a poor, trapped dog, I hated to fess up that he hadn't.

"But he did get shot, twice," Cici announced. "The vet couldn't save his leg, too much damage."

The girl's greenish brown eyes grew wide behind her glasses.

"How did it happen? If you don't mind me asking? I mean, it's not like he looks like a wolf or anything."

I hesitated, wondering how best to broach the subject of Brianna, her murder, and her possible connection to TrapNoMore. Obviously, this particular young woman wasn't familiar with Rett, and according to Cici, that would mean she hadn't met Brianna, either, as they were strictly a package deal.

Apparently, I hesitated too long to get in the first word. Cici took the conversational reins away from me.

"Aimee," said Cici, leaning forward and reading the girl's name off her nametag. "Aimee, his owner used to volunteer with TrapNoMore; I don't guess you met her, seeing how you don't know her dog." Cici gestured at Rett. "She was killed down in the Crazy Mountains earlier this fall, and this guy was shot trying to defend her. Maybe you read about it in the newspaper last week? There was an article?" Cici raised her eyebrows in query.

The girl's eyes almost popped out of her head at hearing Cici's words and she sucked in her breath with an audible whoosh, causing Rett to peer uneasily at her over the table's edge. Her face flushed with excitement, and she took on the raptured look of a teenage fan at, say, a Justin Bieber concert.

"Everyone was talking about this! OMG, I can't believe I'm meeting you! And the dog, nobody knew about the dog! I mean, they talked about him and wondered what happened to him, but no one knew he'd been shot and lost his leg!"

"Who's 'everyone', Aimee?" I interjected. "We'd like to talk with anyone who knew Brianna, just for . . . closure, you know?" I inwardly winced at using the psycho-babble 'closure' word, but we could hardly tell her that we were snooping into Brianna's death, hoping to find clues to her killer, could we? Uncharitably, I thought she'd probably hyperventilate and pass out from overexcitement if I said anything like that.

Aimee wound her long, curly hair around an index finger as she screwed her face up in concentration. "Well, in our organization there are older people, like Bob." She lifted her chin toward the bearded man who was supervising the trap practice, ensuring that no audience members hurt themselves with the nefarious things.

"They're really active in the movement and all, but they're sort of old and fuddy-duddy, you don't see them at face-to-face get-togethers at the bar." Aimee flushed again, suddenly aware that she had maybe disparaged the short, gray-haired lady standing in front of her. I suspect she's one of those girls whose face turns red at the drop of a hat, much to their dismay.

"No worries, you're right! People my age don't really go to the bars anymore." I didn't mention the fuddy-duddy part of the comment, although it had lit the embers of outrage inside me.

"Well, anyway, there's a group of us who are younger, in our twenties, you know; we live here in Missoula and get together to hang out and talk about stuff. We were over at the Branding Iron the night before last, and Vinnie was talking about her, asking if we knew she was dead and all. A bunch of the others had known her, too, and there was, like, a pow-wow session on what might have happened to her."

Aimee shivered her upper body in an attempt to look properly horrified, but the eager gleam in her eye gave her away. Brianna's death and Aimee's vicarious link to a murder only provided a delicious thrill to the young woman. I found myself disliking her more by the minute. Cici was probably getting ready to clean her clock.

A sudden voice behind us diverted our attention and saved Aimee from her very own encounter with ugly.

"Look, dude, it *is* Rett, I told you so!"

Cici and I turned to see two college age men wearing matching, dark-colored puffy jackets with snow on their bare heads and shoulders. They were bending down to engulf Rett in a warm flurry of petting accompanied by manly thumps on his ribs. Despite Deputy Shaw's scoffing skepticism of Rett's ability to rule out suspects, I was instantly sure that neither of these two had been responsible for her death, and I mentally thumbed my nose at the doubting deputy.

The young men left off greeting Rett and introduced themselves with handshakes that were firm but freezing as neither had worn gloves while outside in the snowstorm.

"I'm Jacob and this is Finn," said the taller of the two who sported a mop of shaggy, dark brown hair. Finn looked to be a wrestler, either of people or cows, with his shorter stature and broad shoulders—a wrestler from Ireland, given his name and vibrant red hair.

Both Jacob and Finn utterly ignored Aimee. Good call, boys.

"We were just talking about Rett last night, weren't we, Finn?" continued Jacob. "Wondering what happened to him, 'cuz the newspaper said Brianna had been found dead, but nothing about good old Rett."

"Yeah, we figured if she was dead, Rett was dead, too. So who are you and how did you get him and why are you here?" Finn shot off this string of questions at us in rapid fire fashion, not giving either of us time to reply between queries. I noticed he kept a hand on Rett's back as he spoke, as if in preparation to wrestle the dog away from us if he didn't like our answers. He squared off with us and narrowed his light blue eyes challengingly.

"Du-uuude," said Jacob, jostling Finn's shoulder with his own. "Chill, already. Let's invite these lovely ladies to join us; we can *share* intel, peaceable like."

Turning to us, Jacob went on. "We're here to help put stuff away after the talk is over. That won't take long, and then we can all wander across the street to the Watering Hole for chicken wings and beer; you can tell us the Rett story." His round-eyed, snub nosed, open face looked guilelessly at us in friendly invitation. To his side, Finn continued to glower at us as if "No" wasn't an option.

"Rett, heel." Cici's command, given in a low, firm tone, popped Mr. Rett up off of his butt from where he was lounging at Finn's side. Rett executed a sharp move forward and crisp turn to line himself up on Cici's left side. There, he sat at attention, drilling his round blue eyes into her face, ready and eager for another command.

Satisfied with the outcome of this little pissing contest over the dog, Cici smiled faintly at Finn while answering Jacob. "Sure thing, guys. Beer and wings it is. We'll wait here until you're done and all go over together."

TWENTY-SIX

I FANNED MY WATERING EYES AND DESPERATELY sucked down
enough cold beer to put out a forest fire, but failed to even *dim*
the heat from the Dangerous Dan wing I had blithely popped
into my mouth. I loved Robert Service poems almost as much as
Shakespeare quotes, and had been unable to resist sampling the
Double D's, as Jacob had described them. Maybe Service should
have named his poem *The Poisoning of Dan McGrew*. Or the restaurant could've called them the Sam McGee Cremation wings;
either way I might have had some warning of the internal inferno
to come.

Cici was openly laughing as she handed me a wad of paper napkins across the table to use in Kelly cleanup. Tears poured out my
eyes, and my nose joined in as if in a contest with my tear ducts. To
top it off, the heat in the wings sparked a round of violent hiccups
so I had the fun of convulsing in public as well. Charming.

"Do we need to call an ambulance, boss? Maybe the fire department? Raise your right hand if you want us to call in a rescue,"
inquired little Miss Helpful in a merry voice. I was too busy mop-
ping up to do more than shoot her a filthy glance. It was a down-
right undignified episode for a retired schoolteacher old enough to
be the mother of the other three people at the table.

Well, what the hell. A good laugh is always a good ice breaker, and even Finn had joined in. He had a mischievous grin that combined with his red hair and blue eyes to make his face suddenly attractive, in an off-beat way.

The four of us were at a table in the Watering Hole, which wasn't exactly across the street from the store-front meeting room, but was within an easy walking distance, even for amputee types navigating the now deep snow. More white stuff spilled out of lowering, gray clouds as we walked; the prediction was for an additional six inches overnight, meaning the trusty blue Subaru wasn't going to be pointed back to Helena until well after noon tomorrow, in order to give the snowplows and early morning commuters time to finish up and get out of our way. Thursday afternoon was soon enough to return to Helena.

Aimee had wanted to accompany us to the bar, but Jacob had fobbed her off with a "not this time, love" delivered in an affected plummy British accent and accompanied by a rakish wink. The desire to giggle in coquettish agreement with handsome Jacob trumped her craving to listen with round-eyed, gleeful, ghoulishness to further details about murder.

Sometimes hormone-induced behavior is a good thing.

By the time we had polished off a couple pitchers of beer, and been entertained by the self-immolating Kelly, a feeling of camaraderie had jelled between the four of us. The boys had heard the back story of Brianna and were up to speed on our respective roles in present time; but we hadn't shared any details about our recent discoveries in Missoula. We didn't want to influence their recollections by introducing potential red herrings to the conversation. Any new information from Jacob and Finn should come to light without Cici or I prompting our witnesses.

We learned that both Jacob and Finn had known Brianna through their TrapNoMore work, mainly through the liquid seminars that were held ad-hoc after the organization's formal meetings. They deeply admired Brianna for her ability to drink most of the members of their loose group under the table.

"So you all would get together and get blotto," Cici interjected. "Sounds pretty normal for a bunch college age kids, but was there anything out of the ordinary that you ever saw? Brianna liked to fight, she ever get into it with anyone?"

Jacob's eyes suddenly gleamed with merriment and he pointed at Finn.

"Du . . . .uuuude!"

Finn, his face also shining with suppressed laughter pointed back at him.

"Dawg!"

And the two boys burst into full-fledged, knee pounding laughter that threatened to topple over our beer glasses on the table. When they had laughed themselves out, Jacob leaned back, tipping his chair onto its two back legs. I struggled to not act the teacher and tell him to put the chair back down, pronto.

Jacob and Finn, both grinning from ear to ear, continued to bounce the story back and forth between them like a tennis ball.

"Brianna emasculated that guy!" shouted Finn.

"Tore his balls right off, dude!" agreed Jacob.

"My pair crawled up inside and hid! For days!" Finn snorted.

"He just sat there and took it though, the weirdo." Jacob shook his head.

"Like a puppy dog!" Finn made a disgusted face.

Jacob leaned forward, popping the chair back down on all four legs with a bang. "Dude wasn't wrong, though, I mean his idea was evil and *sick*, but it would work, it totally would."

I raised my hands toward Jacob and Finn, palms up and said, "Spill it, boys, tell Cici and me what you're talking about."

"You tell it Jacob," prompted Finn, still grinning wickedly as he raised his beer glass to Jacob before taking a long pull of its contents.

Jacob took an equally long drink from his, set the glass down, and wiped a little beer mustache off his face before beginning.

"Okay, okay, let's see. This was back in early August, school had just started for those of us going to UM. We had a kick-off meeting for TrapNoMore at the Student Union, and had gone over to one of the bars afterwards. Brianna was there, and so was this guy who had started coming to stuff over the summer."

"What a dickhead!" interjected Finn. "That guy always had to make himself out to be better than anyone else!"

Jacob cocked an eyebrow at Finn and gave him a joking stink-eye. Finn raised his hands in capitulation and quieted down to let Jacob continue.

"This guy sucked, man," Jacob added in agreement. "He wanted to be called 'Dawg' like he was some honcho homeboy, and he always one-upped whatever anyone said, even it was really obvious he was lying. Painful and pathetic to see."

"If you caught a twelve-inch brown on a nymph, then he had caught a twenty incher, with his bare hands," Finn told us. "If you had gone on a five-day backpack trip, well, Dawg had just come back from a ten-day trip. Not only that, but on his trip, he didn't take any food at all, just lived off the land. My god." Finn shook his head.

Jacob cleared his throat and stink-eyed Finn again.

"My bad; go on, bro."

"Anyway, this guy was always trying to get the group fired up to do hands-on activist stuff. He wanted to be arrested in the worst way, kept saying we should join up with the Eco-Liberation Front. On Emasculation Night, he came up with this idea that to be really effective in shutting down trapping in Montana, we should register with the Fish and Wildlife as bona fide trappers and then take advantage of the lax rules about where you can set traps to go out and deliberately, but 'accidently' kill as many dogs as possible. Then angry dog owners would rise up and unite to shut down trapping."

Cici and I goggled at Jacob. This was a *heinous* idea; it made me want to throw up just thinking about it. But deep inside, I had to agree that it was an idea of evil genius, if you happen to believe that the end justified the means. Sacrificing hundreds of dogs would, I felt, cause trapping to be taken off the list of allowed activities, even in Montana, with its long history as a trapping state.

"That's when Brianna jumped in. She didn't physically lay a hand on the guy, but oh my god, did she ever rake him over the coals. By the time she was done, he had a couple of new assholes, and the 'nads? Oh, those were ripped off, chewed up and spat out on the floor. It was uggggly!"

"What a goddamn dipshit," this from Cici, our fount of eloquence. "What did the idiot do? Just sit there and lap it up with a smile?"

"Practically," agreed Finn. "Basically had his tail between his legs, wagging away, rolling his eyes and smiling at her like it was all just a big joke."

Finn pointed at Cici and me, his face suddenly deadpan. "Your friend, Brianna, she could be harsh with people in general, not just with this guy. She was, well, fascinating to hang out with, for a guy, anyway, but she treated lots of people like dirt. I think she got her kicks out of having people crawl back after she put them down. Could be someone, maybe this guy, Dawg, maybe someone else, got tired of it."

"Yeah, I hear you," Cici replied, her voice tinged with sadness and regret. "She was the same in the army. Everyone wanted to be near her, and she shredded them, for fun. She didn't have too many actual friends, go figure."

I signaled the waitress to bring us a fresh pitcher of beer. Jesus, how long had it been since I had been sat at a table with even a single pitcher of beer? It brought back fond memories of being a college student, but as the designated driver as well as the old lady at the table, I felt the need to cut myself off for the night, and wistfully filled my glass with plain water.

"The big mystery, guys, is how Brianna and Rett, and *whomever*," I said as I waved my hand in an encompassing circle. "How did they wind up down in the Crazies? Nobody would drive all the way down there just to shoot someone; there are millions of places around *here* to lure someone into the woods and dispose of them."

I took a drink from my glass before continuing. "We think Brianna had been told there were wolverines down there, and someone was taking her to look for them. And, I don't know, something went awfully wrong and she got shot along with Rett.

"Does this line up with anything you know?"

Finn and Jacob looked at each other for a minute, and then Finn said slowly, "There *was* a rumor going around about wolverines, a while ago. People were up in arms that trappers were targeting them in areas where they really weren't known to be, so Fish Wildlife and Parks hadn't closed those spots to trapping. If evidence showed the animals were there, though . . . then advocate groups could force FWP to act."

"Was Brianna part of the talk? Was this Dawg guy?" Cici asked.

Jacob rubbed his upper lip in thought, kicking his chair back onto two legs again. "Man, it's been a while, I don't really know. But I do know, if that girl had expressed an interest in looking for wolverines, that suck-ass braggart would have been right there, spinning a tale that he knew exactly how to find them." Jacob pointed again at Finn, "Am I right?"

"Would she have believed him though? Would she spend a whole day or more with him on a wolverine mission? I mean, it sounds like she really disliked him," I asked.

Jacob spoke up, "He was dirt to her, but that wouldn't stop her from using him to get something she wanted. She'd *use* people and then drop them like a dirty Kleenex, that's what we're telling you. 'Dawg' had a thing for her, even after she shredded him; he'd have literally licked her boots if she'd asked him to."

Across the table, Finn nodded in agreement.

"What does 'Dawg' look like, anyway?" Cici asked. "You never said."

The boys did their tennis ball thing again, complete with finger pointing to show when the ball went to the other's court. At the end, they had given us a description of a shorter, slightly built man in his later twenties who had long, greasy, blondie-brown hair, usually worn in a ponytail, and a goatee that was wispy enough to be embarrassing.

Cici and I connected our eyes with an electric shock. This was an almost identical description of the Shalimar Stalker, as provided by Adrian!

Unfortunately, the boys didn't know much else about 'Dawg', they had never seen him anywhere else around town, didn't know his real name, or where he worked, or if he was a student at the university. The one other piece of intel that Jacob and Finn had to share was the fact that 'Dawg' claimed not to have a car.

"What a poser! He was all over letting us know that cars were so bad for the environment he wouldn't even have an electric one. Didn't stop him from trying to cadge rides from the rest of us, though," said Jacob. "Joke was always on him, we were always too blasted to drive anywhere!"

Finn poured the last of the current pitcher into his glass and swallowed half his drink in a single go. A belch that he hid behind his hand earned him a whack across the back of the head from Jacob.

"Jeez, get some manners, Finn! No wonder you never have a girlfriend!" admonished Jacob.

Finn flipped him a double bird and started to give a witty Finn reply, but was interrupted by Cici.

"Hey, focus a minute more and we'll buy you another pitcher before we go." Obediently, two sets of slightly buzzed eyes looked her way.

"If this 'Dawg' didn't have a car, then if Brianna did go to the Crazies with him, she would've driven her own, is that what you're telling us? And then he would've driven hers away when he left her there?"

"Shit," Cici now said to me. "The douche bag could've gone any-where! Why would he come back here to Missoula? No wonder no one's found her car."

"Um, he would've at least come back for his stuff, I bet," interjected Jacob. "The guy had some nice things, like his computer." Jacob pointed at Finn.

"His fancy Italian shoes!" Finn pointed back.

"Real leather jacket, from WWII!" Jacob spouted. "Old enough it was okay that it was made from little animal friends!" The boys dissolved into spasms of hilarity that were out of sync with the actual humor of their statements. Recognizing that they had gone beyond the point of inebriation where reliable conversation could be had, Cici and I decided to say our goodbyes and go on our way.

We signaled the barmaid to bring the boys another pitcher, settled up the tab, and left them to their merriment in the warm, dark bar. I was glad we left when we did. As it was, we had to battle our way back through the wind-whipped snow to where the trusty blue Subaru sat buried under an accumulation of snow and ice that had to be removed before we could retreat to the Airbnb for the night.

THE MAN WHO CALLED HIMSELF DAWG, currently hiding in a dimly lit back booth of the Watering Hole hissed *about time*, to himself. At last, the group of pansy asses from TrapNoMore seemed to be breaking up, and he would be able to leave soon without being spotted. It had been a near thing earlier; he had been close to walking out of the bar when the group with the damn dog approached the front door. The man had spun on his heel and gone back to the men's room to get out of sight before they pulled the front door open. Of course they had to sit at a table that was right next to the door, blocking him from an escape.

He had slid into an available, isolated booth, and sat hidden from their view. He cursed the fact that he wasn't close enough to overhear their conversation, but the presence of Brianna's damn dog with his damn nose, meant he had to stay far away if he wanted to remain undetected. He heard the names, 'Kelly' and 'Cici', when one of them had come to grief over the unnaturally spicy chicken wings. He wished they had choked.

He also heard "Brianna" and "Dawg" accompanied by laughter, and his muddy brown eyes burned in outrage as he realized the TrapNoMore boys were recounting the story of his humiliation by Brianna.

Dawg shook his head in disbelief that this mess had washed up on the shores of his life. The damn bitch was dead! How could she and her dog still be showing up to haunt him?

TWENTY-SEVEN

I T WAS SATURDAY, OCTOBER 15TH AND Cici had decamped
from RogerDogs yesterday for Missoula and her new job at
ZooTown Zoo. The place seemed so empty without her, it was
hard to believe it was only two weeks since she had first rolled
into our parking lot. After lunch, feeling out of sorts with my day,
I took a short break from my desk work to wander the kennels
and play with the dogs a little. All work and no play makes for
a crabby Kelly. I felt that I deserved a little of the magic rush of
endorphins that comes from petting puppies, even if said 'puppies' were senior citizen animals.

I made my way slowly around the kennel areas, greeting new-
comers and renewing older friendships as I went. It coulda shoulda
been a Hallmark Moment, but instead I found myself being mowed
over, raked with claws, and assaulted with jumpy-mouthy dogs
exhibiting classic signs of kennel stress.

Being absent since last Monday, for almost five days in all, made
me see residents in a new light, especially the ones who had been
with RogerDogs for more than a few months. How long, exactly,
had Spruce, Walleye and Kanga been at RogerDogs? Frowning
slightly at the frenetic faces and wagging tails, I tried to bring to
mind their intake dates, but the noisy din from the dogs made it

hard to think. Giving up until I got back to my trusty computer, I gave myself over to handing out treats and sharing some happiness, while keeping myself safe from further over-anxious overtures.

Over six months! That's what I found from our computerized records. Spruce, had come to RogerDogs way last spring, and had been adopted out once for four days, but was brought back after 'playing too roughly' with the adopter's elderly Chihuahua. I narrowed my eyes and snorted to myself at that. He's a Lab! Of course he's bouncy! Spruce had lived at RogerDogs for a grand total of nine months and thirteen days.

Walleye, a Pyrenees mix; and the Visla, Kanga, had been at the shelter for six-to eight months.

Time to shake things up, I thought to myself, it's time for an Adoption Event at PetSmart! I spun my office chair around like a mini-carousel while imagined trumpets sounded in my ears. Betty Mills was going to shit a brick; she *hated* putting on Adoption Events. Laughing to myself, I picked up the phone to call PetSmart and see when we could arrange a two-day time slot at the Helena store.

TWENTY-EIGHT

"RED ALERT! RED ALERT! PUPPY BREAKOUT on Aisle Three!" Grace Oberlander's voice rang out from the depths of the store. It was the second day of the October 18ᵗʰ and 19th RogerDog Rescue Adoption Event at the Helena PetSmart; and things had apparently gone to hell in a handbasket over in Aisle Three.

I was manning the office table, which meant I was in charge of the casework files for the dogs, and the 'cash register' which any other day of the week was one of Randy Mills' toolboxes. As much as I wanted to sprint to Aisle Three and see what in god's name was going on, I was trapped at the office table by the need to watch over the goods.

"Grace, what's happening? How many are out and which dogs are they?" I bellowed.

Before I had even finished speaking, I saw a flying wedge of sleek black bodies race across a cross aisle, heading toward the cat supplies area. No! No, no, no, no! The Wild Things were out! Shit, shit, shit, shit!

Two weeks ago, a concerned citizen had brought in a bunch of puppies, maybe four months old, that had been found living down by the Missouri River, south of Townsend. The six young animals were almost identical black dogs that looked to be crosses of blue heeler and German Shepard lineage. They had narrow faces, pricked ears; almond shaped slanted eyes that *gleamed* with intelligence, and a unique bonding between individuals that allowed the merry band to act as a single unit, not unlike a flock of starlings. I had dubbed them 'The Wild Things' on first sight.

We had set up five corrals of mobile fencing thoroughout PetSmart and installed a total of seventeen dogs, including the six Wild Things. The playpen of black puppies was set up toward the back of the store, in part to draw adopters past all the other dogs, and in part as a safety precaution. In case of escape, they were far away from the automatic, sliding glass front doors.

Seven dogs had already been successfully adopted, including all three of the 'long-terms' who had been the spark for the event. This was an excellent outcome, but also meant that seven handlers had gone home, experienced dog people who could have otherwise helped round up the escapees. Waving wildly at the official PetSmart employees behind the cash registers at the front of the store, I shouted, "Loose puppies! Keep the doors shut!"

Just then the swooping phalanx of black bodies rounded the corner of the fish aisle, heading for those same doors, with Grace and J.J. in hot pursuit. Other volunteers, Sue Potter, Sharleen Goodwin and Tracy Alverez emerged from the back aisles to see what was going on.

I abandoned my table and sprinted toward the front doors, almost blinded by the horrifying image of puppies zipping out into the parking lot and beyond, to the heavily trafficked road in front. Please, god, let the doors stay shut!

Perversely, the sliding doors chose that moment to spring open. An incoming PetSmart customer accompanied by a full-grown St. Bernard was approaching from the outside and had triggered the automatic door. I died a thousand deaths as the lead puppy swung the group toward the widening opening and the freedom of the parking lot on the other side.

The St. Bernard saved us.

Just as the Wild Things reached the sliding doors, the enormous dog let loose a deep, rumbling bark and pounced with both front feet at the black river of fur headed his way. The river abruptly changed course.

At the sight of the mountainous dog, the pack sheared away to continue their high speed, joyous flight back into the inner depths of the store. A young female employee secured the front doors behind the bemused man and his heroic St. Bernard, and called to me that she would keep the doors closed until we had re-captured our puppy pack.

With the escapees now safely ensconced at the back of the store, we humans took a moment to regroup and catch our breath.

"Okay, they've had a good run through the store, frisky little so and so's, I bet they're starting to slow down and investigate all the good smells, now. Let's each grab a bag of really good treats and some slip leads. We'll slowly walk through the store—toss a LOT of treats on the floor if you see them and back up. Once they're eating, we should be able to ease up and leash them. I'll stay up here in the front and make sure they don't sneak by to the front doors again."

Grace, J.J., Sue, Sharleen and Tracy each pulled a bag of high value treats from a nearby shelf, and split up to cover the main aisle ways leading to the far back corner of the store, where we hoped the puppies were taking a breathing break of their own. It was a tense few minutes before I heard Grace's voice calling, "We've got them, Kelly!"

The little pack of bandits had indeed decided that they were hungry, but hadn't waited for the RogerDog humans and the bags of treats. Instead, they had helped themselves to three separate, sixty-pound bags of expensive dog kibble stored on Petsmart's bottom shelves in the back corner. Apparently, all six puppies were found buried up to their shoulders in the bags, chowing down as if they hadn't been fed in a week, loose kibble strewn around them on the floor. J.J. and the girls were able to pull them out one by one and get slip leads around their perfidious little necks.

All told, between the packs of treats and the bags of dog food, the rascals had cost RogerDogs over two hundred dollars with their little rodeo, and a certain amount of embarrassment on my part, as the official onsite RogerDogs representative. In the strange way of adopters though, the wild escapade had captured the hearts of three PetSmart customers, including the man with the St. Bernard, and within the next thirty minutes, we were down to only two Wild Things to take back to RogerDogs when the Adoption Event came to a close.

It was a tired bunch of volunteers and dogs who met Betty Mills in the parking lot, where she was waiting to load returning dogs into her jeep. Betty had thoughtfully brought cold drinks and cookies with her, and we had an impromptu tailgate party as we filled her ears with the stories of the day. She gave me a sardonic, 'I told you so' look as she loaded the remaining Wild Things into a kennel and stood back to make room for more dogs.

"Not a total shit show, though," she commented. "You got them all back before any got outside; Grace didn't get herself run over in the parking lot chasing them; and four of the little buggers are adopted, not to mention seven other dogs. I'm real glad *someone*," she fake coughed 'me', "had to stay at RogerDogs to hold down the fort. Remember the first PetSmart Adoption circus we had? I ain't ever bringing my butt inside for one of those again."

I silently agreed. At our very first event, Betty had refused to allow a puppy to be adopted by a shifty character. The beady-eyed, obnoxious man took exception to being told 'No' and unwisely squared up to Betty Mills. The dustup that followed ended when Betty punched him in the nose 'for being an asshole' as she put it. The guy had indeed been a three-star asshole, but even so. Throwing punches in public is bad for customer relations.

Finally the drinks and cookies had been consumed, volunteers thanked profusely, and Betty had departed to RogerDogs with a cheerful wave out the window. I leaned against my blue Subaru and stretched my back out, while closing my eyes.

It would be a perfect moment to enjoy a smoke break before putting myself in the car, if I were a smoker. Pulling my phone out to check messages instead, I idly wondered how many smokers use the excuse of cigarettes just to insert a time-out in the day's business. Maybe the younger generation's manic drive to check cellphones at all possible times of the day was fulfilling this need and keeping teenagers from ever starting to smoke? Huh, and here I had always thought of them only as a classroom nuisance.

Oh, wow. I had silenced my phone during the Adoption Event and with the excitement of the day hadn't checked my messages since the morning. Cici had called several times, and had texted multiple times as well, including twice in the last hour. A voicemail simply said to call her, and the texts merely expressed increasing exasperation that I hadn't gotten in touch yet.

I yanked the Subaru's door open and dropped into the driver's seat, starting the car to take immediate advantage of the heated seat against my tired back. Taking a deep breath and mentally crossing my fingers that the missed communications weren't harbingers of some disaster, I hit the callback button on my phone.

Cici's upbeat and jubilant voice dispelled my worries like cobwebs being whisked away with a duster, and I felt my upper body slump into the warm car seat as tension fled.

"Kelly! About time you called a girl back! I thought I was going to have to drive me and Rett over and track you down in person," exclaimed Cici. "I know you had the doggie Adopt-a-thon thing going, but five minutes out of your day, too busy for that?"

I thought back on the day's events, including the Escape of the Wild Things, and said, "Heck, yes; my day didn't have even five *seconds* to spare! But what's up? You sound like you won the lottery or something." I paused for effect. "If you did, I want you to remember that it was me who bought the winning ticket and gave it to you as a present." I shut my eyes and smiled warmly, even though Cici couldn't see me.

"If I'd won the lottery, Rett and I would be calling you from our beachside condo somewhere in the Caribbean; we'd be so gone our footprints would've come with us," snorted Cici. She then cleared her throat and began speaking in a high pitched, affected English accent.

"Ms. Cici Vargas and her faithful retainer, the dog formerly known as Murphy, would like to extend an invitation to lunch to Ms. Kellan Boyd, said lunch to take place in Missoula at the outdoor patio of Locally Sauced this coming Friday, when the sun is predicted to shine and the temperature should be warm enough for outdoor comfort. All that white stuff from last week has disappeared like it never happened," Cici laughed, and went on in her regular voice, with an overlay of giddiness in it.

"Me and Rett got all sorts of news to tell you, girly, you're going to love it! Can we count on you getting your butt up here, Friday?"

Well, I thought to myself, why not? Boyd had mentioned that he planned to dedicate the next two days to building a corner curio cabinet for a friend. I could leave the heelers at home with him and go to Missoula unfettered, footloose and fancy-free. I'd do lunch with Cici, enjoy the city for the afternoon, and cruise on home in the evening. Heck, maybe I'd even go really wild and stay overnight.

"It's a deal," I confirmed. "Be there or be square. I've got some funny stories to share as well." We arranged to meet up at high noon, and I backed the blue Subaru out of its parking spot at PetSmart with a light heart.

Looking back, this moment stands out as the point where events began to snowball to their final, terrifying outcome. Just as a single, wrong step can trigger hidden cracks underneath a beautiful snowfield, releasing a deadly avalanche that remorselessly sweeps aside all in its path, our celebratory lunch would have far-reaching consequences. But at the time, how could we have possibly foreseen the danger headed our way?

Twenty-Nine

Cici and Rett were seated and waiting for me on Friday, October 21st, when I arrived at the outdoor patio of Locally Sauced. The day was unseasonably warm, for Montana that is, and the patio was packed with Missoulians wanting to sit in the sun with no coats on. There was a pitcher of root beer on the table, as well as a platter of the restaurant's famous Cowboy Nachos.

Cici waved her hand at the food as I finished greeting Rett and took my seat. "I got here about half an hour ago to hold a table, and figured I better order some stuff. The nachos just got here, so they're still piping hot."

I poured myself a root beer and pulled some of the nachos onto my plate, enjoying the sight of the deliciously melted cheese strings that formed as the food changed location. "Mmmm, me love nachos!" I rumbled in my best imitation of the Sesame Street Cookie Monster.

"Hope you don't mind root beer instead of the real thing." Cici raised a glass to me as she spoke. "Me and Rett got to go back to work this afternoon." Cici had a full out smile on her face as she spoke of work.

"Sounds like you're enjoying employment at Zootown Zoo." I made the statement a question by way of an arched eyebrow.

"Couldn't be better, Kelly. I work with the dogs, mainly, but sometimes horses and cats and whatever other critters there are, too. And so far so good . . ." she caught my eye and we finished her sentence together with a shout of "NO SNAKES!"

Other people sitting on the patio turned to give us the eye at our shout about snakes, which made the two of us laugh until we cried. Rett sat up and poked his head onto Cici's lap, rolling his baby blues to her face as he made sure she was okay.

Cici ruffled his ears and told him he was a good boy, then with a small hand signal, dropped him back at her feet in a perfect down, where he continued to watch her closely.

I nodded at the crazy quilt dog. "Rett's looking good, Cici. It's working out for him at the Zoo, too?" I was very impressed with the focus that Rett was giving Cici; he was like a Secret Service agent, on duty with the president.

Cici beamed at me. "Rett does great at work, he's with me all day long, and doesn't need to be leashed at all, not even when we work with the cats. He wanted to chase one on our first day, but I told him it wasn't any of his business. He's been great since."

A waitress wearing black pants and a crisp, white shirt underneath a Mediterranean blue Locally Sauced apron approached our table and asked if we were ready to order lunch. I hadn't had time to look at the menu, but remembered that they served a killer blue cheese, roast beef, red pepper sandwich and on the fly asked for one. Cici held up two fingers at the waitress to double the order.

As the waitress left, Cici's eyes slid off to the side, and the corners of her mouth twitched upward in the tiniest of smirky smiles. "So, Kelly," she began. "I've got some more Rett related news."

Cici extended her hand toward me in a raised 'high five' position and said, "Me and Rett have gotten the green light from that 'SDPT' group in Spokane, Service Dog ParTners!"

My eyes and mouth formed a trio of perfect little O's as I slapped my own half of the high five onto hers. "No frikkin' way! I thought that would be something for maybe in the next couple of months! Way to go! When do you start?"

"The next trainee class doesn't get going until December, so you're right, it won't be for a while. I was a tad disappointed that they said Rett here can't be an actual, official, service dog, but he and I are going to do Companion Dog training." Cici held up her hands in a tamping down gesture to forestall the protest she saw forming on my lips. "It's because of him being a tripod. The coordinator explained to me that the training they put the service dogs through is too demanding for a three-legged dog. With my brain injury and PTSD, I qualify to get a trained service dog from them, but it would have to be some other dog, not Rett.

"Well, I'm not going to replace my buddy; I'd rather work with him as a companion dog. But we get to do the training classes, one of their trainers does classes here in Missoula, and Service Dog ParTners covers that cost. They'll be a great group to work with; got to tell you the counselor I see is pretty pumped I'm doing it. He's also putting together documentation showing I qualify for an emotional support animal, too. With that, rental places can't shut Rett and me out, even if he's not an actual service dog."

I wanted to hop up and down in protest. In my mind, Rett was already doing some of the interventions of a trained service dog, so why not refine his actions through further training? He was laser-focused on Cici, I had seen him nudge her and apply the googly eyes when he noticed her freezing up and doing the Cici Pixilation; he heeled beautifully, and always had his body next to her, ready to stand steady if she needed to brace on him. Also, I could see how much easier it was for Cici to be around other people, with Rett acting both as living buffer, and as a reliable watchdog.

As I opened my mouth to protest, my teacher training took over and clamped my lips shut. Is it necessary? Is it helpful? Is it kind? These questions were part of a 'think-before-you-say' mantra for children in school that certainly was just as applicable to adult situations. My thoughts on the matter hit a trifecta of no-no-no, so Kelly Boyd shut up and held her peace.

Cici hadn't noticed my internal struggle, as she was busy rooting in her messenger bag, pulling out a manila envelope when she found it. She held the envelope against her chest, and looked at me with undisguised merriment.

"So, Kelly," she began in a tone that let me know I was in for some teasing. "Tell me again what kind of dog Rett is, and why you think so. I believe you said a buncha stuff about hair color and genes proving he wasn't a heeler mix?"

I looked at her, nonplussed. I knew I was right, that Rett wasn't a heeler, but from the cat-ate-the-canary smug look on Cici's face, apparently the appellation of 'Catahoula Leopard Hound' was about to be challenged.

"Okay, I'll bite," I retorted. "I said he was a Catahoula, not a heeler. Why?"

"Well, see, the S.D.P.T. lady was explaining how she didn't think a Catahoula dog would be so good to work with, on account of them being hunting dogs; the breed is aloof, can be overly protective, yada-yada-yada, and I kept thinking that Rett was so different from what she was saying. It popped into my head that maybe he wasn't a Catahoula dog after all." She pointed a finger at me and raised her eyebrow. "So you know what I did?"

I shook my head to say 'No'.

"I did the cutting edge, scientific thing, Kelly. I bought a kit and sent in a DNA swab to that company, Embark, to see what's what." Cici slapped the manila envelope down on the table and exclaimed loudly, "Ta-da!"

"Read it and weep, Kelly, he ain't no Catahoula!"

I reached out in slow motion to pick up the Manila envelope while my thoughts whirled around in overdrive. Not a Catahoula! But, but, but, what about the merle coat? The blue eyes? The pink on his cute nose? The hound shaped body? I snuck a quick look at Rett to make sure he hadn't changed since the last time I saw him.

Nope, he was laying on the ground, big as life, with all of those characteristics on full display.

I slid the Embark results out of the envelope and used my finger to underline the text as I read it out loud, so I wouldn't skip around and misinterpret the information. "Thank you for using our services, blah, blah, blah'; based on our databank of 350 breeds, we believe Rett to be a mix of Labrador Retriever (50%), Australian Shepard (45%), undetermined (5%) . . .!!!" my voice trailed off in astonishment, and my mouth hung open slightly as I read and reread the information.

Finally, I raised my eyes to meet Cici's and sputtered, "Labrador! Aussie! No wonder he's so outgoing and friendly!" I looked down again at Rett, and scoped him out, matching his characteristics to the new found breed knowledge. Merle coat, blue eyes, single prick ear: Australian Shepard. Smooth coat, hound face and body, floppy ear: Labrador. Focused work drive: Australian Shepard. Stamina and steadiness: Labrador. Calm and friendly with people: both.

"What about the pink striping on his nose?" I muttered to myself, and reached for my phone for a quick Google. Cici preempted me with a hand placed on top of mine.

"Chill, girl. Way ahead of you. It's called a butterfly nose in Australian Sheperds. There's not a thing about him that stands out as not belonging to an *Aussiedor*." She said the last word with a proud emphasis, and laughed again at the befuddled look on my face.

"Come on, Kel, keep up!" Cici playfully snapped her fingers at me. "Labradoodles, Goldendoodles, Aussiedors . . . it's another designer dog breed." She rubbed her chin and narrowed her eyes in thought.

"You know, Brianna never did come right out and say where or how she got Rett. Aussiedors are expensive dogs, if you buy them from a breeder, but I can't imagine Brianna doing the whole 'buy a dog from a reputable breeder' shtick. Most likely she saw him somewhere, either running loose, or just didn't like how he was being treated, got him in the car and away she went."

At the look on my face, Cici hurriedly added, "Or she could've got him from a shelter, or won him in a card game. Shit, I don't know. He's here now, and he ain't going anywhere except with me!" She gave me a stern look through narrowed eyes, as if she expected me to demand that we turn Rett over to a national lost and found center for dogs. I had no words to say on the topic, however. Let those without blame cast the first stone. I had acquired Leo in a somewhat dubious and shady manner one hot summer day: I had seen a woebegone puppy dispiritedly trailing a homeless man near an onramp for the freeway and had spontaneously handed over the contents of my wallet in exchange for Leo, no questions asked.

The waitress approached our table, just then, loaded down with our mouth-watering sandwiches and chips. All conversation was set aside as we addressed the food with focus and attention that it deserved. We added mocha caramel brownies topped by homemade vanilla ice cream to our lunches, on account of celebrating Cici and Rett's success with the Spokane 'SDPT' group. I don't know about Cici, but I was nearly in a food coma by the time we stood up to leave.

I would walk from the restaurant to where I'd left my Subaru, and check in with Boyd. Most likely he would still be ultra busy with his woodworking project. If so, I'd leave him to it and stay in Missoula for the night. Meanwhile, Cici and Rett needed to go back to work for their next stint at Zootown Zoo. Cici had parked her vehicle a few blocks away, in my direction, so the trio of us crossed the street and walked companionably along the riverfront trail. A breeze sprang up that blew a whirl of dried leaf bits into our faces. I got some in my eyes and stopped to clear things out. Suddenly, I heard Rett make a terrible moaning sound, like nothing I'd ever heard from a dog before. Cici and I both whipped around to look at the dog, who had stopped just behind us, and gasped.

Gone was the friendly, calm 50-50 Aussiedor. In his place stood what could best be described as a werewolf, 100%, complete with blazing eyes from Hell and gleaming daggers of teeth that were ferociously bared to bite. Every hair on Rett's back and neck bristled wildly, as if he were in the process of being electrocuted, and he stiffly popped up and down on his single front leg.

As we stared at him in pure astonishment, Rett shifted the weird moaning sound into a roar that would have made a lion proud. He charged forward as hard as his three legs could go, snapping against the end of the leash with enough force to yank himself and Cici down in a heap.

"What the hell!" Cici yelped. "Rett, you booger, knock it off!"

Cici rolled so that her body held Rett's down, as he scrabbled frantically in an attempt to regain his feet. I followed the dog's eyes, trying to understand what could have sparked this outlandish reaction in him. Several restaurants and coffee shops were across the street, with a number of people seated in outdoor, sunny spots, enjoying the day, much as Cici and I had done at Locally Sauced. Amazingly, no one seemed to have noticed us.

One of those people, soaking up the sun and drinking a coffee, was a slightly-built younger man, with his scant hair pulled back into a ponytail, and a wispy goatee decorated his chin.

The Shalimar Stalker! The man named Dawg! Oh my god, it was him!

THIRTY

"Cici, ohmygodjesus," I grabbed her arm and shook it. "Look across the street! It's *him*! Oh, shit, we've got to call the police." I yanked my purse open and dug hurriedly around for my cell phone.

Cici whipped out a hand of her own and snagged my purse while keeping one hand on Rett's collar as she pinned him down with her body.

"And, what then, Kelly?" she snapped. "If we call the police, they won't do shit, just because some dog growled at a guy, even if that dog's owner was murdered. Isn't that what the precious Deputy Darla told you? We need DNA from this turd. He's right there in front of us! We need to do it!"

"What do you mean?" I hissed back furiously. Damn it, she'd grabbed me so hard I was going to have bruises. "What are you talking about? Get DNA ourselves?"

Cici's face had transformed into features of stone, with dark eyes glittering dangerously beneath her bunched brows, and her breath was coming in short, hard bursts.

"You like Shakespeare, dontcha? Well, here's some for you, Kelly." Cici let go of my arm, rolled off of Rett, and spat, "Cry havoc, and let slip the dogs of war!"

And she set Rett free.

Rett, feeling himself released, surged to his feet, intending to charge across the street and dismember the coffee drinking man. He would've done it, too, if he had four operational legs. Missing his front leg made him lurch awkwardly on his first step, slowing him down just enough that I was able to grab his hindquarters and knock him over. Sorry, Rett.

There was a moment of undignified wrestling between Cici, Rett and myself as I fought to get control of the dog's leash. "Are you INSANE?" I hissed across Rett at Cici. "If he runs over there and bites that guy, the police will come alright; they'll come and take Rett away! They'll kill him! Even if they don't, what about Spokane? A bite history for Rett would ruin it!"

Cici pushed herself to her feet and looked scornfully down at me, her eyes as fierce and as merciless as a falcon's.

"Keep the dog out of it then," she snarled. "We'll send in the Bitch."

With those words, she spun on her heel and surged across the street toward the coffee shop herself. Behind her, on the ground with the snarling, struggling Rett, I gaped at Cici's back. What was she going to do?

Bite him herself?

Hurriedly, I wrapped Rett's leash around the leg of a City Park picnic table, giving me a lot better control of the struggling, howling dog. Once he was secured, I yanked out my cellphone and activated it as a video recording device.

Cici had pulled off her jacket as she crossed the street, draping it over her arm as if she found the day overly warm for its weight. As I started recording with my phone, she walked on an angled course across the coffee shop patio that would take her alongside the suspected Dawg, aiming toward the shop's doors as if she meant to go inside. I saw the man glance slightly at her as she started to pass, and then a lot of things happened, all at once.

Cici appeared to stumble, had she caught her prosthesis on an un-noticed uneven area? The stumble pitched her sideways, toward the man's table, and she put out a hand to catch herself. The table, one of those rickety metal patio tables we all know to hate, promptly tipped over on its side, sending the man's coffee cup flying and dumping Cici on her ass. Dawg and other coffee shop patrons stood up in alarm.

Cici held up a calming hand toward the man, and appeared to say something, I imagined her voice saying, "Sorry, dude". She pulled her legs under her, and at the same time dropped her jacket over the jettisoned coffee cup, undoubtedly meaning to scoop it up and retreat from the scene with DNA and fingerprint evidence. For a split second, my alarm over her fall washed away in a wave of admiration for her sneaky, successful ploy. Then everything went to hell in a heartbeat.

Dawg, far from behaving solicitously, contorted his face in outrage. He stepped aggressively toward Cici, grabbing her roughly by the shoulders and shouting in her face. Not the best thing to do to a trained army vet with PTSD, no sir.

Cici promptly head butted him with a fury that demolished his nose as if it were an overly ripe tomato. Blood spurted everywhere as the other customers, mostly women, backed hurriedly away from the violence.

Dawg let go of Cici to clutch at his wounded nose, giving her space to scramble to her feet and back away from him. She poised her body for action, raising her fists in a combative boxer's stance, ready to take him on again, if needed. On my side of the street, Rett redoubled his vocal output, now screeching, wailing and roaring like a whole pack of hellhounds, as he thrashed wildly against his leash. His high-level conniption fit drew the attention of everyone on the patio, including Dawg.

The skinny young man froze in place, staring in horror at the raging Rett as if he was seeing a ghost. A police siren could now be heard in the distance, rapidly approaching. At the sound, Dawg tore his eyes away from Rett to look directly at me, filming away with my cellphone. Abruptly, he dropped his head and walked rapidly away from the scene, leaving the street to cut to the north alongside the Sweets Bakery Emporium building.

Cici made as if to follow him, but after a single step, turned back to snatch up her coat and the coffee cup instead. Thank god.

By now, a patrol car with lights flashing and siren sounding had pulled up at the curb. I quickly untied Rett from the table and we crossed the road to help explain the incident to the police, and to enlist their aid in collecting crime scene evidence for use in the Brianna Norwood murder investigation.

"WHAT DO YOU MEAN, YOU'RE IN a police car on its way to the station? God dammit! I knew something like this would happen!" Boyd's voice boomed out of my cellphone loud enough for the officer driving to hear, causing him to smile at the corners of his mouth.

"Boyd, stop *shouting*," I said in my best aggrieved-wife tone before primly continuing. "There was a fight at a coffee shop; I filmed it on my cellphone. Cici was there and saw the whole thing, too. We're going down to the station to do *witness statements*! It shouldn't take too long! I'll call you when we're done."

Boyd grumbled out a bunch of words and disconnected the call. I chose to believe that he had apologized for shouting at me and hoped that he believed that our trip to the station was innocent as I had made it sound.

In fact, the police had recognized Cici as a frequent flyer disturber-of-the-peace, and immediately assumed that she was on the wrong side of the coffeehouse confrontation. She had been put into handcuffs and bundled into the first patrol car before even I got all the way across the street. My attempt to intervene and focus police efforts on collecting evidence for an ongoing murder investigation only muddied the waters. Kelly Boyd wound up in the back of a second patrol car, to be hauled down to the police station for explanations. Fortunately, my standing as a retired math teacher, upright citizen and RogerDogs representative, won

Rett the right to ride along with me rather than being consigned to Missoula Animal Control.

I crossed my fingers that all of us would be released after giving statements, just as I had told Boyd. It was going to be bad enough telling him that the coffeehouse fight was related to Brianna's murder without me spending extended time in the hoosegow, maybe even overnight!

By the time we reached the station, I had made use of my continued possession of the cellphone to text Deputy Darla Shaw, alerting her to the new developments. Hopefully, she would be inspired to intervene on our behalf and not toss us to the procedural wolves.

The 'WTF!?' response I received could go either way, really.

THIRTY-ONE

D ETECTIVE TODD JENSEN OF THE MISSOULA police department placed his desk phone back onto its base as he finished a call from his counterpart in Stillwater County, Deputy Darla Shaw. Detective Jensen was a heavy-set man in his early sixties with shrewd, tiny eyes that peered out from his facial wrinkles not unlike the eyes of an elephant. Like an elephant, too, everything about Detective Jensen was gray: gray hair, what was left of it; large, gray mustache, and the suits that he wore for work were invariably gray—and he never forgot anything, to the chagrin of his younger co-workers, who often thought it would be nice if the man didn't have an encyclopedia of all their missteps filed away in his brain. Criminals, too, wished for forgetfulness on Detective Jensen's part, but that never happened.

Detective Jensen sat for a moment, reviewing his knowledge of the Brianna Norwood murder case, and the work his department had done in support of the Sweetgrass sheriff's investigation. No viable suspects had come to light during interviews with her roommates or at her workplace; all information gathered had been duly forwarded to the Sweetgrass sheriff's department, and that had been the end of the involvement of the Missoula police.

Now, almost three weeks later, Deputy Shaw had called him to say two women and a dog were on their way into the station with possible new information about a suspicious male, along with physical evidence in the form of a coffee cup and a bloody shirt—would Detective Jensen run a fingerprint analysis of the coffee cup, and process both it and the bloody shirt for DNA evidence?

Apparently, Deputy Shaw was in a rush to see if fingerprints would match against a partial print from evidence collected at the murder site. Maybe the case would finally have some luck.

Detective Jensen rubbed the back of his neck and tried to ignore the little tingle of excitement that he felt percolating in his brain. Probably nothing, he cautioned himself, most potential clues turned out to be only a waste of time. But the fact was, for Detective Jensen, all bits of information that washed across his desk were akin to wrapped Christmas packages. Who knew what lay underneath the outer wrapping? The *finding out* was still a boy-ish thrill to Todd Jensen and protected him from the jaded burn-out he had seen over the years in other police officers.

Hooding his eyes under his thick gray eyebrows to hide the gleam of anticipation he felt, Detective Jensen walked his bulk downstairs to meet the incoming squad cars with his newfound interview subjects.

I was pleasantly surprised to be met by the lead detective for the Missoula police, and to be politely escorted to an interview room, along with Cici, and Rett, too. My imagination had run a little wild in the police car on ride to the station, and I had fore-seen we would be kept separate from each other, placed into win-dowless rooms that were either too hot or too cold, but certainly smelled bad, and where the chairs had been monkeyed with to be uncomfortable in psychologically disturbing ways.

The heavyset Detective Jensen explained his connection to Brianna's murder investigation. Our statements about the after-noon's altercation with a possible suspect would be taken shortly.

An evidence technician was currently collecting the phone video I had shot; the phone would be returned to me when our statements were taken. The coffee cup was on its way to the lab for fingerprint analysis at this exact moment in time, and Cici's flannel shirt that had been spattered with blood from the man's damaged nose was in the evidence room, awaiting DNA analysis. We would be free to go afterwards; in the meantime, did we need any water?

We demurred, and stayed seated on the perfectly normal chairs in the interview room which was at a comfortable seventy degrees. Detective Jensen exited the room, leaving me with the distinct impression that the three of us would be out of the building within the hour.

An hour came and went, and we were still in the room, without having seen a soul. The room, which seemed so innocuous at first, was revealing itself to be a subtle torture chamber after all. The walls and ceiling were painted the same shade of white, unbroken by any clock, window, or motivational poster. No sound could be heard outside the door, and time passed in slow drips only. It was like waiting in an exam room after a nurse cheerfully claims, 'Doctor will be in soon', only worse.

"This is nuts, I'm going to see what's taking so long," I said, jumping to my feet and stalking toward the door. Cici shook her head at me as if she couldn't believe my stupidity.

"The door's *locked*, Kelly," she said in a voice of doom. "They put you in a room like this and leave you there to sweat. We ain't going to see Mr. Big Shot Detective for a long, long time."

My mouth formed an 'O' of horror. Hours and hours? Boyd was going to freak! Hell, I was going to freak! Of the two of us, only Cici had actual experience in a lockup, but surely this couldn't be right? We had a dog in here! What about potty breaks?

I whipped myself over to the door, prepared to bang on it with all my might in an excess of righteous indignation, until someone responded to my Great Big Noisy Fuss. I stopped just short of the door as my brain caught up with me. We were in a police station, for crying out loud! Obviously, if police stuffed people into locked rooms as a regular policy, they would be well-used to the noise of loud and demanding people. Throwing an indignant, outraged hissy-fit wasn't going to do us any good.

In a spurt of vexation, I kicked the door and pushed down hard on the door's handle for good measure. The handle obligingly disengaged the latch with a loud snap, and the door cracked open, leaving me surprised and fighting to keep my balance. The door hadn't locked behind Detective Jensen!

In hindsight, we didn't need to flee the police station as if we were breaking out of jail. If we had calmer, cooler heads at that point in the day, we would simply have stopped at the station's front desk and left a message for Detective Jensen to contact us at his convenience for witness statements. We weren't under arrest, and were free to leave at any time, the door was never meant to be locked.

But Cici's description of being trapped in an interview room to be 'sweated', and the time spent in that white, sensory deprivation room had skewed our sense of reality, and infused our minds with a bit of panic. Instead of going straight to the front of the police station like upstanding citizens, we scurried down the hall and hid in the ladies' room.

Cici still had her cellphone and summoned a Lyft driver to pick us up two streets away, pronto! Gathering our courage, we walked out the back door as casually as if we were two civilian employees heading out for a smoke. Thankfully, were no legitimate employees taking a cigarette break right then, and we were able to skulk away from the station undetected.

THIRTY-TWO

DETECTIVE JENSEN, IN FACT, HAD FORGOTTEN all about the two women and the dog waiting in Interview Room Number Three.

He had decided to take their statements himself, once the cell phone was ready to be returned to Mrs. Boyd. After putting in a call to IT, requesting that the technician bring Mrs. Boyd's phone to him when they were finished, Detective Jensen settled in at his desk and continued his work on a series of robberies that had occurred in Missoula over the last several weeks.

Some clever but naughty person had figured out how to duplicate the radio signals for automatic garage doors and had been accessing houses through the illicitly opened garage doors. At one break-in, a neighbor had seen a white paneled utility van parked in the driveway and several young men in light blue overalls carrying *in* a few small pieces of furniture, which was a slick move on the burglars' part to give themselves an appearance of legitimacy.

Once the burglars were inside, the houses were rapidly tossed for spare cash, blank checks, jewelry and of course, any drugs they could get their hands on. Several of the break-ins were at houses where an occupant had just filled a legitimate prescription for oxycodone or other controlled substances, leading Detective Jensen to suspect the robbers were intentionally targeting houses on this basis.

Detective Jensen tapped his teeth with his pencil and narrowed his eyes in thought. Could the thieves be lurking in local pharmacies eavesdropping on customer transactions? He grunted to himself. No, it was more likely that an assistant pharmacist or two were tipping the thieves off with customer details for a kickback. Was there a single pharmacy used by the victims? That would be something to find out.

Detective Jensen's thoughts were interrupted by an incoming phone call on his desk phone. With a sigh, he rumbled, "Detective Jensen," and waited to find out what bit of irrelevant bureaucracy was interrupting his work.

The words he heard over the phone flushed all thoughts of the robberies and the waiting women from Detective Jensen's mind.

"This is Agent O'Neill of the FBI. Detective Jensen, a set of fingerprints were just now uploaded to AFIS at your bequest. These prints match with a set recovered from an arson that is part of an ongoing federal investigation. I am on my way to your office to meet with you, please be available."

IT WAS THE NEXT DAY, SATURDAY, October 22nd, before I was able to retrieve my phone from the Missoula police, and to hear about the investigative firestorm that had been lit when the fingerprints from the coffee cup were run through the system.

Boyd insisted on driving to Missoula on Friday night and accompanying me to meet with Detective Jensen in the morning. To tell the truth, I wanted him along for moral support, even if he was clearly unhappy that Cici and I had mixed it up with a suspected murderer. As a precaution, he'd also put the phone number for our lawyer, Al Mowat, on speed dial. Al wasn't a criminal lawyer by any means; he had handled contracts and the retirement sale of Boyd's construction company, but he was shrewd, highly competent, and one of Boyd's best friends. He would be a bulldog in our corner if the Missoula police tried any hijinks.

In a perfect repeat of Friday, Detective Jensen met us at the front desk and escorted us back to Interview Room Number Three. This time, though, the table held a pot of coffee, cups and a tray of assorted goodies that looked as if they came from the upscale Bernice's Bakery. I was happy to see my cellphone waiting as well.

Detective Jensen directed Boyd and me to have a seat and help ourselves to the pastries, as he pulled out a chair for himself. His shrewd little eyes almost disappeared behind folds as he beamed a satisfied smile our way.

"Thank you for coming back in today. Apologies for not ever getting back to you yesterday, I'm glad you and Ms. Vargas didn't sit here all night." His smile grew even wider, as I struggled not to squirm guiltily at the thought of our 'escape' from the station.

"Now, generally, we frown on citizens trying to collect evidence on their own, and must say, if anything like yesterday ever comes up again, please, trust us to do our jobs." Detective Jensen could save his breath. There wasn't anything he could say that Angry Husband Boyd hadn't already covered, more thoroughly—or that Unnerved Kelly didn't whole-heartedly agree with. It was the loose cannonball named Cici who needed talking to, but we weren't going to stir the pot by saying so, no sir. *Give the man my ear but not my voice*, seemed a sensible plan to me.

"But the fingerprints on the coffee cup matched not just the partial print that was found October 3rd, on a shell casing near the recovery site for Brianna Norwood, but also a full set of prints that were found on an empty gas can at the August Rendezvous Emporium arson site."

Detective Jensen paused and gave me a crooked grin as I sat bolt upright in my chair at that news. "So, I see you remember the picture showing Brianna Norwood at that fire.

"The FBI became involved as soon as that match was made,

and things started to happen very quickly yesterday. Now, at first nobody knew the identity of the person those prints belonged to, but with your video, Mrs. Boyd, we were able to winkle a name out of the young lady working at the coffee shop counter. Turns out that the man in the video is a regular at the shop where he always stiffs the workers for a tip, claiming he 'has no cash' as he pays by credit card. He has built up quite a lot of animosity with the staff; they were delighted to throw him under a bus with law enforcement. Gave us Doug Anderson's credit card slip without even asking if we had a warrant."

Detective Jensen shook his head in mock sorrow. "A little common courtesy on his part, and our investigation might have been stone-walled until we could get the proper paperwork lined up."

Here he paused for dramatic effect, helping himself to a raspberry croissant and eating half of it, and washing down the flaky pastry with a liberal swig of coffee, before continuing. I stifled the urge to give him a swift kick-start under the table as Boyd hardened his eyes at me in silent warning to be on my best behavior.

"When the FBI wants a search warrant, they can get it at the speed of light, let me tell you. Agent O'Neill punched some information into his phone on our way to the suspect's house, and by the time the car got there, he had an electronic no knock warrant in hand. We had to hang back for the SWAT team to arrive, but within the hour we were inside.

Detective Jensen leaned toward Boyd and me and his face became very serious.

"We found Brianna's car in his garage."

I froze, staring at the detective as if I hadn't heard him right. Brianna's car was in his garage? What? Why?

"I spent quite a bit of time discussing this with Deputy Shaw, you remember her? She vouched for you and Ms. Vargas, by the way. Said you were perfect pains in the ass, I believe, but that you could be trusted to act in the best interests of Ms. Norwood's murder investigation.

"Deputy Shaw and I believe that Brianna willingly drove to the Crazy Mountains with Doug Anderson, taking along her dog. It's possible that another person went on the trip, too, there would have been room in the car, at least. We'll know more after forensics finishes going over it. We think he shot the two of them and then drove back to Missoula in her car. He doesn't have a vehicle himself, so the garage at his rented house was vacant. The car's battery was dead, with the lights in the 'on' position; we think he stashed it in the garage in a panic and then just left it there, out of sight. Maybe he meant to ditch it later, but with the battery being dead it was just easier to leave it alone.

"If the DNA from the dog's collar, the coffee cup and of course, Ms. Vargas' bloody shirt, matches, we'll have solid proof to tie this Doug Anderson to Brianna's murder, as well as the Washington arson. We should get those results back within the next week.

"Now, when we watched the video from your phone, Mrs. Boyd, we noticed Doug Anderson looks right at you and freezes up for a moment before taking off. Does he know you from somewhere?"

I started to speak, but I had a frog in my throat. After a few sips of my own coffee, I was able to blurt out, "Not me. He recognized Rett, I'm sure of it. I know Rett recognized him!"

The detective continued to stare at me without a reply and Boyd joined him. The silence hung in the room like smoke from a stink bomb that no one wanted to acknowledge. Irritated by their unwavering eyeballs, I snapped, "If you have something to say, just say it! You're both looking at me like I just grew a third eyeball!"

Detective Jensen slowly turned his head to look at Boyd, and then swiveled it back to meet my eyes again. With a look of patience on his face, he folded his hands together on the table in front of him and leaned forward.

"Doug Anderson is on the run today, not three weeks from the discovery of Brianna Norwood's body, smoked out by his chance encounter with you, Ms. Vargas, and the dog. That little episode turned his world here in Missoula upside down and on top of it,

Ms. Vargas quite probably broke his nose." A spark of merriment shone in the depths of Detective Jensen's small eyes.

"We have to assume that he's carrying a hefty grudge, at the least, against you and Ms. Vargas. Doug may look ineffectual, but he's a murderer and an arsonist who, unfortunately, had a very good look at you both yesterday. Until we apprehend Doug Anderson, and we will, you and Ms. Vargas are somewhat at risk. Back a rat into a corner and it's going to bite.

"We aren't releasing your names to the news media, and I strongly recommend that you don't speak to any reporters your-selves, no matter how much publicity you could generate for your dog rescue, Kelly," Detective Jensen sternly said. He didn't quite wag an admonishing finger at me, but I felt my hackles rise anyway. Did he think I woke up and took stupid pills this morning?

Boyd saw the flash of irritation on my face and forestalled any sparky comments from me by jumping in with his own question.

"Do you really think this guy will come looking for revenge? Isn't it most likely that he's gone, vamoosed?"

"He could be holed up in the area, using his connections with ALF and ELF to hide out, or he could be long gone, running to a bigger city like Seattle. With the FBI on his tail, it's just a mat-ter of time before he gets spotted and scooped up, in my opinion. Missoula will be too hot for him to live openly here anymore.

"If Mrs. Boyd and Ms. Vargas keep their heads down and keep clear of crossing Doug's path or catching his attention, I think they are safe enough."

"We're having a sit down with Ms. Vargas later today, and a phone conversation with Mrs. Mills as well, to pass on the same message to them; no reporters, no attempting to locate Doug Anderson on your own. Stay away from catching this guy's atten-tion while we track him down."

The heavyset detective sat back in his chair, watching our faces for agreement. Boyd gave a curt nod to the detective and returned his eyes to the Kelly stare down.

Grudgingly, because I really don't like to be bossed around, I nodded to the two men. I might not be pleased with the detective's manner, but I couldn't argue it was time to step away and sink into blessed anonymity. Murderers and Arsonists and Revengers. Oh, my! No, Kellan Boyd was plenty happy to head down the yellow brick road to home and leave this mess to the professionals.

I only hoped Cici and Betty would agree.

Thirty-Three

Thirty-six days after we first found Brianna's body and eleven days after we smoked out her murderer, Doug Anderson was still at large.

In the first days after Doug Anderson evaded arrest in Missoula, all of us were on edge and jumpy as cats waiting for the other shoe to drop. It seemed like every shadow in the night was Doug, creeping in to wreak mayhem. Betty Mills slept at RogerDogs, keeping an arsenal of weapons within easy reach, and dared Doug Anderson to show his face, while an equally well-armed Randy safeguarded their home.

Cici and Rett refused to hole up out of sight, at Zootown Zoo, with Jana Toski as her only in person contact with the outside world. Instead she and Rett roamed Missoula in their off hours, searching for any sign of Brianna's killer, seeing him in every pony-tailed, scruffy man. She wound up accosting a handful of long-haired college boys and narrowly escaped arrest herself.

Boyd insisted that we take the dogs and decamp to a friend's home in Helena, where we could stay in a 'mother-in-law' tiny house on the property. We lasted three days before returning home, but remained on high alert, posting Sadie and Leo in the yard as guard dogs until their incessant barking at non-Doug animals in the night wore us out.

As the days went by, with no sign of Doug Anderson anywhere, we collectively let down our guard. By Halloween, life had returned to normal and we no longer thought about his whereabouts every minute of every day. It was deeply aggravating that he had evaded arrest so far but it seemed a sure thing that he had fled the area and wouldn't be bothering the likes of us.

We were wrong.

"BOYD! DID YOU BRING IN THE mail yet?"

It was the night of November 8th. We were settled in for the evening, both of us inhabiting cozy recliner chairs in front of the roaring gas fireplace. Boyd looked up from his perusal of Netflix streaming options at the excited, urgent tone of my voice.

"Nope, I didn't get further away than the shop today, didn't seem worth it to flounder down to the mailbox," he answered.

"Well, according to an email notification from the USPS Informed Delivery app, there's a letter in the mailbox from the Arizona carving competition. Boyd! I bet it's your invitation to compete!" I exclaimed excitedly.

Boyd had put his name and bona fides into the hat some months earlier, hoping to be one of the selected chainsaw artists for the New Year's Carve 'Em Up Festival in Tombstone, Arizona. Potential carvers had to submit a curriculum vitae and a portfolio of their three best pieces. With zero competition experience, Boyd's acceptance would be based solely on the pictures of the three pieces he had created to showcase his talents.

My favorite of his three carvings was one that had two otters swimming around a submerged log, in play, while frightened fish dart away. Amazingly, a close inspection of the log shows the head of a large trout peering out from a cavity. To this day, I don't understand how he was able to carve that trout, in situ, with a chainsaw.

I looked at Boyd, giddy with excitement over the letter, and saw a large bear, hunkered into hibernation mode with the TV remote in its paw. As I watched in growing exasperation, *Die Another Day* popped up on our flat-screen TV. Gratuitous sex and violence were being picked above real-life excitement. Men!

Just then, a massive gust of wind slammed into the back of the house, making the glass in the windows boom. Sadie and Leo promptly jumped up from their beds and let out warning barks as they bounced stiff legged around the room, tails raised as battle flags.

The storms of November had come early, with full out winter upon us a full three weeks before normal. Where was global warming when you needed it!

The weather had disintegrated rapidly since the morning, with temperatures plunging into the negative digits, and a significant amount of snow was falling. Most of central Montana was under a severe winter storm warning for the next two days, with high winds, snowfall, and subzero Arctic temperatures making travel extremely hazardous. Citizens were warned not to venture from home, and Boyd was apparently taking this to include walking down our long driveway to the neighborhood's bank of mailboxes.

"It'll be there tomorrow, Kelly, no need to rush around in the dark. If you're feeling antsy, you could use up some energy rustling up popcorn for the movie." Boyd grinned at me and pointed his chin at the kitchen. I narrowed my eyes at him, and he shifted his features into a parody of a hopeful puppy, knowing it never failed to make me laugh.

"Alright, alright, I'll pop us some corn," I said, good naturedly swatting him with a throw pillow as I walked by into the kitchen.

The sight of all the kernels whirring around in the air popper wasn't calming, however; they were a visual manifestation of my ants-in-the-pants excitement over the letter. Did Boyd want to put off opening the letter, in case it was a rejection? Maybe. More likely he just didn't want to haul his butt out into the winter storm. Hmm, should I venture out and fetch the letter myself?

As I sat on the fence, mulling the options, another mammoth gust of wind shook the house. That settled the issue for me; our mailbox is prone to popping open during high winds, releasing our mail to fly away willy-nilly. No way was I willing to sit tight in the house while the important letter sailed off into the night.

I finished with the popcorn, buttering and salting it the way we like it as I put it into a large, sky-blue ceramic bowl that was our official popcorn bowl. I walked back into the living room, past the two heelers who were now burrowed back into their dog beds, and set the bowl on the side table by Boyd's leather recliner chair.

"Don't eat it all before I get back," I admonished him. "I'm going to go get the mail before it gets blown to Wyoming. Be back in a jiffy."

The dogs started to get up out of their beds but I told them to stay put for the moment.

"You could let them out to 'find me', Boyd. Just give me a ten-minute head start." This was a game that the heelers loved to play; one of us would go in advance and 'hide', the dogs would be released to act as tracker dogs, running hither and yon with wild exuberance until the hidden one was found. On a night like tonight, I wasn't planning on actually hiding, but the dogs would enjoy chasing me down on my mailbox trek, at least.

After bundling up properly in a balaclava, wind pants, overcoat, and heavy snow boots, topped off with a wool hat and mittens, I looked like a small, rotund snowman. Judging myself to be safe from the elements, I grabbed a flashlight and started on my mini-expedition to the mailbox.

It never crossed my mind that there could be non-weather-related danger awaiting in the darkness.

A NON-DESCRIPT PASSENGER CAR CREPT SLOWLY DOWN the county road, approaching the Boyd driveway from the north. The car's headlights were off, the driver had found it too hard to see the road what with the light reflected off the heavy, swirling snowflakes, as well as wanting to be secretive in his approach to the house.

The car, with balding tires and front-wheel drive, had given the man quite a few scary moments on his way to the Boyd's; the bursts of fear and adrenaline had added to the man's already agitated state, and he was now cussing loudly and continuously to himself. All thought of simply doing a reconnaissance of their property had flown out the window. Dawg was going in for action, yessir, having dealt with all the shit of getting here.

He glanced over his shoulder into the backseat where multiple cans of gasoline were stored. Sniggering, he thought that soon no one would be cold at the Boyds.

"HOLY CRAP!" I EXCLAIMED AS A gust of wind slammed into me hard enough to send me staggering across the driveway. On my way down the driveway to the stand of community mailboxes that sit by the county road, I had been somewhat protected from the wind by a long ridge that runs alongside our driveway. The ridge subsides where our driveway joins the county road as it loops to the north toward our nearest neighbors. Once beyond its protection I was exposed to the wind's full fury as I scuttled out onto the road. The mailboxes were just ahead, bunched in a wide, level, turn-around spot on the far side of the road's borrow pit.

Not wanting to spend a moment more than necessary in the gale force, I bowed my head and broke into a shuffling jog. I had just crossed the almost invisible ditch, filled with drifted snow, when I heard a car approaching on the county road, going fast, with no show of headlights.

As I turned my head to look at the vehicle in puzzled disbelief, the driver changed course to aim directly at me!

I gave a strangled yelp, and tried mightily to jump backwards far enough to get out of the car's path, but only managed to fall on my butt in the snow. The car would've hit me, there's no doubt, except for the intervention of the ditch and gravity. The driver had chosen to aim directly at me, not realizing that this path would take him off the road into the borrow pit. The car's front left wheel dropped into the snow-filled ditch, dropping the car at an angle that caused the car's nose to sharply impact the bank.

Even in the dark, I could see the airbags activate, swallowing up the driver from sight in billowing white pillows.

"Holy shit!!!" I barked out loud.

What had the dumbass driver been thinking? Driving without lights in a snowstorm on a road he clearly was unfamiliar with, seeing as how he had tried to go cross country through the borrow pit. He had scared the bejeezus out of me, and now I would be delayed getting back to the warm house, damn it.

I picked up my flashlight from where I'd dropped it during my butt flop, and put its beam on the car as I walked over to check on the driver. Was this one of the teenagers who lived further up the mountain with their family? Maybe the retired bareback rider, what was his name? He was no stranger to drinking and driving! I didn't recognize the car as belonging to anyone I knew, though. Was this a visiting friend or relative who made a driving error in the dark? The confluence of driveway, roads and ditch isn't marked at all, and in the blowing snow would be treacherous for a driver who wasn't familiar with the layout.

I was almost to the car when the driver's door opened and the man squirmed out from behind the wheel, unceremoniously toppling into the ditch. I put the flashlight beam full on his face, making him shut his eyes against the bright light. He wasn't sporting his feeble goatee anymore, but I still recognized Doug Anderson in an instant.

"God in hell!" I gasped as I spun around to begin the long run back up the driveway, to the safety of the house.

Thirty-Four

I T WAS THE STUFF OF NIGHTMARES, running uphill while wearing heavy winter wear, buffeted by the wind, boot laden feet churning desperately through the snow. For all my effort, it seemed as if I wasn't actually making any forward progress. I didn't dare risk a glance over my shoulder to see if I was being pursued, and if so, how close the monster was behind me. No, if I stumbled or took a fall, he'd be on me for sure!

A cracking noise split the air to my left, sounding so exactly like ice cracking on a frozen lake that I gasped and expected to fall through, down into dark water, even as my brain shouted that I was running on solid ground. A second crack tore through the air, much closer this time, and I belatedly recognized the sound as the gunfire it was.

The asshole was shooting at me!

I had intended to run up the driveway, all the way to the house, but that would make me a superb target, silhouetted the whole way against the friendly glow of the deck's porchlight. No, I would have to juke and jive to the right, and get into the shadow of Boyd's shop building that lay between me and the house. Once safely in the dark, I'd be able to continue toward the house.

I snapped my flashlight off and ran from the road into the

snow-covered sagebrush, heading for the shadowed darkness of the shop. One good thing about running through sagebrush, you have to constantly change direction in order to dodge the bushes, making you a hard target to shoot at. But all that back and forth slows you down, too.

Desperately out of breath, I reached the shop's back corner without feeling either a punch from a bullet, or a clutch on my shoulder. I staggered along the backside of the building until I reached it's far corner. The shop's door awaited me along the north side of the shop; I floundered around the corner and fell against the door.

"Please, please, please be unlocked," I begged the door, visions of safety, telephone, and readily available weapons dancing in my mind. I had never fired up one of Boyd's chainsaws, much less wielded one, but felt sure I'd be up for the challenge if necessary. The door was thoroughly and unrepentantly locked, however.

Shit!

I gave the door a few fruitless kicks as I tried to think what best to do now.

Was Doug Anderson in hot pursuit of me, or had he fled? God in Heaven, what if he kept going straight up the driveway to the house, to burst in on unsuspecting Boyd while I was floundering around in the dark?

Seized with an overwhelming need to know the bastard's whereabouts, I took a step back toward the corner of the building but hesitated before going around it. What if Doug Anderson was just around that corner? I looked hurriedly around for anything that could be used as a better weapon than the flashlight I had in my hand, just in case he was within striking range.

Aha! Boyd had left some sections of rebar leaning against the shop, and I snatched one up as if it were a sword, before returning to the building's corner for a cautious reconnaissance of my flight path.

No, no, no! There he was, making his way through the sage-brush toward the far side of the shop building. At the sight of him, all the oxygen in the air around me was sucked away, leaving me hollowed out with horror. Doug Anderson wasn't hampered by heavy winter clothing, he was scampering along in a flannel shirt and jeans; he didn't have so much as a hat on his head! He also didn't have any experience running through sagebrush and tripped headlong over a bush as I watched.

Even with trips and falls to slow him down, Doug Anderson was too close to me for escape; there was no way for me to cross the remaining distance to the house without being caught or shot. I would have to hide, long enough for him to freeze to death, or for Boyd to come look for me, but what if the scumbag shot Boyd?

Think, Kelly, think! Was there a way to disable the asshole long enough to let me get away safely?

There were several large logs leaning upright against the side of the shop, stored vertically by Boyd to shed water, ice and snow until he was ready to carve them. The log closest to the building's corner was also next to the air exchanger unit for the shop; if I stood on top of that, and pushed the heavy log sideways, I just might be able to topple it onto Doug Anderson, squashing him like a bug. It seemed like my best chance.

It almost worked, too.

The nine foot high, eighteen-inch-wide log toppled with gratifying ease when I shoved it off balance and gravity took over. My timing was a little off, though. I had waited to topple the log until I saw Doug Anderson appear at the edge of the building, entering the squashing zone, but I guess I was too quick to push the log. Maybe the Valkyrie shriek that burst out of my throat as I launched my attack gave him too much warning. I don't know.

For whatever reason, Doug Anderson was able to throw himself backwards and escape the trajectory of the falling log, by a whisker. With an angry shout, he landed full on his back, like he intended to make a snow angel before chasing me further. The fall temporarily knocked the breath out of him, and he lay gasping in the snow.

The log bounced harmlessly near his feet, and rolled slightly away, down the hill.

I had landed mostly on my own feet, but had to scrabble frantically for solid footing. I still had the rebar in my hand, and with a second shrieking war cry, I leaped wildly at Doug Anderson, whipping the iron bar viciously through the air, meaning to smack his gun hand before he could take another shot at me.

I almost brained Sadie by mistake!

Back at the house, the movie had been at full tilt, covering any sounds of the car crash and gunshots that hadn't already been drowned by the wind. Boyd had finished his popcorn and wandered into the kitchen for a drink, when he remembered that he should send the dogs out on a Kelly hunt. Released to the outdoors, they coursed off the deck steps and flew down the driveway as he headed back to the comfort of the living room and Bond violence, happily unaware of the real-life drama playing out in his very own front yard.

Boyd might have been oblivious, but not so the dogs. They might have smelled Doug Anderson, and they surely would have heard us shrieking and shouting. The two of them came around the backside of the shop at top speed, in a righteous protective fury and tore into Doug Anderson like there was no tomorrow.

Heelers are well used to using their teeth to boss creatures around, and deep in their hearts are delighted with opportunities to do so, but they aren't fighting dogs. Usually their bites are limited to snatch and grab pinches from the back. Catch and release biting as it were.

Not tonight.

Sadie appeared out of the darkness and sank her teeth into Doug Anderson's arm as it were made of soft cheese, and didn't let go. I yanked my rebar swing up, just missing her head, and lost my grip on it. The steel bar whistled through the air as it disappeared into the darkness, downslope from us. Doug Anderson held onto the gun momentarily under Sadie's onslaught, but in the next heartbeat, he was hit full in the back by a high-speed express train named Leo. The impact knocked the gun loose from his hand, to land a few feet away.

I let out a banshee shriek that outpaced both the storm and the Bond action to make it to Boyd's ears in the house, and dove onto the gun. My scream was joined by an even louder one from Doug Anderson as the dogs did some major damage to him.

A thick spray of blood arced through the air, and for a horrified moment I thought they had ripped his throat out like modern day Hounds of Baskerville. Doug Anderson continued to scream and thrash, though, so apparently his throat was intact.

I got my hands on the gun, regained my feet and churned my short legs into motion, running full tilt toward the house once again.

"Run! Sadie, Leo, RUN!" I bellowed, and continued to holler for them as I ran without stopping to the house and Boyd.

THIRTY-FIVE

"**Y**OU THREW THE GUN."

Boyd peered at me in disbelief with dark, beetle eyes, his tone devoid of inflection. Nonplussed, I paused in my recounting of the evening's drama.

"Yes, I threw the gun, Boyd," I affirmed and drew in breath to continue, but Boyd wasn't done with the subject. He narrowed his eyes at me, and then made a weak overarm throwing gesture.

"You threw it. With your little, girly toss. You threw the gun." His voice still expressed flat disbelief.

"Well," I sputtered. "I did better than that!" In fact, I had launched myself into a two stepped, jumping twirl, akin to a figure skater executing a waltz jump just as I learned in long ago youthful figure skating lessons. I had released the gun at the height of the twirl so that it *flew*, gloriously, into the darkness and snow, where it wouldn't be able to harm anyone, anymore.

"Kelly, do you have any idea where the gun wound up?"

What was it with the gun inquisition? Guns to me are like rattlesnakes, dangerous to handle and best left alone. I like snakes, even poisonous ones, but that doesn't mean I'd hold onto one as I ran willy-nilly up a slick, bumpy driveway, pumping my arms and running as hard as I could go. That would be an invitation

for disaster! Nor did I think it appropriate to leave the gun laying around for Doug Anderson to find if he followed after me.
Sending the gun far away, to land hidden in the snow and sagebrush seemed an eminently sensible course of action. Judging
from Boyd's reaction, it wasn't what he would have done.

I waved my hand in the general direction of the open expanse
that lies to the south of our house and driveway. "It's out there.
Somewhere. Down under all the fluffy snow on the ground. It'll
turn up when it melts, or if you want it faster, you can go hunt it
down with a metal detector." I glared fiercely at Boyd, to let him
know I was done with the topic of the gun.

We were holed up with the dogs in our breakfast nook while
a Lewis and Clark county deputy guarded the front approach to
the house, and another watched over us from the back. A bevy
of others were out looking for Doug Anderson and securing his
stranded vehicle.

The house shook as an approaching person stamped their feet
hard on the deck, in an attempt to knock snow off their boots, followed by the sound of the mud room door opening. A man's voice
called out. "Mr. and Mrs. Boyd, officer coming in, okay?"

I jumped to my feet and hustled the leashed dogs into the spare
bedroom, shutting them away as they barked and snarled promises
of destruction to all invaders, policeman included. Sadie and Leo
were still amped up in Superdog mode, ready to attack and defend,
but officers of the law are out of bounds.

"Sorry, guys, it's for your own good," I said as I firmly shut the
door against their wild-eyed faces.

A deputy, wearing cold weather gear, was standing in the
kitchen with Boyd when I came back from the bedroom. He pulled
off his thick, stocking hat and unzipped his coat partway, but made
no move to sit down.

"I'm Deputy Sandusky. I wanted you to know right away that
we have apprehended Doug Anderson and he is in custody." His
broad face, reddened by the wind and cold, creased in a wide smile

at the sight of relief on ours.

"Oh, thank god," I breathed.

"Where did you find him?" asked Boyd.

"Well, he wasn't too hard to find, actually. In defending you, Mrs. Boyd, your dogs caused a pretty significant head wound." He paused and I remembered the horrifying shriek from Doug Anderson as Leo and Sadie ripped into him.

I saw Deputy Sandusky's eyes gleam suddenly with suppressed entertainment. "Yessir, they tore his ear right *off*, along with a good-sized chunk of scalp, so he was bleeding pretty hard. We followed his trail, easy as anything, and found him hunkered under a big sagebrush where it formed kind of a den next to a rock, maybe six hundred yards to the north of this house.

"He's lucky we were able to find him as soon as we did. He'll have some pretty good frostbite as it is, but in another hour? No coat, hat or gloves, wearing only tennis shoes and no socks, in minus fourteen degrees, with a hard wind? He would've been frozen solid before too long."

I wouldn't have been sorry one bit if he had been. And the ear? Good for you, Leo and Sadie! Too bad you didn't get both of them!

Deputy Sandusky took a step back toward the mud room, pulling his hat back on as he did so. "A tow truck will get his car out of the ditch in the next couple of hours; our crime scene and hazmat crew needs to get cans of what appears to be gasoline out of the vehicle before it can be moved."

"What!" Boyd barked in a loud, angry shout. "That asshole was going to burn our house down?" Boyd seemed to swell to twice his normal size as he paced around the kitchen in barely controlled fury. I thought Doug Anderson should be glad he was locked up safely somewhere, and not still available to be found by Boyd.

"Seems like it," Deputy Sandusky replied. "We're guessing that he's strung out on meth right now, and when he saw Mrs. Boyd approaching the mailboxes, he impulsively tried to run her over. Meth doesn't work well with planning and stealth.

"I've got to get back to it, just wanted to give you folks a quick update, so you could rest easy knowing we'd caught him. Also, question for you, Mrs. Boyd; you said earlier that Doug Anderson shot at you, but he didn't have a gun on him when we found him. Do you have any idea where it wound up?"

I told him, and saw the captain make eye contact with Boyd as he silently mouthed, *She threw it away?* Boyd confirmed the silent question with a grimly amused nod. Without another word, Deputy Sandusky exited to the deck and I heard him tell his crew, "It's out there, to the south of the driveway, somewhere. Mrs. Boyd threw it out that way." The crew was too far away for me to hear, but I imagined them repeating the words *she threw the gun?* amongst themselves in a rippling echo.

Clearly I wasn't going to live the gun-throwing down any time soon.

THIRTY-SIX

THE LAST SWEET, TRUMPET NOTES OF 'Taps' echoed across the quiet, pine-scented Montana State Veterans Cemetery at Fort Harrison in Helena, Montana. We stood in a small semi-circle facing the columbarium where Cici would shortly place Brianna's urn, our breath making soft clouds in the freezing air.

Cici and Rett, Boyd and I, Betty and Randy Mills, Deputy Darla Shaw, and both Brad and Jenny from the Search and Rescue team that helped recover Brianna's body from the Crazies made up the funeral entourage. I was pleased that Deputy Shaw was in attendance. We had had our differences, it's true, but she had stood up for us at the end, and it was good to have her present as the representative from the Sweetgrass sheriff's department.

Cici had stepped in to officially claim Brianna's remains, once the coroner's office had released her body. Brianna hadn't listed any next of kin on her military papers which wasn't surprising given her background as a foster child in Pennsylvania. Cici opted to have Brianna's body cremated, feeling sure that the free-spirited girl wouldn't have wanted to be stuck underground in a traditional grave, but had been stymied over what to do for final internment, choosing to wait until 'the right thing' came to mind.

"I really wanted to have a huge bonfire, with her ashes at the top of the pile in a cardboard box. Brianna would've loved that, going out Viking style," Cici had told me. "But I thought we'd probably wind up setting the woods on fire, major oops."

After touring Fort Harrison's national cemetery and seeing the peaceful setting, near the mountains, but out in the open rolling hills, under the big Montana sky, Cici put in the paperwork for Brianna to have a military funeral and internment there. Now buried in December snow, come spring the trees would be filled with songbirds. I liked to think that there would be Swainson's thrushes to serenade Brianna in the evenings with their sweet spiraling calls.

"I would've picked to have her in Missoula, but the veterans' cemetery there is closed for new burials," Cici explained.

The cemetery official unlocked and opened Brianna's niche and stepped back respectfully. Cici walked forward with Rett at her side, holding Brianna's pewter gray urn that was graced with an etching of a soaring eagle rendered by no other than our own Randy Mills. She reverently slid the urn into the niche and turned it so the eagle faced outwards. Cici asked Rett for a sit-stay, and uncoupled the second of two collars that he wore. Ceremoniously, she circled this collar around the neck of the urn, snapped the clasp, and flipped its attached tags around to the front. Brianna's military dog tags were attached, as well as a heart shaped one that was engraved, "Semper Fi – Rett and Cici"

Cici's eyes were wet and shiny as she stood to the side of the open niche, taking in the sight of the gently rolling hills that swoop down and away from the cemetery to the Missouri River.

"Rest in peace, Brianna. Rett and me, we got your back."

With a small nod to the attendant, Cici and Rett rejoined the rest of us, and the niche was closed.

It had been several weeks since Doug Anderson was arrested during his aborted attack on the Boyd residence. We had heard dribs and drabs from the authorities and knew that Rett's blood-stained collar had been definitively matched to Doug Anderson's DNA, and that the gun, thrown by Kelly, was the one used to kill Brianna. In a fury, Doug Anderson had wildly ranted to the deputies about being attacked by vicious dogs and vindictive bitches, confessing that he had indeed shot Brianna and Rett, but claiming self-defense. In his version of events, they had gone to the Crazies to hunt around for presence of wolverines, but argued once they were on the mountainside. Doug insisted that Rett attacked him during the argument, leading Doug to shoot the dog with a gun he had brought along 'for bears'. Brianna had come after him with a knife, and he shot her in self-defense. He couldn't produce the knife, however. Nor could he explain why he had chosen to stuff her body under the rocks on the talus slope and to hide her car in his garage.

Doug Anderson also claimed that, during the snowstorm, his car had simply slid off the road into the ditch at our driveway; he denied that he had tried to run me over with it when he saw me near the mailboxes. The cans of gas in the vehicle? Oh, those were there in case he ran out of fuel while driving.

There was no dodging the fact that he had chased me up the road and shot at me, though. "No comment," was all Doug had to say about that.

The FBI had significant evidence tying him to arson, ALF and ELF.

Justice would be served to Doug Anderson, one way or another, which was deeply satisfying to Betty, Cici and me. The wheels of justice grind slowly but they get there, and in the meantime we could be happy with the rough justice served on him by the dogs: he carries bite scars on both arms and his left buttock, plus the partial scalping and loss of an ear, all compliments of Rett, Sadie and Leo. The police had tried to find his ear that night, in case it could be re-attached, but it was not to be found. I suspect Leo ate it.

Rett carried his head high as he heeled perfectly by Cici's side while we walked back to our cars. There would be a post-funeral wake at our house, and I looked forward to hearing about the upcoming Service Dog ParTners happenings from Cici. I had no doubt that the duo would go from strength to strength with the program. Already, Cici had come so far, pulled by the leash behind Rett into a more normal life instead of spiraling further downward into drink, drugs, and perpetual homelessness.

I could feel Brianna, gone but not lost, smiling down on her old buddies and wishing them well.

New Year's Day found Boyd and me at the Carve 'Em Up Festival in Tombstone, Arizona. I had lost his original invitation during my wild run to the house that snowy November night, which earned me no end of teasing from Boyd. He claims I threw it away into the wind, along with the gun.

But invited he was, and over the three days of the festival, he re-created a beautiful rendition of his otter carving. I felt certain that his piece would win top honors, but those went to a master carver from Finland named Veiti Skinnari, who carved a stag leaping over deadfall. I must admit, Skinnari's work was magnificent. The otters did garner a third prize People's Choice award which put Boyd over the moon.

In addition to the juried work, each day of the festival included a quick-carve contest, held in the afternoon in the open air of a closed off street. The day's competitors were given a raw section of a log and two hours of time to whip out a completed carving.

Boyd's name was drawn for competition on the last day of the festival and he had steadfastly refused to give me even a hint as to his plans for the Quick Carve.

"You'll see it emerge from the wood along with everyone else, Kelly," he told me, thoroughly enjoying my not-so-subtle attempts to get him to spill the beans.

The final day was hot for January, with a full sun shining down on the wide city street when Boyd and the others fired up their chainsaws, sounding like a hoard of mechanical cicadas. At a signal from the official, the chips began to fly and the air filled with the tang of pine sawdust. Some artists were working with their wood in a horizontal orientation, and one grizzled competitor was clearly creating a bench of some sort.

Boyd had chosen to keep his log upright, and he moved swiftly back and forth and around it, dipping and swinging his chainsaw in a smooth dance.

I watched intensely, trying to figure out what he was creating. It wasn't until close to the end of the two hours when I understood, and began cheering, not that Boyd could hear me through the chainsaw's whine and his heavy-duty hearing protection.

Boyd was carving Cerberus, the three headed dog that guards the underworld, and the heads were recognizable renditions of Sadie, Leo and Rett. On the creature's chest Boyd deftly outlined the profiles of three women, each face beneath a dog head. In a final spate of short slashes, the words *Omnia Paratus*, or 'ready for anything', bloomed on the base at Cerberus's feet.

Boyd was paying homage to the Three Musketeers and the dogs!

Boyd lifted his chainsaw with a grin of triumph and gave me a small bow from the waist. As soon as the chainsaw was safely still, I rushed in and squeezed the daylights out of my one-of-a-kind husband who was willing to recognize and celebrate the post-retirement Kelly. I didn't let go even as he whirled me off my feet in dizzying, swooping circles.

"So, Kelly," Boyd spoke directly into my ear, tickling me with his bristly mustache. "Does 'ready-for-anything mean' you'll say 'yes' to a spur of the moment, ten-day trip south of the border for a second honeymoon? 'Cause I've got us tickets, leaving tomorrow from Tucson if it does." He leaned back so that his merrily sparkling brown eyes looked directly into my bright blue ones, which were shiny with unshed tears of happiness.

What? Second honeymoon in Mexico? Am I up for it? Did he need to even ask?

Omnia Paratus, baby!

Ole!

Jessie Moore Photography

BORN AND RAISED IN IDAHO, K.L. Borges moved to Montana in her twenties, where she and her husband raised their three children alongside a series of herding dogs. K.L. Borges was a math teacher at a private Billings high school (Go, Rams!) for a decade, following an earlier career as an environmental engineer. Borges is an active volunteer in the animal rescue community of south-central Montana, a member of the Billings Gem and Mineral Club and is a member of Sisters in Crime. *Murder in the Crazy Mountains* is her first book.